The Queen's Diamond

The Queen's Diamond

Niyah Moore

www.urbanbooks.net

Urban Books, LLC
300 Farmingdale Road, NY-Route 109
Farmingdale, NY 11735

The Queen's Diamond

ISBN 13: 978-1-64556-288-7
ISBN 10: 1-64556-288-3

First Mass Market Printing April 2022
First Trade Paperback Printing October 2020
Printed in the United States of America

10 9 8 7 6 5 4 3 2 1

Distributed by Kensington Publishing Corp.
Submit Orders to:
Customer Service
400 Hahn Road
Westminster, MD 21157-4627
Phone: 1-800-733-3000
Fax: 1-800-659-2436

The Queen's Diamond

by

Niyah Moore

Acknowledgments

I thank God for giving me the precious gift of prose. Without Him, I am nothing.

I used to dream about being a published author when I was a child, and I must thank everyone who supported me while I made that dream come true. If it weren't for social media, and the literary network I connected with over the years, my journey probably wouldn't be what it is.

To my husband, Malcolm, and my children, Cameron, Ciera, Londyn (Rest in heaven), and Miles, you guys are my backbone. You've allowed me to take time away from being your wife and mother to follow my dreams. I am forever grateful.

Thank you to my parents, the best in-laws (in love) in the world, my siblings, and my family for showing your love and support.

I would like to express my gratitude to N'Tyse, the best agent anyone can ask for. Thank you for believing in me and grinding so hard. We've been working with one another for only a year, and in that year, you've done so much for me.

To Carl Weber and the Urban Books / Renaissance Team, thank you so much for my opportunity to shine with y'all.

Acknowledgments

I'd like to give a shout-out to my extensive network of mentors and literary gems. I can't name everyone, but just know that I love you all: Carla Pennington (Pen Twin), Zane, Karen E. Quinones Miller, Shonell Bacon, Shakir Rashaan, Phoenix Rayne, Nicki B, Rikenya Hunter, B. Love, Shan, Diane Rembert, Eric Jerome Dickey, Carol Hill-Mackey, Tee C. Royal, and so many more. Thank you for being encouraging and uplifting. Each and every one of you rocks.

1

DESIRE

2015 – The Beginning of the End

"Bitch, you ain't nothin' without *me*. I *made* you!"

Luxury's words were clear, vivid, and cruel. They hurt as they dug into me like a finger twisting into a bullet's entrance wound. I would've liked it better if he had taken a knife to my skin than spoken those punishing words. He knew everything there was to know about me, every perceived flaw, every vulnerability, so I didn't understand why he was talking crazy. At first, I thought he was just talking like that because he was drunk and high. He usually knew exactly where to apply pressure and how to get underneath my skin, but never to a point where I felt worthless. I was such a confident woman, but now he had me second-guessing myself.

Am I nothing without him?

To think that his pressure made me into a diamond, but now he was trying to crush me. How could he annihilate a diamond like me? Diamonds were supposed to be the hardest natural material in the world. I learned quickly that *hardest* didn't mean indestructible.

"You hear me, bitch?" he said. "You ain't shit without *me*!"

Luxury's words were ringing in my ears like a gong, reminding me of my forgotten pain, my worst memories, and of the times I had felt most abandoned. Here I was, at the height of my professional music career, shining, without a care in the world. Overnight, I had become a star with his guidance, but he hadn't made me. He wanted me strapped at his side like his 9 mm pistol so it would be hard for me to leave. He thought those words would remind me of everything he had ever done for me.

With his hands gripping the collar of my black mink coat, he dared me to fight. He wanted a boxing match, and part of him was craving it, but I didn't want to fight. I just wanted to move on with my life, because this Luxury and Desire thing wasn't working anymore.

"Luxury," I breathed out, and my breath turned into fog. That was how cold it was that winter night. We were standing right in front of his Hellcat in the parking lot of Square Eights Club. Tears welled up in my eyes as I pleaded, "Please, let me go."

He smirked at the way I pleaded. My pleading only made him feel more powerful.

"Hell nah, bitch! I ain't lettin' you go. Get yo' ass in the car right now. You out here playin'." He ground his teeth together as his jaw moved from left to right. The E-pills he had popped earlier in the night made his jaw do that.

How we had got to this point ran through my mind like a speeding bullet. Before we'd left Square Eights, a nightclub where I had a paid appearance, the night had been Gucci. We had smoked a few blunts and had had a few drinks, but after a couple of pills, he had started feeling himself a little too hard. I'd been ready to go by then, because he was in some bitch's face like I wasn't standing there, trying his hardest to make me jealous. His level of disrespect had risen to a new height. He had never tried no shit like this before, because he already knew how I felt about other bitches.

When I'd bolted out of the club, he'd been on my heels.

That was when I'd stood in front of his car and screamed to the heavens, "I'm done. I can't take this shit anymore, disrespectful-ass nigga. I'm gone."

Blame the liquor for giving me the courage to finally let off what I had been thinking, but now that my truth had spilled out of my mouth, I couldn't take it back.

I had turned to walk away to hit up Uber to pick me up, but he'd snatched my ass up so quick, my cell phone had hit the concrete. I wasn't used to Luxury lunging at me, tearing me apart with no holds barred, as if I had crossed some invisible line in the sand, so I hadn't understood what was going on at that moment. There were too many witnesses outside, so I hadn't thought he would be stupid enough to put his hands on me. It was clear to me now that either he didn't give two fucks or he was too high to pay attention to his surroundings.

Run, a voice screamed inside my head. I needed to break free and run like hell to anyone for help, but he had a tight grip on my neck. Out the corner of my eye, I spotted a group of drunk women heading to jump into a Lyft parked right in front of the club. No sooner did I think I could scream to get their attention than he backhanded me. The smack was as loud as a clap, and it stung my face. I was no longer intoxicated; it felt like he had slapped me sober.

"Bitch, you think I'm playin' with you?" he shouted. "Get yo' ass in the car! You ain't goin' no fuckin' where. Don't make me say it again."

I could feel a small cut where his pinkie ring had caught me right below my right eye. I staggered backward, clutching my face. He grabbed my neck again to make sure I wouldn't run. I felt more pain as the second blow came for my abdomen. A sudden gush of pain jolted throughout my body. My stomach ached, and my legs began to weaken. His hard fist hit me in the head again, and this time, I fell from the force of it on the ground. His fist kept cracking me in my face, snapping it back with the strength of his blows. My head reeled as it slammed into the concrete.

"I poured everything into you! Now you wanna up and leave? Mothafucka, it don't work like that," he yelled.

He kicked me while I tried to curl up into a ball to protect myself. I didn't remember how many times he kicked. I just remembered thinking, *Why is Luxury trying to kill me*?

2

DESIRE

Rewind to 2012 – Young Street Dreamin'

Tyga's "Rack City" sounded as my alarm on my HTC One X to wake me up.

It was 6:00 a.m. on a Saturday, and I had to get up to go to Saturday school. I still couldn't believe they had ordered me to attend school on a Saturday as a way of punishing for ditching too many classes that week. This shit was stupid, not to mention it was my eighteenth birthday. If they thought I would spend my birthday handwriting dumb essays, they were gonna have to think of another form of punishment.

Slowly and reluctantly, I pulled back my purple sheet and uncovered my face. I blinked, closed my eyes, and blinked again. Streaks of sunlight coming through my window blinded me as I opened my eyes. Kicking the covers on the floor, I sat up, dragged my feet off the bed, and rubbed my eyes with my knuckles. I stretched, reaching toward the ceiling, and yawned.

I turned off my alarm on my phone and looked around my junky room. I needed to fold the clean clothes that were spilling out of the basket and put the dirty clothes that were piled high in the corner in the washer, but I didn't feel like it. Laundry was always the last thing on my mind and one of the many things my mom complained about. Today was my birthday.

"Happy Birthday to me," I said to myself dryly.

I wasn't excited about my birthday, because we were in the midst of hurricane season. It was tax-free storm-supply week at the stores, so that was what my parents were focused on. I checked the weather report, and it was devoid of hurricanes, so I didn't want to waste a beautiful day in Saturday school.

"Nope, I ain't going," I mumbled to myself.

We had only three more weeks of school anyway. I wasn't about to waste my time.

My bedroom door swung open, making a whooshing sound, and my mom barged into my room like she was the Miami PD.

Why can't she just knock for once? I thought as I scowled at her. While scratching my messy head, I realized I could've been naked or something. But she wouldn't care even if I was naked. I didn't pay any bills, so I had no say about anything around here. This was *her* door and *her* room. I couldn't wait to move out. I didn't know why she was on me so tight all the time. She acted like she paid bills. She didn't pay for shit, either. She didn't even have a job.

My mom had been born and raised in South Florida and had lived in different parts of the region. She looked like she could be my older sister. Her long, curly black hair was pulled into a high ponytail, and she had a scarf tied around her head like Tupac. There was always a deep scowl on her face, her nose was usually turned up, and her big eyes always looked like they were going to pop out of her head. Curse words flew out of her mouth every single time she addressed me. I didn't get what I did that made her hate me so much.

I stared at her through half-opened eyes, waiting for her to say something.

"Get up and get yo' raggedy ass ready for detention," she barked.

I can't get a "Happy Birthday"? Why I gotta be raggedy?

"I ain't gotta go," I answered, rolling my eyes.

"What you mean, you ain't gotta go? You ain't got no choice. Get yo' ass up right now."

"But, Ma, it's my birthday," I whined.

"I don't give a shit if it was Jesus's birthday. Hell, I know what today is. You the dummy that keeps fuckin' up in school. It's bad enough I get a call from the principal yesterday, talkin' about you missing some credits. Did you know you ain't graduating? Huh? You know that, li'l bitch?"

I wasn't shocked that she called me out of my name. But I didn't know I wasn't graduating. I knew I had a couple of Ds and Fs, but damn. My heart sank into my stomach as I smacked my lips. "What? Man . . ."

"Man, my ass, Desirae. You and this li'l funky, half-ass attitude is really starting to work my last mothafuckin' nerve. You better start actin' right. I mean that shit. I ain't raising no dummies."

I took a deep breath and exhaled as I swiveled out of bed. Standing on my feet, I glared at my mother. She was always nagging and tripping. "You be on that bullshit," I mumbled.

"What you just say?" She stepped farther into my room, with her hands on her wide hips. "Speak up."

"Nothin', Ma. Dang."

"Oh, I heard you. You think you are grown now? You turn eighteen, and now I be on that bullshit?"

Feeling my insides boil, I screamed, "I am *grown*."

"Well, get yo' grown ass on up outta here, then. See ya. Wouldn't want to be ya."

Storming out of my bedroom, my footsteps thudding loudly against the wood floor, I yelled at the top of my lungs, "*Papi*."

She was behind me, walking fast. "Tell your papi. He 'bout sick of ya fast ass, too, but he acts like he too scared to tell ya that. Out here fuckin' on these nasty-ass boys all the time. You think we didn't know that, huh? He out in the backyard with your brother. At least Javier knows how to help around here, unlike your lazy ass."

"Jav is a grown-ass man. He needs to start paying some rent, don't ya think? Why you ain't sweatin' him like you sweat me?" I slid open the sliding door in the dining room, and the crisp morning air chilled my body. I screamed, "Papi!"

"What?" he asked as he kept trimming the bushes.

My papi was born Diego Fernández and had been raised in Cuba. His family were poor coffee farmers, but they were hard workers. When his family moved to Miami's Little Havana, his father started a coffee factory that sorted, washed, dried, milled, and bagged Cuban coffee beans. Grandpa became the coffee plug, with his connection to Cuba. That little coffee factory grew, and our family brand expanded all thanks to my papi. In South Florida, people thought Cuban coffee was superior. People loved drinking dark-roasted blends from small cups.

When Papi met my mom, it was love at first sight. He loved her black ass. He was seventeen years older than her, and Javier was already three years old. He wasn't my papi's son, but my papi took care of him like his own because Javier's dad was in prison, serving a life sentence for trafficking cocaine from Colombia. Papi was a good man. He wanted his family out of the ghetto, and he gave us the world. Once business took off, he moved us to East Little Havana, where the houses were nicer, and we had grass to play in.

"Papi, Ma is tryin' to kick me out."

"Tell him why I'm kickin' yo' ass out," she hollered, opening the sliding door wider so Papi could see both of us. "Diego, I'm tired of Desirae's mouth. She's in here talkin' too much shit."

"Don't talk shit to your *mamá*," he replied nonchalantly, keeping his eyes on those bushes.

He was used to me and Mama going back and forth, and most times he had my back, so I didn't understand that he was so quick to take her side this time just to shut her up.

Javier's fat ass brought the lawn mower from the garage and positioned it on the grass.

"Don't you cut that on, Javier," Mama ordered.

Javier wore a confused look. "Why? What did Des do now?"

"She lost her damn mind, that's what. You need to have a talk with your sister before her hot ass ends up on the street, sellin' pussy," Mama said. "Her mouth tryin'a write a check her ass can't cash."

Javier didn't respond as he put his headphones on. His iPod Nano was the only thing he cared about. He walked past us into the house. He never, ever had the big brother, little sister conversations with me. We didn't get along like that, and we were only five years apart. How was he going to give me any kind of advice when he had never left home? He couldn't even take care of himself at twenty-three years old, with his big, grown, overweight ass.

Papi stopped what he was doing and walked closer to me. "Are you getting ready for school?" he asked, finally looking at me through his thick glasses.

"No. I don't have to go. It's my birthday."

"You think because it's your birthday, you deserve a pass?"

"Yeah," I replied, with my arms crossing my chest. "Who wants to spend their birthday at Saturday school? It's not mandatory. Hell, I'm not graduating, anyway, so what's the point?"

"*Mierda*," he cursed in Spanish under his breath. "You know you won't get a pass this time," he said to me firmly. "Get dressed, and I'll take you to school."

My mouth nearly dropped open, because he never talked to me that way. "This ain't fair."

Mama blurted, "If her ass would've been where she was supposed to be, she wouldn't have Saturday school in the first place."

The sound of her voice was irritating my soul. "Ma—"

"Ma, what?" She was close to my face now. "Get yo' ass in that shower and get ready for school. I'm not gonna tell yo' triflin' ass again. If I find out you didn't go, you might as well not come back here."

My whole body felt tight. It was like this pent-up aggression that had been building from her constantly nagging was now surfacing. She was picking at me, and I wasn't feeling it. "Well, I'm not going to school, so I might as well leave now, then. I don't need you all up in my face, either." I stormed down the hall toward my room, making my bare feet slap against the hardwood floor. "I'm not about to spend my birthday at school. Y'all got me all the way twisted."

"Ooh, Diego, I'm telling you, I'm gonna punch that li'l girl in the face!" Mama stormed.

"No, you shouldn't have to do that, Paula. Let me talk to her."

"Her mouth is so reckless. She's not going to get away with this. Believe that, baby. Humph. I ain't got time for this li'l girl."

"Now, just calm down," Papi said. "I said I'll talk to her."

"I can't calm down. What's talking going to do? I'm supposed to let her talk to me any kind of way?"

"I didn't say that, Paula. She acts just like you. Where you think she gets it from?"

"Nah, Diego. She thinks she's grown. She ain't even graduating on time. Woke up eighteen years old, and now she thinks she can talk to me any kind of way. No, sir. I'm tellin' you and everybody up in here, there is only one queen up in this bitch, and that's me. She done crossed the line."

I slammed my bedroom door to drown out their voices. I didn't want to hear her mouth. Papi usually stuck up for me, even when I was wrong. Things were changing, and I figured the only way they would appreciate me was if I was gone. I threw off my extra-large sleeping shirt and put on my bra. I wasn't going to Saturday school, and that was it. I was going to spend my day the way I wanted. Since my family wasn't celebrating my day, I was going to do whatever I wanted.

When I was growing up, I used to imagine leaving home for college, with my mama in tears, begging me not to go, and my papi being proud that I was leaving the nest to go to college. I would pack my small car with boxes and my suitcases, and then I would watch them wave at me from my side mirror as I drove away. Now that was nothing but a dream. How could I think about college when I wasn't graduating from high school on time? My GPA was barely a 2.0, and I hadn't applied anywhere. I had already made up my mind that college wasn't for me.

I packed fast, anger fueling me. I wrapped my toothbrush after I brushed my teeth. After I had my bags packed and all the money I had out of my piggy bank, which was about seventy-five dollars, I texted my best friend, Mina.

Me: Mama kicked me out. I got nowhere to go. The bitch is crazy.

Mina: You know you can stay here. You coming now?

Me: Yeah.

Mina had always said that I could stay at her apartment. She had graduated last year and had a job. I didn't know where she was working these days, because she always quit after two weeks and then would be working somewhere else. The main thing was she was paying her own bills and didn't have to worry about school anymore.

When I came out of my room, Papi was still working on the yard, and Javier was mowing the lawn. When I reached the living room, Mama was standing in the middle of the room, smoking a joint.

"You better leave all your keys right here on this table." She pointed with her pinkie finger as she held on to a joint with her thumb and pointer finger. She hit the joint hard and blew out a cloud of smoke. "Car keys too."

"Huh? It's my car. Papi bought it."

"He got the car 'cause he thought yo' ass was graduating from high school. Since you so muthafuckin' grown, get yo' own shit, bitch."

With tears burning the back of my eyes, I reluctantly tossed all my keys onto the coffee table. I didn't look back as I walked ten blocks to Mina's apartment complex.

I was sweaty and out of breath by the time I made it to Mina's complex. The humidity itself had taken my breath away. She saw me coming from her balcony. Mina was wearing Daisy Duke shorts and a pink half shirt that showed off her belly button, and she was barefoot. Her lip gloss was popping as she sipped her bottle of Coke with a red straw.

Mina was my best friend, and she was so sweet. She was five feet, three inches of pure peanut butter–brown curves. Mina was a beautiful Afro-Cuban girl. She was born in Cuba and had come over as an illegal immigrant with her entire family. We had been best friends since I started high school, and she was the only person I told everything to. She'd been a grade above me, but she hadn't had any friends, and neither had I. When she'd graduated last year, I'd felt lost, so I'd skipped school to hang out with her.

Ever since Mina had got her own spot a few months ago, I had hardly gone to school. I liked being over here. My mom always hated on me for being here. Mina had three older brothers and a couple of uncles who were in and out of prison, and Ma swore up and down I was fucking one of them. I was fucking, but not any of her brothers. That was just nasty. I was comfortable around them because they were like my brothers too. Mina had a big heart and always let her family crash at her spot whenever. She kept her door open for family no matter how crowded it got.

"Wait . . . Hold up. You walked? Why didn't you call me?" she yelled down to me from her balcony. "I would've picked you up."

"The bitch took my car." I wiped my forehead and exhaled. "You got a whip?"

"You see that Chevy right there?" She pointed to a red car that looked brand new. "Didn't I tell you?"

"No. You must've thought you did, but you didn't."

She giggled. "Oh. My fault."

"Sammy gave you a pay raise?" I asked, wondering how she could afford rent, a light bill, and now a brand-new car.

"I don't work at Sammy's no more . . . That wasn't paying shit. I got something else poppin'."

"Oh, okay . . . You gonna tell me what's poppin'? I need a job."

She sipped her soda and didn't answer about hooking me up with a job. "Happy fuckin' Birthday. You are now officially an adult. How does it feel to be eighteen?"

I couldn't smile, because I was too hot. Now that I wasn't walking, sweat was forming all over my body, especially under my boobs. "You gonna let me in or not?"

"You look hot and mad as hell," she laughed.

"Girl, I'm over this shit. I had to walk all the way up over here. You got another Coke? 'Cause you making that shit look really good." I sighed as I walked up the stairs to her front door.

She smacked her lips, disappeared into the apartment, and opened the front door for me a few seconds later. "I should have one bottle left in the fridge. Now that my uncle NuNu is staying here again, we can't keep nothin'. I need to go grocery shopping, but I do that on Saturdays, as you know."

As soon as I was inside and that freezing air from her air conditioner hit me, I felt relief. I went to her refrigerator, and it was empty as hell. She had an empty pizza box, an empty jar of Welch's grape jelly, and that one unopened bottle of soda. I took it and closed the fridge. I unscrewed the cap and took a few gulps. I burped from the bubbles.

"Where can I put my bags?" I asked.

"Come on. Let's put them in my closet."

I followed her to the back of the untidy two-bedroom apartment. There was a big pile of clothes on her couch and a sink full of dirty dishes, but Mina kept her bedroom spotless. She was a neat freak, but only when it came to her bedroom. I handed her my suitcases, and she put them in her closet with the mirrored doors.

"So, what's up? You graduating or not?" she asked.

"The fuckin' school called and told my mom I ain't graduating. I think I'm a few credits short."

"But you can always make those up in summer school. That's what you're going to do, right?"

I rolled my eyes. One thing about Mina was that she always said to stop fucking around and get my diploma, but I didn't see the point of that.

"I'm too far behind to finish up this summer. I probably gotta go to continuation school or something."

"Damn it, Desi. You're that far behind? I told you to go to school, but nooo, you just had to be with your boo."

"Now you sound like her," I scowled, feeling irritated.

She took a deep breath and exhaled. "Well, since school is not on your list of things to do and you say you need a job, how about you come and work with me?"

"You gone tell me where you work and what you do and whatnot?"

"Sit down on the bed real fast," she said.

"Why?" I gulped the soda.

"Just do it."

I sat on the corner of her bed and watched her go into the top of her closet and pull out a shoebox. "You work at a shoe store?"

She looked at me like I was crazy. "Hell nah. Shut up and listen." She opened the box and showed me that it was full of money bundled with rubber bands. "I have three more boxes like this. I made all of this in four days."

My eyes nearly popped out of my head. "Doin' what?"

"Nothin' but dancin'." She shrugged. "You got some money on you?"

"I took all my money out of my piggy bank. It ain't much, but I can eat with it for a few days. Wait, so you're dancin' or strippin'?"

"Dancin'." She took a bundle of money without counting it and said, "Here. Take this."

I took the money reluctantly while asking, "Where you strippin'?"

"I'm *dancin'* at the Queen of Diamonds. You ever heard of it?"

"Nah . . . So, you be *dancin'* naked?" I asked, trying to imagine taking off my clothes for strangers.

"Sometimes . . . Hey, how long you need to stay?"

"I don't want to go back home, not for a while, anyway. She told me if I don't go to Saturday school, then don't come back, so I really don't know."

"You know you can always stay as long as you need. I gotta dance tonight. You should come, and if you think you can hang, I'll talk to Queen about you."

"Okay." I started to count the money Mina had given me, while she returned the shoebox to the top of her closet. I paused when I was midway through the bundle of bills. "We still going to the beach?"

"Hell yeah."

"Cool," I said.

"You ain't invite Montego?" she asked with a smile.

Montego was my so-called boo, and he was a year older than me. We were off and on so much because he was so childish and played too much. I was mad at him because he hadn't called or sent a text to tell me Happy Birthday, as if I wasn't important. Plus, I had heard he was fucking bitches all over Miami. I couldn't stand a cheating-ass nigga.

"Nah, I ain't talk to him."

"It's always the light-skinned boys that act like that," she said and laughed.

I laughed, shaking my head. "I don't know what skin tone has to do with it, but he's so stupid. Speaking of boos, you tell Zay to meet us up there?"

Xavier, aka Zay, was Mina's boyfriend. They had been in a relationship for only six months, but they acted like they had been together forever.

"He's on his way over here now. We're riding with him to the beach."

I nodded, but then my mind went back to her new gig. "So . . . how you be dancin'? You be all on the poles and shit?"

She stuck her tongue out and then replied, "Yeah, but you'll see tonight."

I was curious, but then I realized I hadn't finished counting the money she had handed me. I added up the rest of the twenties, tens, and fives. "Mina, this is four hundred dollars."

"I know. Does that give you a li'l motivation?"

I shrugged. I wasn't a virgin or nothing like that, but I had never been in a strip club before. I liked to get naked when Montego and I got down, but how did she expect me to get naked in front of a roomful of strangers?

"Why you lookin' all scared?" she asked with a scowl.

"I ain't scared."

"Yeah you are. You ain't about to be dancin' tonight, so you don't need to be scared. All I said was to come and watch, but if you want to make some money, then cool. I got you. I've seen you naked before. You got a bangin'-ass body. You got a phat ass and nice juicy titties, your stomach is flat, and you can shake and twerk your ass better than me. *And* you cute as fuck. Dudes stay gettin' at you everywhere we go. We always talk about all the nasty shit you do for Montego all the time. This ain't no different."

I was a freak; I liked having sex and dancing, but with Montego only. Nobody else. I knew I wasn't ugly, so I didn't need her to tell me that. I was five feet two, with curves in all the right places. So many niggas tried to get at me regularly, but I didn't fuck around. Montego wasn't my first, but he had been the only one for two years.

"Yeah, but with my boo, it's different. So, wait . . . You do nasty shit at the club?"

"You gotta be a freak to do this, period. Girl, the nastier and the freakier, the more money you get, but we ain't even about to talk about this right now. I'm about to get changed, because Zay will be rollin' up in a minute. You got your bathing suit on already?"

"No. I'll get changed right now."

"Matter of fact, take off your clothes for me."

"For you?" I asked with a frown.

She smacked her lips and rolled her eyes. "How many times I've seen you naked before? Shit, we've had sex in the same room how many times now?"

"Yeah, but I didn't look at you. I was too busy getting mine."

She rolled her eyes again and waited for me to get naked. "If you can't take off your clothes for me, then you sho' can't take them off for strangers."

I took a deep breath and hopped up from her bed. I removed my jean shorts, tank top, bra, and panties and kicked them away from my feet. She folded her arms across her chest and scanned my body, as if she had forgotten what it looked like.

"Turn around," she instructed.

I turned around fast and put my hands on my hips.

"Damn, yo' ass got a li'l bigger since the last time I saw you," she noted. "Montego has been bending that thang over, huh?"

"Somethin' like that," I replied, turning back around to face her.

"I can tell." She walked closer to me and put her hands on my shoulders. She guided me to the full-length mirror that was hanging on the back of her closet door. "Look at yourself. You're beautiful, Desi."

"Thank ya, thank ya." I looked at myself. I knew what my body looked like, but I tried looking at myself to see what she was staring at. There wasn't anything about my body that I didn't like. "Okay, I'll go to the club tonight, but I won't make no promises 'bout strippin'. My daddy might kill me." I grabbed one of my bags from her closet to get dressed.

"A'ight. Deal. You know, it's crazy how you don't care anything about your mama's feelings, but you still want to be an angel for your daddy. Straight-up Daddy's girl."

"You know it. Hey, can we get a fresh fruit batido when we get to the beach?" I asked, digging in the bag for my bathing suit.

"Yeah, yeah. I got you. It will be my birthday treat. Hurry up. I think I just heard him pull up."

The bass from the sound system in Zay's car was faint, but I could hear it. I rushed into my bathing suit, threw my jeans and tank on over it, and grabbed my purse.

"I got the towels and sunblock in my beach bag," Mina said. "You got your sunglasses?"

"Shit. I left them at home."

"I got an extra pair," she said, reaching into her top dresser drawer. "Let's go."

We loved South Beach. It was only about twenty-five minutes away, and we always had so much fun there. Underneath a mist that swirled thicker than air freshener lay warm sand, sand that shifted underneath the pressure of my bare feet. I didn't need to look down at the sand, only feel it. The feel of it always took away any worries I had.

I looked out past the sand at the ocean, and it was alive with constant motion as a scatter of people jumped in and splashed around. I inhaled the salty smell. It was a fragrance that summoned surfboards, half-naked men and women, and their dogs. The sound of the ocean gave me internal peace. These waves were never the gentle kind that rolled up the beach the way I had seen in the movies. And they weren't the crashing kind, either.

These powerful waves moved smoothly but then died within a few feet. South Beach could've been anywhere, but it wasn't. This was my home, and I had been coming here ever since I was a small child.

I got out of my jeans and tank, stood still, facing the breeze, and soaked it all in as I sipped my fresh fruit batido through a straw. I savored the mango sherbet, vanilla ice cream, fresh mango, milk, and honey blend. It was the best, and ever since I was a kid, Papi had always got us a batido before hitting the beach. The beach didn't feel like the beach without it.

"Zay, can you put this sunblock on my back?" Mina cooed before she sipped her coconut and pineapple batido.

You couldn't wipe the smile off his face as he happily obliged. Zay was tall, with a baby face. He wore a fade, and his skin was smooth, dark, and chocolate, much like Hershey's Special Dark. He was wearing basketball shorts and nothing else except a pair of worn white Jordans that needed to be thrown away. I didn't see how Mina even dated a nigga with fucked-up shoes. I wouldn't be caught dead, but he was cute. His skin was dripping with sweat already, and we had just got there. His abs were glistening as he took off his backpack.

"Baby, don't you think Desi got a bangin'-ass body? She should work at Queen of Diamonds with me, huh?"

I snapped my neck at her. Why was she putting me on blast? I looked at him to see what he was about to say. His eyes danced all over my body, as if she wasn't sitting in front of him, getting rubbed down with sunblock. I gave him a dirty look when our eyes met.

He smirked, "She cool, but with that attitude, she ain't gone make no money."

Mina burst into laughter.

I rolled my eyes, lay on the beach towel, using my purse as my pillow, put my sunglasses on, and sipped my shake. I wasn't about to be bothered by them.

Mina said, "Montego should really be here."

"I don't want to be around him today."

"Hmmm. Well, if y'all gone be together and you decide to dance with me, you gotta tell him. If he ain't with it, you gotta dump his ass for good. Too many bitches up in there let these niggas beat they asses 'cause they all in they feelings about them dancin'."

I sighed and sipped. Mina was acting like I had said I would do it. I hadn't said yes or no.

"Look, don't act like you don't need a job," she said.

"Mina, I said I'll check it out. I gotta think about it, you know?"

"Okay. I'll shut the fuck up. You'll love it, though."

I took a deep breath and tried my best not to think about it, but all I could think about was how I would look dancing naked. The thought freaked me out.

3

DESIRE

The Queen's Diamond

I ain't about to lie. Walking into the Queen of Diamonds for the first time had my heart racing. It was much like the feeling I had had when I watched porn for the first time at sixteen. I'd never forget when I saw a dick for the first time on-screen. My very first scene was a white housewife giving the plumber head. Then I had started waiting until my parents went to bed to watch Porn Hub. It was like it had felt good to watch and please myself, but I had always felt dirty and guilty. That guilt was what I felt walking up in Queen's. First, we weren't old enough to even be up in there. The age limit was twenty-one.

On our way there, Mina had handed me an ID and said, "For the record, I'm twenty-one, and so are you."

I'd stared at the ID and frowned. "Uh-uh. This Spanish lady looks nothing like me."

"They ain't gonna ask for it, but just in case they do, that's you."

I had shaken my head. She'd already made sure my tits were sitting up and were exposed in a tight-fitting black minidress. She had also told me to make sure my makeup was extra heavy. I had done what I was told so that I wouldn't stand out awkwardly.

We had got there a little after 10:00 p.m. I wasn't sure what Queen of Diamonds ever expected to go down there, but whatever it was, they were prepared for anything and everything shady. Men and women security guards were in vests, fully armed, as they stood at the front.

Like Mina had said, they didn't ask me for my ID. They let us go straight in, and it could be because I was with her. This place was fuckin' huge. The bar area was larger than any bar I'd ever seen. Though it was early, it was packed. We passed so many VIP sections, they seemed endless. Mina found me a seat near the front of the stage.

"Enjoy the show. Zay should be here soon. Save this spot for him," she told as I sat down.

I nodded, without words, and she left me sitting there alone. I tried not to look around nervously, but I couldn't hide my emotions. I was like a fish out of water. The music was pumping so hard that I could feel it throughout my entire body. There were some dancers onstage, doing what looked like magic tricks. I felt like I was watching some Cirque du Soleil shit. I looked up, and damn, I had never before seen a pole long enough to reach heaven. That was how tall the pole was. A chick climbed to the very top, and it seemed like she was climbing forever, and then slid all the way down. She blew my mind.

Everything Mina had prepped me for about Queen of Diamonds was right on target. These bitches were some of the baddest bitches, and they smelled so good. I was expecting the place to smell like straight hot booty and fishy coochie, but nope, they were on their shit. They were thick, curvy, and talented. I relaxed more and more by the second.

Five minutes later, my phone started vibrating. I dug my phone out of my purse. It was Montego blowing me up. I rolled my eyes and stared at the screen as his call went to voicemail.

I sent him a text: What nigga? I'm busy.

Montego: I just wanted to tell you Happy Birthday. I see you on Instagram, lookin' good.

Me: Well, you wouldn't have to look at me on Instagram if your ass had shown up at the beach. It's over. We're done.

Montego: Like that?

I couldn't believe this nigga was hitting me up now, when I had only two hours left of my birthday. *The fuck?* I angrily tossed my phone into my purse. I was not about to let him ruin what was left of my day.

Before Mina could hit the stage, someone sat in the seat I was saving for Zay and said with a Southern drawl, "What ya fine ass doin' up here by yourself?"

I looked over at the man in shades. His skin was the color of a caramel candy. His hair was faded into these thick-ass ocean waves on the top, and his facial hair was well groomed into a shadow beard. He was smoking a fat blunt. I couldn't see his eyes behind those shades, so I continued to look at him from head to toe. He was tall, close to six feet, which I liked. Wearing nothing but designer everything, he had bundles of cash in his hands. He wore a thick gold chain with the diamond-encrusted letters *MB*, and he had a fully iced Rolex on his wrist. He was built strong and had broad shoulders, as if he worked out daily.

When he smiled, a pair of the deepest dimples made me swoon instantly.

Who is this fine-ass muthafucka right here? I thought to myself.

"Um, excuse me, but this seat is taken," I said, remembering I was supposed to save it for Zay.

"Huh?" he asked, leaning his ear toward my mouth. His cologne was overpowering but smelled delightful at the same time. "I can't hear you, baby. Speak up."

"I . . . I said this seat is taken."

"I know. It's taken by me." He blew out smoke in the opposite direction.

"No, for real, for real. My friend is comin'."

"I'll move when she gets here. Till then, this my seat." He paused to stare at me through his shades. "This ya first time, huh?"

I didn't say yes or no. "My girl is dancin' tonight, and I'm just here to see her."

"Ya *girl* girl or ya girlfriend?"

I scowled. "Nah, I don't roll like that. My patna."

"A'ight, li'l mama. You got a sweet Spanish accent. You Latin?"

"Yeah, half Cuban."

"*Cubana*. I dig it . . ." He licked his lips and inhaled his weed.

I thought I would choke from the smoke, but the ventilation was really good in this place. I looked around, and a lot of people were smoking.

Zay walked up a few minutes later, but as soon as he saw who was sitting next to me, he stood at the end of the stage instead of trying to nab his seat. Zay looked like he knew exactly who this guy was and wanted no parts of him. His reaction had me looking more intently at this fine stranger.

"Is that ya nigga?" he asked, nodding his head toward Zay.

"Nah, that's my girl's boyfriend. That's his seat I was saving."

"Hmmm," he said but didn't move. "I think I know ya girl. Exxxotic."

"Who?" I was confused, but then I paused because I remembered Mina telling me she had a stage name. She had said it so fast that I had forgotten it. "Oh yeah, Exxxotic."

"She's up next, I think." He removed his shades to reveal his deep, dark, and sexy eyes. He was even finer without the shades. There was something about the way he licked his lips that had me staring at him.

I couldn't stop staring. He had the kind of face that stopped you dead in your tracks. Those eyes were looking through me as if he had X-ray vision. I guessed he might've been used to my kind of reaction, because he didn't seem surprised that I was staring at him that way. It was as if a woman's intense gaze was an everyday thing for him. Once I realized he was staring at me the same way, I felt my face grow hot. I was blushing so damn hard.

"You drink?" he questioned.

I shook my head coolly. "I don't drink, but I am thirsty."

"Whaaa?" He looked like he ain't ever heard anyone say that. "A'ight, well, mo' fa me." He motioned to the topless waitress who was walking by, and she walked up to him. "Bring me Henny with a li'l ice, and bring her a . . ."

"Can I have a Sprite?" I said.

The waitress nodded and walked to the bar.

I looked around to see if he was rollin' solo, but I couldn't tell. There were people everywhere. He seemed like a very private person, and he had that godly thing about him, like he had superhuman powers. I knew instantly that I wanted to experience them firsthand.

"What's ya name?" he asked.

"Desirae. And you are?"

"Luxury."

I blinked hard because I had heard of him around the city. I also should've realized he looked familiar, and it dawned on me that I had seen him on social media. Now that he was in front of me in the flesh, I could see that this nigga didn't fake it for the Gram. He was everything he put out there. I was already following him on Instagram and Twitter.

"As in Luxury like the Monnahan Boyz?"

He nodded. "The one and only, baby."

One of the biggest dope boys was sitting in my face. He stayed flexin' online, flashing his money and cars. Bitches stayed trying to holler at him, leaving the craziest thirsty-ass comments.

"Oh, okay. I follow you on Instagram," I revealed.

"Do you?"

"Yeah."

He pulled out his phone. "What's your name on there?"

"Desi_Rae."

He found me on Instagram and hit the FOLLOW button. "I'm following you now."

I nodded, trying to play it cool, but on the inside, I was too excited.

Just then, the waitress brought his Henny and my Sprite with a slice of lime.

"Thank you," I said.

"No problem," she said.

As I took a sip of my Sprite, the DJ announced, "Coming up to the stage . . . You playas better get yo' money out right now. Make some noise for ya girl Exxxotic."

I slowly turned my eyes to the stage. I did a double take because my best friend was giving me so much life in her white outfit, which hugged her body in all the right places. She looked so beautiful and sexy that she took my breath away.

Luxury sat his drink on the cocktail table on the other side of his seat, and his money started raining all over that stage. My jaw dropped, because other niggas were following his lead. I drank my Sprite as I watched in awe. Mina peeled off her clothes layer by layer. The more clothes that came off, the more money that flowed.

"You act like you ain't never seen this much money befo'," he uttered.

"I haven't," I admitted.

He put one of his fat stacks in my hand and replied, "Show ya girl some love."

My hands were shaking as I put my glass down near my chair. I didn't know what to do. Was I supposed to toss the money like in the music videos, let the bills fall one by one, or stuff some into Mina's G-string? Now Mina was rolling her body, popping her ass, doing pussy poppin', and executing shit I didn't think she could do. I was so impressed. I looked around at how everyone else was tossing money on the stage, and I imitated them.

"That's it, baby," Luxury said with a chuckle.

I loved the way his voice sounded when he called me baby. I wanted him to call me baby forever.

I continued to look around, and all I could see was ass, ass, and mo' ass, cash and mo' cash. Mina danced as if she wanted every bitch and nigga up in there to feel her presence. She demanded their attention, and she got it. She didn't give a fuck, and I wanted to be just like her. I was craving that attention she was getting from Luxury. My breathing became heavier as my nipples started getting hard. I was turned on. Watching one of Queen's diamonds had me ready to jump on that stage at once.

Once her routine was over, Mina hurried over to us and said to Luxury, "You know it's my girl's birthday, right?"

I tried not to blush while his eyes gazed at me as if I was a treat he couldn't wait to taste.

"Is that right? Happy Birthday, li'l mama."

I smiled. "Thank you."

"You thinkin' 'bout getting up there like ya girl?" he asked as Mina waved at us and then dashed to the other side of the stage. He was paying close attention to the fascination in my eyes.

"Hell yeah," I said without giving it much thought. I watched for Luxury's reaction to see if he liked that idea, but I couldn't read him.

"Hmmm . . . I got the perfect name for you if you do." He rubbed his hands together.

"You do? What's that?" I asked.

"Desire."

"Desire? That sounds too much like my actual name."

"I know, and that's why it's perfect. You'll have every nigga wantin' or, better yet, *wishin'* they were yo' nigga."

The way he said it made me wonder if he was wanting or wishing he could be my nigga. I liked the way the name Desire sounded as it left his lips. It was the perfect play on my name. I nodded, all while imagining what my life would be like if I made this kind of cash.

For much of the night, I sat back and watched Mina work the room for lap dances. The few times she disappeared into what they called champagne rooms, Luxury and I carried on a conversation.

"Hey, come with me to VIP," Luxury said into my ear when Mina finished her last lap dance.

"Okay."

I followed him through the crowd to the section that was for exclusive people only. Men and women were acknowledging Luxury as they passed us. Everyone loved him; they were drawn to him. I took note of the way they hung on his every word, as if he was the alpha and the omega. They wanted to be close to him, just like I did. If he wanted to, he could have more friends than hours in the day, but he told me that he chose to keep his circle small. According to him, his brothers, Frill and Lavish, were the only ones he trusted.

He told me a lot about himself that night. At twenty-two years old, he was a natural thug, though he considered himself to be a businessman. Luxury had made a name for himself sellin' drugs in the streets, but he wanted to be done with that. He had dreams of being at the top of the music industry. In fact, he proclaimed himself to be the next Birdman in terms of leaving the drug game alone and running an independent record label. I loved that about him. I could see him doing everything he dreamed of.

I honestly thought he would get my number that night, but he didn't ask for it or hint about it, which had me in my feelings. He wound up leaving the club without my digits.

As we left the strip club, Mina walked beside me, her hand on my shoulder, as Zay followed behind us, smoking a cigarette.

"Girl, don't even trip. If you start working here, you'll see Luxury all the time. He's a regular," she said.

I hoped so, because I was infatuated with him already.

"When can I start?" I asked her.

"You can audition tomorrow night."

4

DESIRE

2015 – Twenty-One and Lovin' It

For three years, I became many men's and women's desire, especially once I upgraded my body. I enhanced my breasts to a full, luscious D cup and had my ass shaped like a ripe peach by the best plastic surgeon in the city, one of the best investments I could've ever made. The money just flowed right on in like water. Everybody loved my new body. I changed my social media account names to DesireHer. My Instagram and Twitter stayed on fire. Niggas were hopping into my DMs on Twitter left and right. It got to a point where I couldn't read them all.

Once I started averaging four thousand a night, I was feeling myself. I moved out of Mina's spot, which was getting too crowded with all her uncles and brothers always needing somewhere to stay. My new place wasn't in the best neighborhood, but on the inside, it was plush, and it was all mine.

Renting was cool, but my dream was to own. Before long I had the money to put a down payment on my dream penthouse overlooking South Beach, but they were talking about I didn't have the credit. Who needed credit when I had money? It didn't make sense to me. Mina had told me to get a man, so he could buy me a house in his name. But I didn't need a nigga to do shit for me.

I hated niggas that thought that every bitch needed their name on shit in order for her to have anything in life. These niggas stayed flexin', and when they figured out you really didn't need them for shit, they started talking to you crazy. I wasn't impressed by any nigga, because I could do everything for myself.

Since the day my mom had kicked me out, I hadn't talked to her. I had called to see about my dad, but once my mom had found out I was working at Queen's, she'd wanted him to disown me. Papi loved me too much to cut me all the way off, so we would meet up for lunch whenever he could. My papi's love for me would never die. I couldn't trip on my mom, because she had hated me since birth.

Papi wanted me to go back to school and get a GED. He even prayed that I went to church with him, but for what? I was a stripper, yes, but that didn't make me a bad person, right? Why did I need to go to church? And why did I need to go back to school? I had been dancing since I was eighteen, had been saving my bread since then. Three years of stacking. I had niggas and bitches traveling to Miami to watch me and shower me with cash. They loved me, so quitting was out.

Dancing wasn't just a job to me; it was fun, and it gave me so much joy. I took a shot of liquor here and there, but I wasn't into drugs like the other girls. Dancing gave me a natural high. I admitted that I wasn't the friendly type with those bitches up in Queen's. I didn't befriend any bitches up there, because I didn't trust them hoes. I had watched too many of them get into fights over stupid gossip. Mina was the only one I wanted in my corner. She kept all my secrets.

Mina was still grinding and twerking to make her ends meet. She and Zay had a two-year-old daughter now, and they were talking about getting married soon, but I hadn't seen a ring yet, so who knew when that would be. They were in love, but it was strange how Zay didn't give a damn what she did to make money. She would fuck if they paid enough. He would be right there afterward, collecting. Shit, I couldn't give my hard-earned money to nobody. I wasn't built to have a pimp as a boyfriend.

As far as my love life was concerned, I didn't have a man by choice. I wasn't stuntin' no niggas unless his name was Luxury. That was the only nigga I wanted, and nobody could compare to him. My infatuation grew every time I saw him. I wanted him so bad. It didn't seem like he liked me like that, though. He never requested a lap dance from me. He would toss money when I was onstage, but that was it. That was the only kind of attention he gave me.

The last time I saw him, he was in VIP, but then he disappeared too fast. I never knew when he was coming up there. Some nights, I would stare at the door, hoping he would walk in. I dreamed he requested a dance and I ground on him while whispering why he should fuck with me.

After three years, I really needed to stop trying to get his attention, because that shit wasn't working. Since I couldn't have Luxury like I wanted to, I fucked whomever I wanted when I wanted, but I was absolutely not interested in tricks. I never fucked for money. I wasn't a prostitute. I never fucked nobody up in that bitch, period. Not knocking those hoes who were down for the shit, but I simply felt like I made enough money without having to lie on my back to get it.

On my twenty-first birthday, I didn't want to go to work, but my other plans had fallen through. As it turned out, the one night I wanted Mina to hang with me, she couldn't find a damn babysitter, and so she couldn't leave the house.

"What am I supposed to do now?" I asked while looking in my closet for something to wear. "We supposed to be going out tonight. How come Zay can't watch her?"

"Girl, he ain't even here. Look, go make some money and then get some dick or somethin'. I'll make it up to you, I promise. See you tomorrow." She hung up before I could beg.

Get some dick? Dick was the last thing on my mind. The two niggas I let slide through every now and then had brought me birthday wishes. One had given me roses, and the other had given me a teddy bear. I had thanked them with a kiss, had made up a lie about being on my period, and had sent them on their way. I could go out by myself, but I wasn't in the mood for that.

Making some money didn't sound like a bad idea. Instead of going to bed, I decided to get in the shower. I washed every inch of my body with Caress Daily Silk body wash. I loved the way it smelled. I took a thirty-minute shower and got out. I tossed on my black joggers from Pink, a black halter top that said BITCH, and black and red Jordans. After I threw my hair in a sloppy bun, I grabbed my purse and keys. I texted Mina as I was going out the door.

Me: Going to work 'cause you suck, sucka.

Mina: I love you too, bitch. We'll celebrate this weekend. Night.

I rolled my eyes and left my apartment. I hopped into my car and headed to the club. When I walked into Queen's, Rich Homie Quan's song "Flex" was playing. I walked straight to the back to change into my yellow two-piece, which accentuated my ass perfectly, and let my hair down. I was ready to hit the floor. After I locked my locker, I started to walk out of the dressing room.

Just then Syn strutted toward me, naked, and said, "Hey, Desire."

"What the fuck you want, Syn?" I snapped.

"Damn, bitch. What's your problem tonight?"

Syn was five feet one, a short, thick bitch. She was beautiful, with her hair as red as cherry Kool-Aid, and niggas loved it.

I let out a long sigh. "It's my birthday, and I should be out partying. Instead, I'm stuck here."

"You talk to Queen about taking the night off?"

"I had the night off, but I don't have shit to do. Mina couldn't get a babysitter, and that fucked up my plans."

"Damn, that sucks. Well, shit, make that money, boo. And Happy Birthday. How old are you?"

"Thank you. I'm twenty-one," I answered, letting my real age slip out. Shit, I was supposed to be twenty-one three years ago. "I mean, I'm twenty-four."

She laughed. "Don't act like everybody ain't know you were only eighteen when you started shaking yo' ass on that stage. Girl, everybody was eighteen when they started taking off they clothes for money."

"Oh . . . Is it poppin' out there tonight?"

"You know it's always poppin'." She paused. "Luxury is out there," she said with a grin. "He just told me to come get you, and that's why I came back here."

"He asked about me?" I scowled, finding that hard to believe.

"Yeah, he did. I was giving him a lap dance, and he said, 'Get Desire.'"

"Like that?" My eyebrows rose in doubt.

"Straight like that. He's over in his usual VIP section, near the bar."

"His brothers with him?"

"You askin' too many questions, bitch. Go out there and find out."

I rolled my eyes and walked out of the dressing room. I scanned the place as I walked, but when I reached Luxury's usual spot, he wasn't there. Where did he go? Did this nigga ask for me and then leave? I took a deep breath and exhaled, feeling irritated from his shenanigans.

Some dude signaled for me to give him a lap dance, and I didn't hesitate, because I didn't see Luxury's ass anywhere. The stranger put the money in my thong, and I went to work. I rolled my hips slowly to Future's "Where Ya At." When I felt his dick get hard, I knew he had better pull out some more money before the DJ cut to the next song.

Out of nowhere, I heard Luxury's voice. "Fuck. You workin' that nigga like you a muhfuckin' pro. Ooh-wee."

I looked up at Luxury with a smirk on my face. If he had come to see me more often, he would've known that I was a pro. The DJ cut the song, and my three minutes were up. I got up from the guy's lap as he placed a few crumpled twenties in my bra. I smiled down at him before my eyes landed back on Luxury.

I was hoping Luxury would request a lap dance of his own, so he could really see what kind of tricks I had up my sleeve, but when he didn't say anything, I walked away. He was playing games and wasting my time.

"So, you just gone walk away from me?" he called.

I turned around and faced his fine ass. "I haven't seen you in so long, I almost forgot what you look like."

"Ah, now you got jokes? It's been a minute, but I ain't forgot about ya. Ain't it your twenty-first birthday?"

I tried my best not to look surprised that he had remembered my birthday or even how old I really was, but I guessed I didn't hide my shocked expression too well, because he gave me the biggest grin, with those deep-ass dimples begging for my affection. He took a bundle of one hundred-dollar bills out of his pocket as he walked toward me.

"I came to give you a birthday present." He placed the money in my free hand. "I know you've been working your ass off for the past three years. You've been holding your own. Niggas can't get enough of Desire. I told you."

Flipping through the bundle of bills, I bit my lower lip. There were at least forty Benjamin Franklins. This was one night of work, without busting a sweat or popping my pussy for him.

"Damn," I said under my breath, but he heard me.

"Let's get out of here. You down?" he said.

"Yeah," I heard myself say, still in disbelief. "Let me get changed and tell Queen I'm out."

"I'll be at the front."

I walked to my locker, changed back into my joggers. I took out Queen's percentage from the lap dance before putting the rest of my money in my purse and locking my locker. Then I left the dressing room. Once I reached Queen's office, I knocked on the door.

"Come in," I heard her say.

I walked in, and Queen was standing there with Rob, one of the bouncers. Queen looked as if she had been cussing his ass out. She was always cussing somebody out. Queen, nine times out of ten, was an unpleasant woman. She was not that old, but she was straight from the old school and had the mind of a pimp from the seventies. The strands of her short blond wig limply framed her aging face. Her forehead was wrinkled and had many peaks and trenches, caused by years of constant frowning, and her eyes permanently harbored a glare full of disdain. Her entire face always looked drained of any signs of joy and amusement.

Those who thought Queen was nothing but an old-ass woman would quickly be reminded why they called her Queen. She would beat anybody's ass with that steel bat of hers, and I had been a witness to that a few times. I didn't fuck with her. I made sure to stay on her cool side. Matter of fact, I liked to think that I was one of her favorites.

"You changed your mind about working?" she asked, glaring at my dressed-down attire.

"Yeah, other plans surfaced. I did one lap dance, though. Here you go." I tried to hand her the money, but she rejected it as she put her hand up.

"It's your birthday. Go, get out of here, and enjoy it."

"It's your birthday?" Rob asked.

I happily put the money in my pocket and nodded. "Yeah."

"Happy Birthday, shawty."

"Thanks, Rob. See y'all later." I stepped out of Queen's office, closed her door behind me, and walked to the front of the club. I waved bye to a few girls on my way out with Luxury.

"Desire," Luxury's deep voice said as soon as we were out of the club and in the parking lot.

I didn't look at him, but a smile spread across my face.

"You can smile, but ya can't look at me? Who does that?"

"Luxury, what I need to look at you for?" I asked, feeling shy, with these butterflies swirling in my stomach like crazy.

"Look at me," he said in a gentle yet demanding voice.

I slowly looked up at him.

He didn't say anything.

I smacked my lips. "I'm looking at you, and now you ain't got shit to say? Boy, you play so fuckin' much. I can't stand you."

He chuckled a little. "A'ight. I see you got a mouth on you. You just rolled with a nigga, and I ain't even tell you where we going. You trust a nigga like that?"

"Where we going?"

"Shit, I don't even know yet. I didn't think you would even roll with me. You're big-time now. What you want to kick it with li'l me for?"

I sucked my teeth and laughed. "Wow . . . okay. I think you know exactly where you wanna take me."

He smirked and bit his lower lip all sexy-like. "Maybe."

Suddenly, I felt the need to go off on him. "Why you don't say hi to me when you come up here? You don't even request me. You gave me my stage name the first night we met, and you've barely talked to me since. It's been three years, Lux—"

"When I come up here, it's mostly for business. This is where my brothers get their inspiration for their music, but don't think I haven't been seeing you doing your thing. I'm tryin'a get to know you better and find out what's inside that pretty li'l head of yours." He unlocked the doors of his all-black Hellcat. He opened the passenger door for me.

My baby got manners, I thought. I got into his car, and he went around to the driver's side without closing me in. I shook my head and pulled the handle to close the door myself. *Well, a few manners.*

"Lavish is having a kickback at his house," he said as soon as he started up the car.

The Hellcat was loud when it roared. With its supercharged V8 Hemi engine, the Hellcat had power, and the sound of the engine instantly turned me on. Luxury reached into the middle compartment and pulled out a Glock and tucked it into his waist.

"Couldn't bring my shit with all the metal detectors up in that bitch. I keep my thang on me at all times."

I nodded, because most niggas around here were always strapped.

"You want me to go with you to Lavish's li'l kickback?" I asked him.

"Yeah. Is that good with you?"

I didn't want to feel salty, but I was disappointed. I had thought he wanted to go to dinner or somewhere nice so we could finally be alone. I stared at my joggers and sighed, "I'm not even dressed for all that."

"Look in the backseat." He turned on the light on the ceiling so I could see into the backseat. A white box with a red bow was sitting there. The box looked a little big for one piece of clothing. "That's for you."

I looked at him. "Okay, wait. How did you even know I was working tonight?"

"Why you think Mina couldn't get a babysitter? I told her to make sure you made it down here tonight."

"Oh, so that was you? My own best friend was in on it and didn't say shit to me about it."

"I wanted to surprise you." He reached into the backseat, grabbed the box, and put it in my lap. "Open it."

My hands were shaking. I wasn't expecting any of this. I pulled the top off the box and pulled out a hunter-green halter jumpsuit. It was cute as hell. Underneath was a pair of ankle-strapped silver stilettos.

"Did Mina help you pick this out?"

"Nah. What? You think I don't know how to shop for a woman?"

"I don't think any man can unless he's gay."

"Hell nah, I ain't gay. I know what will look good on the li'l Spanish mami. If you roll with me, you will wear only the finest and flyest."

I bit my lower lip and put everything back in the box. "Where am I supposed to get dressed? Right here?"

"Let me run you home really fast so you can get dressed. Little Havana, right?"

"Wynwood."

"I thought you lived in Little Havana. What side of Wynwood?"

"I stay near Biscayne. I'm from Little Havana, but that ain't where I live. Just drive, and I'll show you the way."

He turned up some music for the ride. I nodded my head. I had heard the song on the radio many times. The Monnahan Boyz had had their first radio hit, and the beat was hard. I loved it. It took about fourteen minutes as I guided him to my complex. He pulled up to the curb and turned down the music.

"I'll be waiting right here. I got a call to make," he said.

"Okay." I thought he would want to come inside, but there he was, on that weird shit.

"Don't take long," he ordered.

I snapped, "I won't. Are you always such a bossy ass?"

"Always." He smiled.

I shook my head, hopped out, entered my building, and walked briskly to my door, which was a little way down the hall.

Once inside my apartment, I headed into my bedroom and plopped the box down on my bed. I went into my bathroom and washed up quickly, hitting my hot spots. I put on some lotion, deodorant, and perfume before slipping into the jumpsuit. I snapped off the tag carefully and put on the shoes. Everything fit perfectly. I shook my head, thinking about how Mina had managed to keep this from me. I grabbed my phone out of my purse and called her on speakerphone.

"Hello?" she said, sounding as if she was wide awake.

"Bitch, you are so fired. I thought yo' ass was tired."

"The baby is asleep, so I decided to watch a movie with Zay. Wait, where you at?"

I pulled my hair into a high ponytail. "I'm at home, getting dressed. Why didn't you tell me Luxury wanted to kick it with me tonight?"

She laughed. "Ah, so he showed up? What he get you?"

"Fuck all that. We supposed to be best friends, and you hid this from me, bitch."

"I sure did. Just in case that nigga didn't come through. I wasn't in the mood to hear you bitchin' and complainin' if he pulled one of his disappearing acts. Hurry up and tell me what he got you."

"This fly-ass jumpsuit and silver stilettos. I'm glad you told him my size, 'cause the shit fits perfectly. And he gave me four bands."

"What? He asked me only your shoe size. He ain't say he was gonna do all that. Wait, where he at right now?"

"He's outside, waiting for me."

"Girl, you better hurry up. I'm hanging up right now. I don't need you calling me, talking about how Luxury left yo' ass."

I frowned as I wet my hair with the brush and water from the faucet to smooth my ponytail into a bun. "He would leave me?"

She laughed. "You got a lot to learn about Mr. Luxury. His time is precious, and he has no patience, so get yo' ass up outta there right now."

Before I could respond, she hung up. I brushed my hair quickly into that bun at the top of my head, making sure not a hair was out of place. I grabbed my purse and locked up my spot. When I got back into the car, he was sending a text message to somebody.

"Hope that didn't take too long."

"Nah, you straight." He looked up from his phone to gaze at me. He didn't smile or anything. He just stared.

"Thank you for everything . . . the money, the outfit," I said.

"I know it's not much, but you know, I loved the surprised look on your face. That made my night." He started up the car and pulled away from the curb.

I tried my hardest to stop myself from smiling so broadly, but I couldn't help it. I smiled so much, my cheeks were starting to hurt.

5

DESIRE

Lavish's Pad

Luxury pulled up to what looked like a mini-mansion. We got out of the car after he parked. I followed closely behind him as he walked up to the front door.

"Why you back there?" he asked.

I shrugged, feeling my insides turn over. I needed a shot of something, but I didn't like to drink like that, not even when I took my clothes off every night and danced. The girls at the club thought I was a super freak because I could strip sober. It was just a job to me. I saw how liquor had them looking sloppy and loose. Niggas took advantage of drunk hoes, and I had vowed that would never be me. I didn't need a reason to be taken of advantage of, so I knew my limits.

He gently pulled my arm so that I was standing beside him. "You nervous or somethin'?" he asked, ringing the doorbell. Before I could answer, he said in the sexiest tone I'd ever heard, "Don't be nervous, babe."

The massive front door opened, and the smell of weed hit me in the face. I tried not to look as if I smelled a skunk's spray, but that shit stank so bad.

"Hey, Luxury is here," Frill announced, with his blunt hanging from his lips, and a few dreads hanging in his face. "Come in, bruh," he said before slapping hands with him. "What took ya ass so . . . Yo, is this . . . ?"

"Desirae," Luxury said, stepping inside. "You know her, don't you?"

I followed him inside the house, thinking it sounded weird for him to call me by my real name. Honestly, I hadn't heard anyone call me by my actual name in years.

"You mean Desire," Frill said, correcting his brother. "Yeah, I know her."

It was crazy how Frill had been all up in Queen's, and yet he was still underage, only nineteen. Two years behind me, he had been only sixteen years old when I first started dancing. He had requested me once, and I had given him a lap dance. People went crazy for him because he stood out as the better rapper when compared to Lavish.

Frill led us to the living room. Music played in the background but was not too loud. His dreads French braided to the back, Lavish was sitting on one of the couches, smoking a weed-filled hookah with three other chicks.

"Hey, everybody, this is Desire," Frill announced. "Desire, you already know Lavish. That's Lala, our stylist . . . That's Nia, our barber. And that's Egypt, our personal assistant. These our homegirls."

Everyone said, "What's up?" The ladies smiled, but I felt a little awkward. Though Frill had said these bitches were their homegirls, the guy to girl ratio was now off: four bitches and three niggas. I took a good look at these "homegirls" to see which one was supposed to be there for Luxury.

Lala had golden brown skin and long, flowing jet-black hair, and baby hairs swirled around her hairline. She was dressed in distressed jean shorts and a green-and-white sparkly shirt with the words *Pretty Girl*. She was puffing on that hookah, looking at me.

Nia was about the same shade of brown as Lala. She was rocking a cute blond bob that was parted down the middle. Everything about that bob said she was a hairstylist. It was one of the best lace-front wigs I had ever seen. She was wearing an airbrushed purple and blue jean jacket and had a black bra on underneath it, and she also sported black spandex booty shorts. The way she was all up on Lavish, I could tell she was fucking him.

Egypt was light skinned and had a short wavy cut. Her hair texture made her look mixed. She was wearing a yellow spandex dress with spaghetti straps. Her toenails matched her dress. She reminded me of a young Mariah Carey, especially her face. The way she was mugging me had me staring right back at her. She might've been the one who had a thing for Luxury, but I couldn't tell yet.

"You can have a seat on the couch right here," Luxury told me. "You want a cocktail or something?"

"What y'all got?" I asked, feeling like I really needed a little something to take the edge off.

"I'll bring you something," he replied and then walked with Frill to the kitchen, which was only an island away.

I sat down on the empty couch.

"Hey, I been sayin' she's sexy as fuck. That ass, though," I could hear Frill say to Luxury. "You know that's my crush right there."

"Cool it, li'l nigga. That's me. I already told you that." Luxury went through the cabinets to find some cups. When he saw them, he went to the freezer for some ice.

"That's you? Since when?" Frill scoffed.

"Since now, bruh. You gotta find you a new crush now."

I smiled on the inside. Luxury was putting a claim on me. That was sweet, but I hoped he didn't think an outfit and a couple of bands was all it would take. Shit, he had made me wait for three years, so I was going to make him work a little harder if he wanted to claim me.

"How long you've been knowing Luxury?" the assistant, Egypt, asked me.

I fluttered my eyelids as I looked at her. I was about to give her a smart-ass answer, but I didn't get a chance.

Luxury responded from the kitchen, "We've known each other for three years. Hey, it's Desire's birthday, so show her some love."

"Happy Birthday," Lala and Nia said in unison.

With a fake smile on her face, Egypt replied, "I don't usually see her at kickbacks or parties with you. I was just asking."

Luxury acted like he didn't hear her.

"Don't you work at Queen of Diamonds?" Lala asked after taking a puff of the hookah.

I nodded without speaking.

"Okay, that's where I heard your name. You're a stripper." Lala snapped her fingers. "I thought you looked familiar."

"The best muhfuckin' stripper Queen's got right now. Happy Birthday, Desire," Frill shouted and then downed a shot. "Lav, why you ain't talkin'?"

"Nigga, I'm enjoyin' my high." Lavish lit a blunt and took two drags. He stood up and walked over to hand it to me. "Happy Birthday, though, young stunna."

I put my hand up. "Thank you, but I don't smoke."

Lavish shrugged and exhaled smoke. He stood there, glaring down at me. "Where ya girl Exxxotic at?"

He always requested her when he was at Queen's, and from time to time, they fucked. Everybody at Queen's knew this. Mina had admitted to giving him a blow job a couple of times to pay a few bills.

"She's at home with her family tonight," I said, trying to make sure he understood that what happened at the club stayed at the club.

He didn't respond as Luxury handed me a brownish-pink drink in a transparent plastic cup.

"What's this?" I asked.

"Henny and Red Bull mixed with a splash of cranberry."

Luxury held a cup of straight Henny as he sat next to me.

"At least you drink," Lavish said after letting some smoke exit through his mouth and nose. "I was about to say, Luxury why you bring this square-ass bitch up in here?"

The three women laughed like what he had said was so funny.

I rolled my eyes and took a sip of my drink. I had never had this mixture before, and it was good. I tried not to take offense to Lavish calling me a square-ass bitch.

Luxury said, looking into my eyes, "Don't let this fucked-up-ass nigga or any nigga get you to do some shit you don't do." His eyes moved from my eyes to my plump lips. Then they traveled to my titties, my small waist, and my thick thighs. "You fine just the way you are."

I smiled at him.

Lavish said, "We goin' downstairs or what? Y'all niggas playin'."

Frill yelled, "Hell yeah. I got some heat to lay down. Let's go."

The girls hopped up from the couch and followed Frill and Lavish to a door just past the kitchen.

"What's downstairs?" I asked. My mind instantly was on some freaky shit. I'd seen some orgies pop off out of nowhere before, but I wasn't down with no dungeon freak-type shit.

"The studio," Luxury informed me.

I felt relieved and excited at the same time. Who wouldn't want to see the Monnahan Boyz in their element?

"Luxury, you rap? I ain't never heard you on a track before," I said.

"Nah, I'm the CEO. I don't rhyme. I'm the nigga with the most money. Remember that, baby."

I nodded and sipped my yummy drink. I was feeling a little buzz. "I heard the fuck outta that. I likes that."

"I know you do, baby. Come on."

When we got downstairs, loud music blared through the speakers. Lavish had a bomb-ass studio. It wasn't one of those "just starting out" basement studios. I had been in plenty of those in my day. This was some professional shit. The girls were dancing as Frill was rapping in the booth and Lavish was sitting at the board. Luxury and I sat on the couch and bobbed our heads. I had thought it would be hot down there, but the AC was pumping, and it felt good.

The girls were shaking their asses and snapping their fingers as they danced.

Nia pushed her blond hair behind her ear and said, "Come on, Desire. We know you know how to shake that fat ass."

I shook my head and enjoyed my drink, which was nearly gone. I wanted a refill but didn't say anything. I crunched on the ice.

"Who gone get up in here and spit?" Frill asked to the beat. "E?"

"You know I can't rap," Egypt shouted and laughed. "That's why I'm the assistant. I leave the rapping to the rappers."

"Get in here, birthday girl. Let's see what you got," Frill called.

I hopped up. I had played around a lot in the studio with this one dude I had dated the year before. I had freestyled a few times. I didn't think I was good, but I was feeling myself. I handed my cup to Luxury. I sashayed over to the booth, stepped inside, and put on the headphones.

"Okay, y'all, don't laugh at me," I said into the mic, with a serious face. "I ain't done this in a minute. Let me see if I still got it."

Everybody was already looking like they were ready to laugh at my first line.

"Give me a dope beat, Lav," I said, looking at him.

"A'ight," he replied and put on the next track.

The hard-hitting trap sound came through the speakers. Closing my eyes, I pretended that no one was in that booth but me. I nodded my head for a few counts before I started.

"Aye yo, I'm the new baddest bitch in the game. She goes by the name d-e-s . . . i-r-e. And ain't no other bitch as fine as me. *Yo quiero estar contigo. Tu quieres estar conmigo.* Money, money, money always on my mind. Gimme a can of Sprite with a twist of lime. My flow be bringin' all the boys to the yard. I am such a fuckin' lady, let me do my curtsy. Fuck a dry-pussy bitch 'cause she stay thirsty."

I tossed off the headphones and walked out of the booth, laughing my ass off. I was the only one laughing. Lavish was nodding his head as he played it back. I hated the way my voice sounded. I shook my head as I sat down next to Luxury.

"Look what y'all made me do. I sound goofy as hell," I said, then laughed.

"Nah, you killed that shit," Frill said. "You rap before?"

"Kind of, but I . . . just be fuckin' around."

Luxury was staring at me as if he was impressed. "Hey, Spanish mami got hidden talents. Not only can you entertain with your dance moves, but you also know how to rhyme. Why you stop? You should've kept goin', baby."

"Nah, I don't really like to rap."

"I liked that Spanish part, though," Luxury said.

I giggled. "You did? What I say?"

"I want to be with you. You want to be with me." He nodded. "That shit sounded sexy as fuck."

"You speak Spanish?" I asked in surprise.

"*Muyyy poco*," he answered, overpronouncing the words.

I laughed again. "Yeah, okay. I see you."

Suddenly, the music was cut off. Lavish spun around in the chair and looked dead at me. "Desire, you got heat, playing around or not. We need our first female on this label. There ain't too many females killin' the game, and it would be dope as fuck if we had another out of Miami, *and* you speak Spanish. We would kill the fuckin' game."

I shook my head. "Come on. Now, y'all straight pumpin' my head up. It wasn't all that. I just let off whatever came into my head."

"That's what makes the shit hot. What if Frill writes a song for you? Will you record it? At least try it out?" Luxury said. "Lav can produce it, and Frill can be featured on it."

What was he talking about? I was just joking around, but by the looks on everyone's faces, they truly were feeling it.

"Can I think about it?" I heard myself say.

I had never thought about rapping or being a rapper for real, but it was something I could think over, especially if that meant I would get to hang out with Luxury.

"Yeah, but don't keep us waiting too long," Lavish said. "Let Luxury know when you ready."

"Okay."

Luxury looked at his watch and said, "A'ight, y'all. We about to roll out."

"Bye," the chicks said and waved.

Luxury stood up from the couch and grabbed my hand. After I stood, he gave Lavish and Frill a hand hug. I made sure to grab my purse before we headed up the stairs.

"Where we going now?" I asked.

"Let's go chill at my place. Is that cool?"

"I'm down."

"Yeah, you always down, huh?"

"All day, every day. Down like two flat tires."

He chuckled. "You so goddamned cute. Let's ride."

6

DESIRE

Livin' in the Lap of Luxury

I would always be down so I could be with him. I wanted to get out of these clothes, get comfy, and lie down. The liquor had me feeling sleepy, and I yawned as we got in his car. We drove for only about eight minutes as he lived up near the next freeway exit. When he pulled up to his house, I couldn't stop staring. I thought Lavish's pad was nice, but Luxury's crib outdid his brother's by far in terms of its size.

We got out of the car and walked up the stairs to his front door. As soon as he unlocked the front door and we stepped inside, I took off my shoes and left them at the door.

I smiled. "Your house is nice."

His marble floors and that staircase with the crystal chandelier that hung from the high-ass ceiling had me in awe.

"Thanks. I just copped this, like, a few weeks ago. It's taking some getting used to because it's so big, you know."

I followed him up the stairs, looking around as I went. I wouldn't mind spending all my spare time here if he wanted me to. Once we were in his bedroom, I smiled. It was everything I imagined a king's bedroom would look like. King-size bed, sixty-inch flat-screen on the wall, brown suede sitting bench in front of the bed. Blown-up pictures of the Monnahan Boyz onstage were plastered on the walls.

His bedroom smelled so good, just like his cologne, but my clothes stank from all that weed smoke.

"Is to cool if I take a shower?" I asked him.

"Knock yourself out." Luxury took his gun out of his waist and placed it in the top drawer of his dresser. He went into his bathroom to turn on the light for me. Then he invited me in, handed me two towels and a white robe, and left me alone.

I wished he had stayed to shower with me. I could've said something to that effect, but he left the bathroom before I could muster up the courage to ask.

Before I got undressed, I took a picture of myself in his bathroom mirror and saved it. I was tempted to post it on my Instagram, but I didn't want him to see it, so I didn't do it. I was just so excited to be with Luxury in his house. I already knew we were about to fuck. Well, at least that was what I wanted to do. I was ready to put it on him. As bad as I wanted to text Mina right now, I was going to have to give her the full scoop in the morning.

I took off my clothes, jumped in the shower, and washed with his silky shower gel. It was a man's fragrance, but I didn't care, because I wanted to smell like him. I turned off the water, stepped out of the shower, and dried off. Then I put on the robe and walked into his bedroom.

Luxury was lighting a candle on a chocolate cupcake with a sliced strawberry on top.

"Awww," I said. "You gone sing to me?"

"I can't sing for shit, but, uh, Happy Birthday. You gonna blow out the candle?"

I stood in front of him, closed my eyes, made a wish, and blew the candle out. I picked up the strawberry and put it into my mouth. He popped a bottle of rosé champagne and poured some into a flute. As he handed it to me, I caught sight of a nightie lying in the middle of the bed.

"Is that what you want me to wear?"

"Yup."

"This has been the best birthday, hands down. You definitely surprised me."

"I meant to holla at you a while ago." He kept his body close to mine.

"And say what?"

"When I met you, you were too young for me, but I thought you were fine as hell. I wanted to see what you were about first before I got your number."

"Oh, like if I was one of those girls fuckin' and suckin' dick for a dollar?"

He smirked. "Nah. Well, I wanted to see what you were made of. I ain't never heard no bad shit 'bout you or seen no shit I ain't like. You work hard, and I've watched you even when it seemed like I wasn't. You have every right to be happy about your accomplishments."

"I am happy. I need my job."

"Nah." He shook his head, staring into my eyes. "The only thing you *need* is me." He stared deeply into my eyes now. "You like taking off your clothes for money?"

I shrugged. "I make a shitload of money doing it. Look, I know people look at me crazy, but—"

He cut me off. "What if I told you I have a way for you never to step foot in the strip club again, unless it's for your own pleasure? You definitely wouldn't be stripping if it were up to me."

"But it's not up to you."

He squinted his eyes. "Why are you so guarded? You don't like to open up to folk, huh? I'm not sure if it's because of your past or whatnot, but after seeing you rapping in that booth tonight . . . Real talk, I see so much potential in you. You're too talented, and you don't even know it."

I drank some champagne and hummed as I went over to his bed to look at the lingerie. It was a short see-through black gown with lace panties and bra. I looked to see the size of the bra and discovered this nigga had my exact size.

"You had all this planned for me?"

He nodded and drank straight from the champagne bottle. "I already had intentions of making you mine. I was just waiting for the right opportunity . . . You know, I've helped my brothers become stars, and I can make you one too. We can make millions together."

"Don't you already make millions?"

"Not yet, but I'm so close, I can taste it."

I gulped the champagne until the flute was empty. After placing the flute on one of the bedside tables, I removed my robe and let it hit the floor. I stood there naked, waiting for him to come and touch me.

His eyes never left mine as he said, "You wanna know what else I see in you?" He didn't give me a chance to reply. "You've been through some shit, but you ain't never hit rock bottom before. It won't take much to break you, but you like to pretend that you're strong. There's shit you can't handle, but you think you can. It's dangerous in these streets. You ain't seen the dirty side of the strippin' business. You ain't never been raped or taken advantage of, and to be honest, you have put yourself in situations where you could've been. I know that ain't the life for you. I think you deserve more than what you've been giving yourself . . . Put the robe back on."

Feeling embarrassed, I put the robe back on and folded my arms across my chest. I lowered my head, not knowing what to say.

He came over to me and lifted my chin so that I could look into his eyes. "Don't you ever lower your head, baby. I want you to imagine more for yourself. Fa sho', yo' body is making you money right now, but what about in five or ten years? You think your titties will still sit up perky?"

"They better. If they don't, I'm suing the doctor. Easy." I pulled away from him and took two steps back.

"You sho' got a smart-ass mouth, don't you?"

"Whatever," I replied, feeling confused as to why he had invited me to come here.

"A lot of women would kill to have the face and body you got. It will make them even more envious when you become famous. I'm attracted to you, so don't think I'm not. I'm also attracted to what we can be—a power couple, the ghetto version of Will Smith and Jada Pinkett."

I hummed and said, "That sounds nice."

"You don't believe it, though. What's your dream?"

"My dream?"

"Yeah, your dream. What do you want out of life?"

"My dream is to own a penthouse apartment overlooking South Beach, a white-on-white Range Rover, and to have more money than I can count."

"And you can have all of that. Listen, if I don't make you a star in the next six months, then you can stay at the strip club and keep doing what you're doing."

"Sounds good. You want to know what else I dream about?"

"What?" he asked, looking deep into my eyes.

"You. I dream I belong to you." As soon as I said it, I almost felt like I hadn't. Luxury was unpredictable. Not sure how he would take it, I watched his reaction.

He bit his lower lip and then drank from the bottle. He nodded, as if he liked the sound of that. He took two steps toward me and slid his hand into my bathrobe. He palmed my bare ass. "You belong to me now, you know that?"

I shook my head slowly. "Nah, I belong to *me*. You gotta earn all of this, playa."

"You don't think I earned it tonight?" He smirked, with one eyebrow raised.

"What? 'Cause you gave me a night's pay, an outfit, shoes, and lingerie?" I scoffed.

"Don't forget the cupcake and the bottle of rosé." His hand was still on my ass, and he gave it a squeeze.

I laughed, and so did he. His laugh was adorable.

"I'm serious, Luxury. Don't get me wrong. You've shown me so much love tonight, but if I'm gonna be yours, I gotta be the only one."

"You don't think I know that about you?"

"So, you sayin' you ready to be my man?"

"I'm already your man. Stop talkin' crazy."

I felt his fingers travel to the inner folds of my pussy. I spread my legs so he could get in there better. I moaned as two of his fingers played with my clit.

"I want a taste," he whispered in my ear.

I shivered, feeling the anticipation throb between my legs, as soon as those words left his thick lips. I was wet as I took a deep breath. I didn't want to control the sensations taking place between the sweet folds of my pussy. Just hearing him say what he wanted had me on the brink of exploding.

"I *need* a taste," he said, but he didn't wait for me to say anything.

In one swift motion, he picked me up and carried me to the bed, then gently placed me on my back. I watched him as I listened to my breathing become heavier. Luxury pulled off his shirt and tossed it on the floor. Keeping his eyes on mine, he spread my legs apart. As soon as two of his fingers pushed inside me, I drew in a deep breath.

"Mmm," he moaned as he sucked on the same two fingers that had been inside me. He pushed my legs farther apart. His tongue made rings around my clit.

I felt a head high instantly. "Ooh," I cooed.

My pussy had got eaten plenty of times, but Luxury was making love with his tongue. His hands slid under me and palmed my ass, then pushed me forward so he could be completely submerged. He moaned, sucked, and licked at my clit. He inhaled my juices as if he was so fucking thirsty and I was quenching his thirst. With my ass still gripped firmly, he twirled and swirled that velvet tongue to make figure eights. After each figure eight, a moan escaped my mouth. I was feeling pure ecstasy. He stuck his tongue deep inside me, and I grabbed the back of his head. I arched my back and lifted one leg to rest it on his shoulder. My orgasm came upon me too fast. I couldn't hold it in.

"Don't you dare hold that shit in. Come on my muh-fuckin' face," he demanded as he continued to suck on my swollen clit.

"Mmm," I moaned as my juices seeped out with each wave that came over my body. He was pulling it all out of me until I let it all go.

I was trying to catch my breath when he went to his dresser. I heard him fumbling with a condom wrapper. He took off the rest of his clothes. Before I could catch my breath, he was on top of me, giving me deep kisses. My body was on fire, as if he had set a match to my ass. As soon as he was inside me, the intensity from what his tongue had already done had me ready to cum. I clutched his back with both hands. He moved in and out, looking into my eyes. I was coming again.

"This pussy is mine," he declared.

"Yesss." *Finally*, I thought to myself. "It's all yours."

I had one of the most powerful orgasms, one that I had never experienced. As much as I wanted to jump on top of him and ride that dick until neither of us could move, I let him do his thing. The way he pumped and stroked, I couldn't do anything but tremble. We were both sweaty. As soon as we came together, he climbed off me. He pulled the condom off and got out of bed. He went to the trash can in the bathroom and threw the condom away. Next, I could hear him taking a piss.

"See what happens when we get intoxicated," I called to him.

"Only the best things, baby." He flushed the toilet, washed his hands, dried them, and then returned to bed.

He bent down and kissed me, slipping his tongue into my mouth, before he pulled on my bottom lip. "Mmm. Your lips are everything, li'l mama."

I pushed him on his back, and then I grabbed his shaft and ran my tongue across the head. "I bet they feel like everything right now too."

"Hell yeah," he said, then exhaled with a moan.

I worked him with my tongue before putting him all the way in my mouth. I could do this all night long.

I woke up in Luxury's bed, my hair all over my head. The sun was fighting to shine through his closed thick-paneled shutters. I wondered what time it was, but it didn't matter. Mornings, I usually slept in. I didn't really function until the late afternoon. Working nights did that to me. Luxury was still asleep next to me, and as I stared down at him, I still couldn't believe I was here with him. I propped my head on my hand, and I admired how handsome he was even while sleeping.

As soon as he fluttered his eyes and opened them, I said, "Wake that ass up."

"Not yet." He pulled me to him so I could rest on his chest. "You in *my* bed. I get up when I'm ready. Now, if we were in your bed, then maybe I would take orders from you. Next time, I'm sleepin' at yo' spot."

"What makes you think there will be a next time?" I teased.

He peeked at me through one eye. "I already told you that you belong to me, so stop playin'."

I giggled and rubbed his washboard for a stomach. The thin hairs that made a trail down to his belly button had me running over them repeatedly.

"You cooking us breakfast?" I asked.

"Sounds good, but, uh, I don't cook. If you want breakfast, just tell me what you want, and I'll have Egypt go get it."

I shook my head, because I wasn't trying to see no bitch. I would be damned if the next bitch delivered breakfast to my man. "Nah. I'll just cook us breakfast."

"Let me find out you can cook, but shit, I ain't got one pot to cook in, and I ain't got no groceries, so that's out."

"How you gone have a bomb-ass kitchen like that and no pots or pans? I don't want to order out. I want to cook in your nice brand-new kitchen. I should be the first to break that bad boy in."

"Hop up real quick," he said to get me to give up my position resting on his chest.

I sat up, naked. I hadn't had a chance to put on that cute little nightie he'd bought me. As soon as that robe had been pulled off, there hadn't been a need to put anything on.

He climbed out of bed and went to his top drawer. He was wearing his boxers. I hadn't realized he'd put them on, but then again, it seemed to me that I had fallen asleep before he had. He went through his wallet, came back over to the bed, and handed me his debit card.

"The car keys are on the table by the door. Don't take my Hellcat. There's a car in the garage. Go buy whatever. This breakfast better be all that too. Don't be for real burnin' shit up. I'm going back to sleep. Wake me up when it's done."

He climbed back into bed and lay on his side, facing me. I planted a kiss on his lips before easing out of bed. I put his card next to my purse and headed to the bathroom to wash up.

"Bae, there's a brand-new toothbrush in the medicine cabinet," he called after me. "If you need something to wear, take a look in that closet on the other side of the bathroom."

"Okay."

I went to the medicine cabinet first to get the toothbrush. After brushing my teeth, I took a quick shower. Then I went into the closet, and when I turned on the light, my jaw nearly hit the floor. The walk-in closet had a vast array of women's clothes with Chanel, Balmain, Fendi, and Givenchy labels. Louboutin, Gucci, and Balenciaga shoes were neatly arranged on shelves that ran from the ceiling to the floor. I looked at the shoe size. My size. I checked the tags of the clothes. My size again. Then I noticed a case of jewelry with a glass panel. I peered through the glass and saw women's watches, rings, bracelets. What the hell was all this? I walked briskly out of the closet and out of the bathroom. What kind of games was he playing? I started imagining that a woman lived in this house, and I felt jealous. He had me fucked up if he thought I was about to play dress up in the next bitch's shit.

Luxury was snoring lightly. I didn't want to wake him up, but I had to know what was going on.

I walked right up to the bed. "Luxury."

He stopped snoring. "Huh?"

"Why the fuck you got some bitch's clothes and shit up in here? Who the fuck you live here with, nigga?"

"What? Baby, them yo' clothes and shit."

My heart felt like it hit the bottom of my stomach. "Mine? You bought all that for me?"

"Are you going to the store or not?"

I felt giddy with excitement. I wanted to run, to shout, to tell the world what Luxury had done to make my birthday weekend special. I couldn't wait to tell Mina. This tingly feeling ran straight through me. Nobody had ever done anything like this for me in my life.

I jumped on the bed and showered his face with kisses. "What am I going to do with you? All these damn surprises."

"I already told you what's up. Now, get yo' ass up and hurry back, 'cause now you got a nigga's stomach growling."

"When I get back, you better be out of bed."

He chuckled, then turned serious as he shouted, "Go."

I hopped off the bed and jumped in the shower. I washed up within ten minutes. I got out and dried off. I put on lotion quickly before running into the closet. I found a cute pair of Gucci joggers and a matching T-shirt. I shook my head, with a huge smile on my face, because we weren't even an item yet, but he had picked things for me that he wanted me to wear. I slid into a pair of sandals. Everything was mine. I felt like I was in a dream. If it was a dream, I didn't want to wake up.

I went back into the bathroom to fix my hair. There was an unused brush and comb sitting on the counter. I smiled when it dawned on me that he had thought of everything. I turned on the water, wet the brush, and then ran it over my hair to slick it into a ponytail. As soon as I was done, I went back into the bedroom. Luxury hadn't moved, and I didn't want to bother him. I grabbed the debit card and my purse and headed down the stairs, smiling the whole way. I couldn't wait to tell Mina everything. I took the car keys from the table and opened a few closet doors in my search for the door to the garage.

When I swung the third door open and found the garage, I stopped short. Before me was a black-on-black Benz with a red bow on it.

"The fuck?" I squealed. "Is he fuckin' kiddin' me?"

To think he had done all of this before getting a piece of ass. What kind of nigga did shit like this? I walked over to the car and took off the bow, then tossed it to the side. I opened the driver's door and hopped inside, feeling like a little girl. Before I could figure out how to raise the garage door, it started opening. I looked up to see Luxury walking toward the car in a pair of black joggers.

"Start it up," he said as he stood near the open car door. "It's a push start, so push that button."

"I know," I replied, pushing the button. Tears came to my eyes, and I almost started crying. "Thank you for all of this. I don't even know what to say."

He smiled and nodded his head. "Say you love me."

I swallowed the hard lump that had formed in my throat. Had he read my mind? I had been in love with Luxury since the first time I laid eyes on him. Three years of fantasizing and yearning to belong to him, and now my heart was on fire. My whole body felt feverish.

"I love you, Luxury."

"Tell me how I know that. But you wanna know something?"

"What?"

"I love you too, Desirae." He bent down and placed a kiss on my lips.

I sucked his tongue, and he sucked mine before he pulled away.

"Awww. Don't tell me, you a mushy nigga." I laughed.

"I ain't gone lie. I got the softest spot for you. So, what store you going to?"

"Most likely Walmart. One-stop shopping."

He nodded. "Understood. Now, hurry back with yo' fine ass. You lookin' right up in that whip. Hey, the home button on the mirror is programmed to open and close the garage."

"You think of everything, don't you?"

"I do, and don't you ever forget that."

"I see you trying to turn me into a psycho, Luxury. I'll probably kill yo' ass for fucking with another bitch."

He laughed, shaking his head. "Ain't no other bitch, period. Never will be as long as you're with me. I've been waiting for you since you were eighteen . . . Don't think the psycho shit is one-sided. I'll kill somebody before I let them even think they gettin' they ass all up in my good pussy. That's my shit. *Mine*. Got that?"

I smiled, because he was turning me on. "I got you, baby."

I closed the door to the car, rolled down the window, and adjusted the mirrors before backing out.

I thought about calling Mina as soon as I was away from Luxury's house, but this was the kind of shit I had to tell her in person. I quickly made my way to Walmart. I got a set of pots and pans, the things I needed for breakfast, plus the important shit every house should have, like seasonings, dishes, and eating utensils. As much as I didn't get along with my mom, she had taught me how to cook and clean. I didn't go overboard with shopping, but I had exactly what I needed. I was back to his place within an hour.

As soon as I pulled into the garage, Luxury walked in to help me take the things in the house. He was dressed as if he was going somewhere.

"You get everything you need?" he asked.

"Yeah. You got plans?"

"Nah. I just took a shower. I'm ready for this grand breakfast you bragged about."

"I didn't brag. I said I would cook."

"Don't be coming in here with some croissants, muffins, and juice, talking about that's breakfast, either."

"Don't do me like that. That sounds like some hotel continental breakfast bullshit."

He laughed. "Okay, we'll see."

I smiled as I entered the house with my hands full. While he grabbed the other things out of the car, I started putting things away in the refrigerator and the cabinets. Every cabinet was empty, so it wasn't like I had to find where he wanted me to put stuff. As soon as the box of pots and pans was inside, I opened it, pulled everything out, and washed a couple of pots.

He took out a tray of weed from the pantry and started rolling up on the other side of the island. He eyed everything I took out of the bags. "What you about to make?"

"Why? Are you a picky eater?"

He smirked and said, "I am. I hope you ain't making something I don't eat."

"Oh God. What don't you like?"

"Tell me what you making, and I'll let you know if I like it."

"*Ensalada de frutas* with mango, pineapple, and melon, cheesy grits, fried eggs, aka *huevos fritos*, ham slices, bacon, and honey biscuits."

"I like fruit salads. Don't do nothing fancy with them grits for me. Just make them plain, and I'll add my own sugar. Scramble them eggs, 'cause I don't do fried. I don't want no ham. That bacon gotta be crispy. You making them biscuits from scratch?"

"Nah. Pillsbury Grands!" I replied, pointing to the can. "With yo' picky ass."

He shrugged. "Can't help it."

I laughed at him.

It was at that precious moment that I felt the love inside me burning too hot. Luxury consumed me quickly. The fuel of this new romance was sweet affection. This foundation was meant to be durable, was something that would last, but things started moving from there way too fast.

7

DESIRE

Best Friends Are Forever

"So, what's up with you and Luxury?" Mina asked as soon as I stepped foot into the apartment she shared with Zay and their daughter.

"Damn. Can I get all the way in the door first? Hella anxious, bro."

She closed the door behind me. "Don't play with me, bitch. I've been blowing yo' ass up all day. I couldn't wait to hear this."

"I know. I wanted to call you so many times, but I didn't want him to hear me. I've been a little tied up." I flopped down on her red leather couch.

Her living room was set up so that her couch was facing her big-screen TV. Her walls were a creamy off-white. Most of her pictures were of beautiful African women wearing gold jewelry and bold prints.

"Judging by that big-ass grin, I'm guessing your birthday blew your mind and Luxury blew that back out."

I laughed hard. "Mina, he fucked my mind all the way up. That's what he did."

"How?" She sat on an arm of the couch and folded her arms across her chest.

"So, we went to Lav's. I already told you about the cash and the outfit."

"Yeah."

"So, we leave Lav's and go to his place. His house is pretty much a mansion. I go to take a shower, come out, and he's got a cupcake lit with a candle, champagne, matching bra and panty lingerie set on the bed. Shit, in the morning he tells me to go into the closet and, bitch, this nigga had a whole wardrobe for me, including shoes and jewelry, and I ain't talking about no cheap shit. All designer shit. Then . . . Go look out your window. I made sure to park right where you can see."

Mina got up from the couch and looked out the window. "He bought you a Honda Civic?"

"No! The car parked in front of the Civic."

"Desi. He bought ya ass a Benz?"

"Yeah, and it's brand new, never been owned by anyone. It ain't a Range, but it's still a nice-ass car."

"Aye, aye, aye," she yelled in celebration as she put her hands on her knees and made her ass bounce in a circle a few times. "Okay, I see you, Luxury. He's at you hard as fuck." She stepped back from the window and looked me up and down. "So, um, I noticed you just skipped right over the sex part. What's up with that? I need all the freaky-ass details. Don't act all shy now."

"There's nothing to tell. Once you hear one sex story, you've heard them all. Plus, I don't like discussing my sex life with my man."

"Your *man*? He told you that, or you just claiming him like some crazy-ass stalker?"

"Bitch, I ain't no stalker . . . He said he loves me."

Mina smiled big at me and started twerking again for a second. She stopped and laughed. "Yas, bitch. Girl, this just keeps getting better. You tell him you love him back?"

"Of course I did."

"Of course you did. You've been in love with him since day one."

Mina's front door opened, and Zay walked in. That made us stop talking. One thing about Zay was that he hated hearing girl talk and gossip. I wished his ass had stayed wherever he was, so I could tell her about how Luxury and I had fucked on the kitchen counter after he said my breakfast was the best. I really wanted to talk to my best friend, and Zay was fucking shit up. As usual, Zay didn't speak, and I wasn't about to talk first.

"Where's Zyla?" Mina questioned, noticing he didn't have their daughter with him.

"She's with my mom." He sat down at the kitchen table and coolly tossed a bag of coke on the table. "Aye, you remember that nigga you've been fucking with behind my back?"

Looking like a deer caught in an oncoming diesel truck's headlights, she said, "I . . . I . . . I'm not fucking round with nobody."

"Fuckin' liar. You always fuckin' around. You think it's okay to be texting this fat-ass nigga behind my back and shit? And don't tell me he's payin' for the pussy, 'cause I know he ain't payin' for the pussy. You still fuckin' this nigga."

"Boy, bye," she replied with a scowl on her face. "You sound stupid as fuck right now."

"Don't lie. I know you fucking the nigga I get the blow from behind my back, bitch. You such a ho. God damn! He talkin' about he can fuck you for free. Now, why would he say that to me? You always fuckin' shit up. I should kick ya muthafuckin' ass."

Mina's eyes were filling with tears.

I wanted to beat this nigga's ass for getting at her like that. She had told me she was tired of his ass, but for some reason, she was staying with him. All the nights she had cried on the phone and told me how fucked up he was, she had never told me she was fucking with anybody. She had made it seem like she had no choice but to fuck these niggas for money, because Zay wasn't paying for shit. He sat back like her fucking pimp. He made me sick.

He went on. "I'll kill this nigga straight up, Mina. Don't let me see that nigga anywhere around here! We got into it, and that's why I took Zy to Mom's. He's talking big shit, like he wanna pull up, so I told the nigga to pull and see what happen."

"It ain't all that serious. I'm not fucking around with nobody. Is my child staying the night over there?"

Ignoring her question, he yelled, "Fuck that fat-ass nigga, Mina. You want to hit this shit before I bag it up?" He created two lines and snorted one.

"Not right now. Put a little to the side. I'll probably need a li'l zoom before I walk into the club tonight."

I didn't judge her or Zay. Coke was their thing and had been for a little while. I didn't touch cocaine, because I didn't see the point. All that sniffling and messing with the nose seemed crazy to me. Plus, Mina was always complaining about how her nose was itchy and how she kept sneezing. I didn't want those problems.

"Well, I gotta get home," I said. "I'm sleepy. I'll see you tonight."

Mina nodded at me. "A'ight, girl. You rolling with us tonight, or you driving ya fancy new whip?"

"I'm driving, so I'll meet you up there."

"Okay," she replied.

"Bye, y'all." I grabbed my purse.

"Bye," she said.

Zay didn't say shit to me, with his rude ass. So I ignored him and headed out.

I couldn't get Luxury off my mind, and I couldn't find the words to describe what I was feeling. That man was a beast in the sheets. I thought I would be feeling like a straight ho, having given it up our first time kicking it, but I didn't, because he didn't make me feel like one. He was all I could think about all day. Every time I thought about him, I would shake my head and smile.

I wanted love to feel like this all my life, but I also wanted to be independent. Luxury seemed like the type who would leave me wanting for nothing, and I wanted a relationship where we could be us without letting anyone get in our way. This was like getting on a teeter-totter at the park. I had to trust that Luxury wouldn't jump off and send me crashing down to the ground. Together, we needed to balance one another out to ride successfully. Was I overthinking this shit or what? How did I know that Luxury wasn't playing with my emotions? He could've pulled this move on other bitches. He didn't seem like the tricking type, but only time would tell.

I had a good two-hour nap after I left Mina's house, but as soon as I woke up, he was the first person I thought of. I picked up my phone to hit him up, but I didn't want to seem like I was jocking him, so I decided to wait for him to call or text me.

Feeling hungry, I left the house and picked up a ham and cheese sandwich from my favorite spot in Little Havana, then cruised around while I ate it. I washed it down with a large cup of freshly squeezed lemonade. After I finished the sandwich, I checked my phone, and still no text from him.

Did he just hit it and quit it? I wondered. Nah, he wouldn't have bought all that shit if it was just about some pussy, I decided.

When I got home, I ran a hot bath with bubbles. My phone finally chimed as soon as I got in the water. I had a text, so I dried off my hands with my towel before picking up my phone, hoping it was him.

Luxury: So, this how you do? Just fuck me and leave me. I see how it is.

I smiled as I replied: I didn't want to sweat you. What you doing?

Luxury: You can sweat me whenever. Come to the studio. You remember where Lav lives?

Me: Kind of. Shoot me the address. What time?

Luxury: Nine.

Me: I gotta be at the club by ten. Will we be done by then?

Luxury: Probably not. Why you going to the club, anyway?

Me: That's where I work, remember?

He called me instantly.

I picked up. "Yes, Luxury?"

"I got something better for you to do and you'd rather strip?"

I didn't know how to answer. Working at Queen's was the first and only job I had. It paid very well. I couldn't just quit like that. I didn't want to be in the strip club for the rest of my life, but I wasn't ready to leave my job. There was something about Luxury that made me want to do whatever he wanted me to do, but then again, I had my own mind.

"I've been thinking about it, so don't get mad," I told him.

"I'm not mad. I'm confused, though."

"Don't be confused, baby. I haven't decided yet. I need a little more time, if that's okay with you. Plus, I thought you said I won't have to quit until the music takes off."

"But you have to be in the studio, and most studio sessions are at night."

"Okay . . . I can always work them both until that time. I'll meet you at the studio at nine."

"A'ight. Hey, what you doing right now?"

"I'm taking a bath, thinking about you."

"Is that right? Come open the door."

I paused and laughed, but he wasn't laughing with me.

"Wait. You're outside right now?" I said.

"Yeah, so come open the door with ya sexy ass."

I stood up and got out of the tub. I grabbed my towel and wrapped it around my body. I rushed to the door and looked out the peephole. Luxury wasn't lying. He was standing there, looking so yummy in his black Fendi sweatsuit, dick print on blast. I bit my bottom lip to hold in my excitement and opened the door.

"If you give me a house key, I won't have to interrupt your bath ever again," he said, ending our call.

"A key to my place? But I don't have a key to your spot."

He held up a house key and dangled it in front of me. "Yeah, you do. You might as well move in now." He placed a kiss on my lips and walked in. "With them big, juicy-ass lips."

I laughed, closing the door behind him. "Don't you think we moving too fast? I mean, we just hooked up last night." I led him into the living room, and we both sat on the couch.

He placed the house key on my coffee table since I hadn't taken it from him when he dangled it in front of me. "You think three years is fast, baby? You love me, and I love you, right? Or was you just saying it for shits and giggles?"

"No, I'm in love with you, Luxury. I don't say shit for shits and giggles. You act like we've been dating all three of them years."

"You've been knowin' a nigga for three years, so same difference."

I shook my head. "If you say so."

"Aye, how long you about to be? I'm hungry, and I want to take you out for dinner before we go to Lav's."

"Not long. I gotta wash up. I'll be dressed fast. We goin' on a date?"

"If that's what you want to call it. Wet your hair and wear it curly. I saw you wear it like that one time. I like it like that."

"Okay, Papi," I teased. He was sure acting like he was my papi. Demanding and bossing me around. It was cute, though.

On the way to the restaurant, I recorded myself on Snapchat as a Monnahan Boyz song was blasting. I rapped the lyrics, pointing at the camera, with my nails poppin'. I posted the video and saw how good I looked with flowers from the flower filter wrapped around my head like a crown.

"Why you didn't put me on your li'l Snap?" Luxury asked.

With a smile on my face, I looked over at him. "I didn't think you wanted to be seen with flowers around your head." I started laughing. "I mean, then all my followers will know who I'm fuckin' with."

"You don't want everybody to know who you fuckin' with? I want the world to know who I'm fuckin' with."

"Okay. Well, then, the next Snap I post, I'll make sure to have you in it."

"Bet."

Just then a Snap message came through from the bestie.

Minaboo4life: Bitch. I see you. You look cute in Luxury's ride.

Me: Thank you, boo.

I locked my phone and tossed it on my lap just as we arrived at the restaurant. Luxury pulled up to the front entrance so the valet could park his car. We got out and walked into the restaurant, a popular Italian place. I looked around as we were seated. It was the fanciest place I had ever been to. I almost felt out of place, but when I noticed how comfortable Luxury was, it made me relax. He looked as if he had been here lots of times. The restaurant overlooked the Atlantic Ocean and had a champagne bar. I studied the menu, and I couldn't decide what I wanted to eat. Everything sounded good.

While I was looking over the menu, Luxury said, "Come sit on my lap. Let's take a picture for my Snap and Gram."

I was cheesing all hard again. "You ready for that?"

"I meant what I said. You my girl, right?"

"Yup, I am." I got up from my seat and sat on his lap.

He took out his phone and lifted his camera for a pic. As I smiled for the camera, he placed a kiss on my cheek and snapped the pic. I giggled as I sized up the photo.

"Ooh, we cute," I said, then stuck my tongue out.

He leaned into me and sucked my tongue all sexy like. This nigga was a straight freak. I loved it. I giggled, putting my hand over my mouth bashfully.

"This is going straight on my shit right now," he said.

"That's to let all them bitches know you're mine, right?"

"Ain't no bitches, but yeah, you can say that."

I got off his lap and sat back down on my chair. Next thing I knew, he tagged me in his photo. Before I could decide what I wanted to eat, his Instagram was getting notifications like crazy, and his hashtag relationship goals were starting to trend that fast.

"Baby, you trying to make us go viral?" I said.

"I wasn't trying to do nothing but show the world my beautiful chick."

"I heard the fuck outta that."

He turned serious for a moment and said, "I need you to know that whatever you decide about this rappin' shit, I'll still fuck with you. Even if you don't want to do it. I don't want to make it seem like I'm telling you what to do, you know."

"I know," I said, smiling. "I trust you, Luxury. I know you just want what's best for me."

"What's best for *us*," he said, correcting me.

"Yeah, what's best for us . . . So, are you serious about us living together? When you want me to move in?"

"Tonight," he replied.

"What? No, seriously. I'm on a month-to-month lease, so I gotta wait until the end of the month."

"Nah, you really don't. Your rent is paid for the month, right?"

"Yeah, but they need notice."

"Not on a month-to-month. Long as you're out of there when the month is up, you're straight. Unless you just want to stall."

My heart was racing. This was a big move, but what would be better than waking up to his fine ass every day? "A'ight. You know you don't have to do all that you're doing for me, right? I almost feel like you tryin' to save me or something."

He chuckled as he scanned the menu, ignoring what I'd said. "They changed this shit up. I'm looking for the shrimp linguini."

"It's at the bottom of page two. I was just looking at that. This shit is expensive."

"Don't worry 'bout prices when you're with me."

I settled on the shrimp linguini, as well, after looking through the menu one more time. I put it down and continued to gaze around the restaurant. It was a beautiful place, from the chandeliers to the swirled crème floor. When I was done, I looked at Luxury. He was staring right at me.

I smiled. "What?"

"You're so beautiful."

I blushed and looked away, shaking my head. "Thank you."

"You're welcome."

The waiter appeared, and we ordered.

Right after the waiter left our table, I looked at my phone, because it was blowing up. "Now I'm getting all these requests to follow me."

"Good. You gotta get your social-media fan base up. I know you got your followers from all the half-naked photos and from dancing, but just watch how shit changes for you."

I nodded, feeling excited and nervous all at the same time. I had some shady females from time to time getting at me, because they were on some hating shit, but now I was going to get a taste of that celebrity hating. I had thick skin, but I was going to have to have even thicker skin.

Over dinner Luxury and I talked about the studio, music, and his plans for us. After dinner, he paid the tab, and we walked out of the restaurant. I was so stuffed. I shouldn't have eaten that whole pasta dish, but it was one of the best I'd ever had. The shrimp were big and seasoned perfectly. The pasta was so yummy that I had to eat it all.

Luxury reached for my hand, and I gave it to him.

"You extra mushy," I said. I laughed while I looked down at our hands, feeling awkward.

"I guess you ain't used to a nigga showing you the right kind of attention. You rather I toss you my dollars for shakin' yo' ass, huh?"

I let his hand go, feeling offended. "You for real?"

"I'm dead-ass serious. Look, I ain't tryin' to offend you. I'm just saying, you think it's weird if a nigga wants to hold your hand?"

"I didn't say it was weird, Luxury. I'm just . . ."

"Not used to real affection. I get it. Hey, don't sweat it. Let's get to this studio." He unlocked the car, and we climbed in.

His silence on the way to Lavish's spot made me feel bad. He was so sensitive. We were still getting to know one another, and I wanted to understand him.

"I'm sorry, Luxury," I said after we'd gone a few miles.

"I said, 'Don't worry about it.'"

"Are we good?" I asked, feeling as if I didn't know what else to say.

"Yeah, we straight. I just won't try to hold your hand no mo'."

I smacked my teeth and grabbed his right hand. "I want you to hold my hand." I held his hand in mine and brought the back of it to my lips. I gave the back of his hand the sweetest kiss I could.

He bit his lower lip, and a grin crept onto his face. "Aye, I forgot to tell you. We got a show coming up in Atlanta in two weeks. You should come."

I had never been anywhere outside of Miami. Atlanta sounded like fun. "I'm down. I gotta let Queen know I'll be gone."

"You might as well tell Queen you're quitting while ya at it."

I sighed. "Fine. Luxury. I'll quit. If this shit don't work, I can always go back."

"It's gone work. Just watch. You'll never have to dance ever again."

8

LUXURY

Love Without Limits

The first time I met Desire, I thought, *What's her pretty, young ass doing in here*?

She looked every bit of eighteen no matter how much makeup she had on. She looked scared as fuck to be up in there. Despite her tender age, she was one of the most beautiful girls I had ever seen. I wanted to give her everything she wanted even then, but she wasn't ready for me, and I wasn't prepared for her.

I waited for the perfect time, which just so happened to be when she turned twenty-one. I had to make sure my loose ends with other bitches were cut and burned. I had to come correct. Too many niggas, including my brothers, wanted to holler at her, but I could see the way she felt about me every time she looked at me. She wasn't stuntin' no nigga but me.

My life was good. I loved my life. I was quite blessed to be able to help my brothers with their rapping, and I could leave the dope shit behind with this music label. I wasn't about to take anything for granted. Lavish, Frill, and I were blood brothers, same mom and same dad. Our so-called dad had bailed out on the fam when we were little, so our mother had raised five bad boys by herself. Talk about strength. We'd grown up in the ghetto, in one of the most broken-down parts of Miami. Shit, we'd slept on mattresses on the floor.

With the money we were making, we had bought our mom a beautiful three-bedroom house in the suburbs. Her backyard faced the water, so she could look at the flamingos and shit. She'd cried the day we handed her the keys to that house. She couldn't believe that we would take care of her that way. It was the least we could do. Frill lived with her so she wouldn't be lonely, but he was over at Lav's so much, you would think he lived there.

Money had changed a lot of things in our family, had turned things real ugly. Before the music business had come the drug business. We'd lost two brothers behind drug money. Our youngest brother, Travis, had killed Frill's twin brother, De'Vonn, over a funky two hundred dollars. Whenever I thought about it, it seemed crazy that he had destroyed his own flesh and blood, like De'Vonn was just another nigga off the street.

Travis had been only fifteen years old at the time and had been tried as an adult. He would be in prison for the next eighteen years, and I had nothing to say to the nigga ever. None of us had shit to say to him except Mama, because Travis was her baby. Mama was the only one who acted like what Travis had done wasn't cold-blooded. She made all kinds of excuses for him, said he felt bad about what he had done. I hoped the guilt he felt ate at him for the rest of his life. Before he was killed, De'Vonn had been on his way to becoming a big star in the industry with us. Not a day went by when I didn't think about my little bro.

Losing my brothers had left holes in my heart. Having Desire in my life was like replacing these missing pieces to the puzzle. Desire's head and her pussy game were top-notch, and that could be why I was feeling so crazy about her. She wasn't no dummy, either. I never wanted her to leave my side. I didn't want her to strip, because I felt it was a waste of time. A woman like her didn't need to be up there taking off her clothes for a buck. She had that star quality, and she didn't even know it. I was about to change her life for the better.

I looked over at her as she rode with me over to Lav's. The way she had kissed the back of my hand made me feel soft as velvet. I had never allowed myself to fall in love with anyone, but my heart was open for Desire. I wanted to be in love with her. For three years, I had sat back and watched her. I had had to know she was the one, without any doubts. Though I hadn't said much to her during those three years, her actions had spoken volumes. I'd never seen her sloppy drunk. I'd never heard about her givin' up the pussy for money. She was the complete opposite of her best friend, who was topping Lavish off every chance she could get, and that was what I loved about Desirae. She didn't allow her surroundings to influence who or what she wanted to be.

I parked in Lav's driveway, and we got out of the car. Her walk was mean as her hips swished from left to right. I couldn't keep my eyes off her. She turned to see why I wasn't walking behind her.

"Come here, sexy," I said, biting my lower lip.

Without hesitation, she came to me.

Yeah, I like that submissive shit. I wrapped my arms around her. As I kissed her lips, I slid my hand in the front of her jeans. She moaned but immediately pulled my hand out.

"We can't be doin' this in front of Lavish's house," she scolded.

"Why not?" I asked. "We the only ones out here."

"How you know? Plus, I can handle whatever you want later."

"Damn right . . . I love you more and more by the second."

"I love you too, baby," she said, leaning in to kiss me again.

When we kissed, she moaned, and the sound was like music to my ears. She moved her lips to my neck, rolled her tongue over my skin.

"I thought you said we can't be doing this out here," I whispered in her ear.

She pulled at my Louis Vuitton belt buckle, and as she unbuckled my pants, I pulled her to the side of the house, which was draped in shadows. My baby was so fucking sexy. I had a real one by my side. We were Luxury and Desire, and it couldn't get any better.

9

DESIRE

Pain Is Inspiration

My first official studio session with the Monnahan Boyz was insane. The beat, the hook, the verses, the song, which we called "Real," were fire. It took about three hours to finish the song top to bottom. The engineer mixed and mastered it to perfection. Luxury couldn't wait to get it out. I had to admit, I sounded like a real rapper. I didn't think I could sound like that, and Lav didn't have to tune my voice, either. With the ad-libs and voice doubles, my voice was everything.

"Now, that's what the fuck I'm talking about," Frill hollered.

"You ready to be a star?" Luxury asked, with the biggest smile spread across his face, those dimples as deep as ever.

I felt a little excited, yet I was nervous at the same time. Was I ready to be introduced to the world? I had never once thought that I would be in this kind of spotlight.

"This is def a hit," Lavish said after blowing out smoke. "Keep that shit on repeat. I'm about to post a sample on the Gram."

My cell vibrated my hip, and I saw it was Queen.

"Damn," I said, looking at my phone. I had forgotten to let her know I wasn't coming in.

"What?" Luxury frowned, seeing my worried look. "Who's that?"

"It's Queen."

"You gotta answer?"

"I should. I forgot to call in. I'll be right back." I stepped out of the studio and answered the call as I was walking up the stairs that led to Lav's kitchen. "Hey, Queen. Sorry I didn't get to call to tell you I wasn't coming in, but—"

"Desire, I'm not calling about that."

"Oh . . . ? What's up?"

"It's about Exxxotic."

The way Queen's voice sounded made me pause. "Okay . . . You looking for her? She told me she was going to the club tonight."

"No . . . she . . ." Queen paused, and she was sniffling, almost as if she was crying.

"Queen? What's going on?"

"Somebody . . . shot her about an hour ago. I've been trying to reach you."

"What?" I felt my heart drop into my stomach. "Wait, is she all right?"

"No. She and her boyfriend were gunned down out front. The paramedics did everything they could. They're gone."

My knees buckled, and I hit the floor.

I woke up to Luxury shaking me. "Desire, wake up. Wake up, baby."

Everyone was standing around me.

"What happened?" I asked, putting my hand on my head.

"I don't know. I came in here to check on you, and you were on the floor, totally passed out."

"I must've fainted."

"You faint like this often?" Egypt asked.

"No," I said as Luxury helped me to my feet. Then I remembered what Queen had told me about Mina, and it brought me to tears. "Queen just told me that Mina and Zay . . . Someone shot them outside the club tonight. They're dead."

Everyone groaned.

"Fuck. Are you serious?" Luxury asked.

I nodded, crying. "I gotta call her family. I . . ." My legs felt wobbly.

Luxury held me up. "Just sit down for a minute." Guiding me over to the kitchen table, he asked, "They got beef with anyone?"

"Zay was saying something earlier today about Mina fuckin' around with the nigga he gets his coke from, but I don't know. Zay was into a little of everything."

"You talking about that nigga Fat Man Bo?" Lavish asked, his eyebrows furrowing on his forehead.

I shook my head. "I don't . . . Wait, Fat Man Bo? The fat, ugly, greasy nigga who owns that pool hall?"

"Yeah. That's who Zay got his blow from. I heard she was fucking around with him, but I've never known him to get down like this, though," Lavish commented.

Luxury said, "Listen, everything will be okay. I'm here. Just breathe. I got you."

I couldn't believe my best friend was gone, and she was my only friend in the world. My whole body shook as my tears blurred my vision. My emotional pain was flowing out of my every pore. A cry escaped my mouth, a cry so raw that everyone had tears in their eyes. I held on to Luxury so that my violent shaking wouldn't cause me to fall on the floor. Everything in that house was a blur. I felt only pain, pain so searing that it was enough to break me, pain sufficient enough to turn my heart into a cold brick.

"Let me get you home," Luxury said.

Black filled the edges of my vision, and the only thing I could hear was my own heartbeat. My breath came in ragged, shallow gasps. Seconds, even minutes, passed, and I was still crying. It was like I could hear Luxury's voice, but I could not move.

10

LUXURY

The Pool Hall

I took Lavish and Frill with me to go holler at Fat Man Bo the next night. I wanted to hear his side of the story because although no one could confirm he was the one that had murdered Zay and Mina, the streets were talking. Everyone knew about the little argument between him and Zay. No one was talking to the police, because they knew what the consequences would be. No one fucked with Bo. He instilled the kind of fear that a mob boss did.

We had heard that Bo and his pack of goons were hanging at his pool hall, so we pulled up on him. On any other day, we wouldn't pull up on him like this, but this was serious business. We didn't have any beef, and Bo and I had respected one another when I was in the dope game.

As soon as we walked in, I could hear him talking a gang of shit to his minions. We followed his voice to the back, where the bar was. Bo looked a lot like a fat black version of Lurch from *The Addams Family*, but bitches loved his big black ass. His loud, obnoxious laugh roared above the trap music and the sounds of people playing pool.

"The muhfuckin' Monnahan Boyz. What brings y'all down here? Ya tired of trickin' off ya money in that pussy shack?" Bo asked with a deep grimace.

"You know it ain't trickin' if ya got it, right?" I asked.

"That's what that nigga T.I. said seven years ago, and everybody still livin' by that bullshit. Sound like an excuse to be stupid if ya ask me." He popped his collar.

"Hey, you mind if I holler at you for a minute? Alone?" I asked.

Bo took a hard look at us before he looked at his boys. He motioned with his head for me to follow him, and then he headed toward the back, in the direction of his office.

I gave Frill and Lav the hand signal to stay put, and then I followed Bo.

"What's good?" he asked after we stepped inside his office and he reached out to close the door.

"I should be asking you that same thing. Tell me that wasn't you that was shooting outside Queen's last night."

He replied without blinking, "It wasn't me."

I clasped my hands together and said, "Here's the thing. My girl lost her best friend in that shooting. I'm just trying to figure out what happened. That shit wasn't no random thing. That was an execution. I heard you were fucking around with her, and her nigga didn't like the shit. I heard he popped off at you and told you to stay away from her."

He popped a toothpick in his mouth, bit down on it, and sucked his teeth. "Nigga, you got some balls walking up in here, accusing me of some shit I didn't do."

"I ain't accusing you of shit, Bo. I know you and ole boy had a falling-out over Mina. Tell me you didn't pull up and end them like that."

He grunted, "Nah, that ain't my style. We didn't fall out over his bitch. I don't get at niggas over bitches."

"So, what happened?"

"Nigga, you workin' for the police now or what? You wearing a wire?"

"Fuck outta here. The day I become a snitch is a day I kill myself. Come on, man. You know me better than that, or at least I thought you did."

He observed me for a moment in silence before he said, "The fuck boy was supposed to make good on a deal, but he failed. That don't mean I was the one to give him what he deserved."

"What you mean, he failed?"

"I fronted the nigga a key, and he couldn't pay me back, claimed some shit went wrong on his end. He offered his bitch to pay off his debt. I fucked her for months to work that off. I was more than lenient. The pussy was good, and the head was superb. Truth be told, she couldn't leave a real nigga like me alone."

"Sounds to me like y'all worked that shit out."

"Nah. He asked me to front him another key, and I did, but I wasn't taking his bitch's pussy as repayment, because I was already hitting it for free. I wanted my mothafuckin' money. He talked real slick, warning me to stay away from her. Hey, it's unfortunate what happened last night, but, uh, it wasn't me."

I nodded. "I hear ya. Mina didn't deserve that, though. Zay's business had nothing to do with Mina. Now my girl is broken up over the shit."

Bo sat down at his mahogany desk, leaned back in his black leather chair, and chewed on that toothpick. "Like I said, that wasn't me. I don't know shit about who did it, either. How's the music business?"

"I can't complain. I ain't in the streets no mo'."

"I know. That made mo' room for me." He grinned and paused before he said, "You said you fuckin' with Mina's best friend?"

"Yeah."

He stood up and went over to his safe. Once he got it open, he pulled out a few bands. "Let her know this is to help pay for her funeral, and send my condolences."

I put my hand up. "It's good. The funeral is covered. Thanks, though."

Bo shrugged. "A'ight. Let me walk you out."

I opened the door and walked out, and he walked behind me. I didn't say anything else to him, and he didn't say anything else to me.

I nodded at Lavish and Frill. We walked out of the pool hall and got in my car. I started it up and pulled out of the parking lot.

"The fuck he say?" Lavish asked from the passenger's seat, lighting his blunt.

"He said he didn't do it."

"You believe him?" Frill questioned, flipping his dreads out of his face.

I shook my head. "Fuck no. Bo may not have pulled the trigger, but he ordered the hit."

"Over some pussy?" Lavish scoffed. "Shit, I was fuckin' the bitch, too, so he gone kill me next?" Lavish inhaled smoke.

"Nah, they had some other shit going on, but he claims he didn't do it and don't know who did. That's that," I said.

"What you tellin' Desire?" Lavish asked.

"Nothing. Tellin' her is gonna do what? The first thing she's going to do is want revenge."

It was my job to protect Desire. It was better for her that she didn't know anything about my conversation with Bo.

11

DESIRE

It's Too Hard to Say Goodbye

The day I buried my best friend was one of the hardest days of my life. That morning the sky became a charcoal color, and rain started pouring down, as if the day itself knew it was a dreadful one. During Mina's memorial service, I was a mess. Though I struggled to hold back my grief, I couldn't stop crying and thinking about what had happened. As I allowed my tears to flow, I silently held down my head. I felt so bruised inside. I was numb, empty, as I walked behind Mina's white coffin at the end of the service. I found myself saying goodbye when she was already gone. My soul was unwilling to acknowledge the finality of her death. I would never be able to look at her face again or feel her embrace, see the warmth in her eyes, or be surrounded by her love. I was glad when it was all over.

I had read on news sites that Zay's and Mina's bodies had been riddled with bullets before they could even walk into the club. Some niggas had executed my friend, and nobody knew anything. Luxury had told me Fat Man

Bo didn't have a clue as to who would do this. It was going to be up to the police to figure out this mystery. Luxury not only tried to get to the bottom of what had happened, but he also paid for the funeral and burial, which he didn't have to do. I thanked God for him. He made sure Mina had a proper service and repast, and he also comforted me as much as he could.

Going to Atlanta for the Monnahan Boyz' show was what Luxury felt I needed. Our song was spinning on the radio, but everyone's reaction to it was unexpected. People loved the song. It was their jam. Luxury wanted me to get onstage to perform it with the Monnahan Boyz, even though I was dealing with losing my best friend. I just hoped I wouldn't fuck up the lyrics.

We got to the venue in Atlanta hours before the show, so we could get in a rehearsal and have time to chill. I was drawing blanks backstage, and it almost sent me into a panic attack. I had to remember to breathe. Somehow, I was sure the words would come back to me once I was onstage before a live crowd.

I looked like a million bucks in that one-piece sparkling bodysuit and thigh-high boots Lala had picked out for me and Luxury had approved of. One thing I could say about my man was that he knew fashion and had a great eye for making me look good. Luxury posted pics of me all over his Facebook, Instagram, Twitter, and Snapchat. I loved the way Luxury's eyes roamed up and down my body, a sign of his approval. Once I got on that stage, the energy from the crowd pumped me all the way up. It was like my pain from losing Mina was gone temporarily. When I rapped my part, Luxury went live from his phone.

After the show, we changed our clothes and went to some club. I was still feeling the buzz from performing. I couldn't wait to do it again. We went straight to the VIP. Drinks were flowing. I glanced around the section. The black couch was filled with beautiful women, enough for Lav and Frill to flirt with. Thick clouds of smoke were in the air from the blunts they were smoking. Cool air was fighting to circulate with all the bodies in the room, and I felt hot.

Exposed skin was everywhere. A few chicks were grinding on one another, smacking asses. As the beat was bumping, I started thinking about the days when Mina and I would dance onstage together. I missed her so much. If only she were still alive, she would've been able to see me do my thing. I felt the tears spring to my eyes.

"I got you another shot," Luxury said, handing me a shot of Cîroc.

We stood next to each other, since there wasn't a seat to be had in the VIP section at that moment. As I downed the drink and placed the glass on the cocktail table, I couldn't help but feel that if I didn't get out of this sad, depressed state, I was going to fuck up what Luxury had planned for me. I hadn't recorded another song, and Luxury was on my ass about it. Since Mina had died, I hadn't stepped foot in the Queen of Diamonds, so he didn't have to worry about me going back. I was trying to figure out how to feel like myself again.

"Thank you," I said, then forced a smile through my tears.

"You know I'm proud of you for getting out there tonight, right? I know it ain't easy."

"It ain't. The reaction from the fans was crazy."

"I told you. Soon crowds will be chanting your name. Hey, did you see that another picture of us went viral? We are officially a meme, babe. We're everybody's relationship goals now. Do you know how many followers you have now?"

"I haven't had time to check it out with all that's been going on. Since I made my page public, like you told me to do, I haven't been keeping up."

"You're at eight hundred ninety-four thousand followers."

"What?"

He pulled up my Instagram to show me. "See. You're blowing up, and you ain't even know it." He chuckled.

Out of nowhere, a brown-skinned chick with straight hair down her back walked right up to Luxury. I frowned, watching her.

"Hey, I saw you from over there, so I had to come over and say something. You're Luxury, right?" she said.

He looked at her. "Yeah. Who you?"

"I'm Trina," she said, as if he was supposed to know that.

"Nice to meet you, Trina," he replied. "This is Desire. You heard of her?"

She shook her head and didn't look at me. She looked as if she was trying to see if he remembered her. The way she was standing there looking at my man bothered me.

"It's nice to see you again, Luxury," she purred. When she put her hand out to shake Luxury's hand, I nearly lost it.

"Bitch, you betta—"

Luxury put his hand on my chest and nudged me back. I scowled, looking at him as if he had lost his mind.

"Hey, this is my girl. So, no disrespect, but I'm taken," he explained.

Trina rolled her eyes and nodded, as if she already knew that. "That's cool, but I was hoping you needed one more to join your party."

I tensed up again, and Luxury placed his hand around my waist. "Nah, we good, Mama."

As she walked away, she said over her shoulder, "Too bad."

"I was two seconds away from throwing my drink in the bitch's face," I growled.

"You gotta kill that. There's about to be a lot of hoes, and I don't need you fighting and getting thrown out of clubs. You know I am all about you."

"I know."

"Good." He caught my eye. "Hey, you ever had a three-way?" Luxury asked.

I shook my head, wishing I had another drink. "Nah. Never."

He pulled me close and whispered in my ear, "Well, that makes two of us. I ain't interested, so you ain't gotta worry about that." He kissed me long and slow as he took hold of my ass with both hands. "You looked so fuckin' sexy on that stage, much sexier than you do when you're stripping."

"Is that right?"

"Yeah. I've seen so many naked women, titties, and pussies. That shit doesn't move me. A woman who is confident and about her shit, like the way you rocked that stage, that's what gets my dick hard. I love a woman with power."

My hand traveled up his tattoo-covered arm. I looked up to see that broad giving me the stink eye. I squeezed him tighter and rolled my eyes at her.

"Baby," I said. "I need to sit down. These fuckin' boots are killing my feet."

"A'ight. I'll make room on the couch. Hold on."

I watched him walk over and tell the bodyguards to free up some space on the couch. Within seconds, we were sitting close to each other on that couch. I felt like I was the only woman in the room, because Luxury didn't look at other women. These hoes were everywhere, serving legs, breasts, and thighs as if they were at Popeyes. Like he'd said, that shit didn't move him. Luxury always exuded sex appeal, and that night was no different. The throbbing between my legs confirmed I was going to fuck him good all night long.

"I'm Different," a song by 2 Chainz, started playing. That was my jam. I straddled Luxury and started twerking. Lavish and Frill had their phones in their hands and were recording my lap dance. Out of the corner of my eye, I saw that Trina, the same female who had bothered us before, had made her way over and was standing in front of us.

Is this bitch crazy? I stopped dancing, looked at Luxury, and saw that he had donned an expression of annoyance.

"Luxury, you act like you don't remember me," Trina said.

"The fuck he need to remember you for?" I barked as I hopped off Luxury's lap. "He told you to step, bitch."

She rolled her eyes, as if I was irrelevant. "So, you really gonna act like you don't remember me, Luxury?" she asked. "I think you actin' brand new 'cause you got yo' li'l half–Puerto Rican bitch here with you."

I was used to people confusing my Latin heritage, because most didn't know any better. I had been called

Mexican, Dominican, Puerto Rican, but they never, ever guessed I was Cuban. This stupid ho wanted his attention so damn bad. I was about to swing on her, but Luxury had given the bodyguard a hand signal, and he was moving straight toward her.

"I need you to leave this area," the bodyguard told Trina.

"Aw, hell no, Luxury. Really though? This how you treat me now? Fuck you, nigga. Fuck you!" She stormed out of the VIP area, and the bodyguard roped it back off.

"You know that raggedy-ass ho?" I asked.

He shrugged. "No."

"She acting like y'all fucked before, so don't lie to me."

"Ain't nobody lying to you. I think she's confusing me. Maybe she fucked Lav and don't remember."

Lavish heard him say that and began to laugh. "I might've. It's possible."

"Yeah, okay. Y'all don't look that much alike," I said, folding my arms across my chest. "You know what? You ain't gotta explain shit to me."

Luxury smirked and let out a low chuckle.

I cocked my head to the side. "What's so fuckin' funny?"

Luxury grabbed me and pinched my cheek before kissing my lips gently. "You so damn cute when you're mad. My baby got a li'l temper. Let's get out of here, 'cause I'm ready to get you up out of your clothes for that lap dance."

As soon as the hotel door was closed, Luxury started hungrily kissing my neck and rubbing my nipples through my dress. I moaned as he sucked my neck. A few seconds later, he had his hands up my dress and was removing my thong. I stepped out of it. He cupped my ass as his lips moved over my dress to my hard nipples. I arched my back and pulled him onto the bed. Luxury hovered above me while I took off my dress and bra. He pulled his clothes off next. I got on my hands and knees. He pushed inside me from behind. I opened my legs wider to give him better access. With each moan, I felt like I was losing a piece of myself. The deeper he went, the deeper he went into my heart.

"You got me ready to beat that pussy up," he said.

I liked when he talked nasty like that. I liked it when he pulled my hair. I liked the way he smacked my ass. When he put his hand around my throat, I loved that shit.

He flipped me around so he could grab my throat with one hand as he fucked me. His grip was tight, and I loved it. I gasped for air, but I couldn't find it. I was getting light-headed, and my orgasm was rising through my body. He was so deep in the pussy and was breathing hard, with his eyes closed. Right when I felt like I was choking, he eased up his grip, but he was pounding me hard and rough. In the throes of passion, I was bucking and screaming. He was hitting all the right spots at the right time. My screaming was at the heavens. With every stroke, my pussy overflowed. A shiver ran through me, and when we came together, we collapsed in one another's arms.

Luxury eased off me.

"Nooo," I whined. "Where you going?"

"I gotta piss."

I whined as I watched him walk to the bathroom. I loved his naked body. He had the perfect body. Not too slim and not too muscular. He had nice legs, and those abs . . . I could just stare at him all day.

I heard him pee and then flush the toilet. He washed his hands and stood in the bathroom doorway. He stared at me, as if he was in deep thought.

"Why you looking at me like that?" I scowled.

"We should get married. Yeah."

"What?" I laughed.

He wasn't laughing or smiling. I stopped laughing and ran my hand over my hair. We had been living together for only a little over a month. I had just turned in my key a few weeks ago, and now he wanted to get married? This roller coaster I was on with Luxury was moving at the speed of light.

"We're getting married," he said.

"Already? What's the rush?"

"I'm not talking about right now," he said, noting my worried expression. "I mean, like, one day. I'm gonna surprise you. I'm not gonna tell you when, but I'll propose the right way." He got back in the bed with me and pulled me close.

Holding him close to my heart, I closed my eyes and imagined that I was already his wife. If he wanted to get married without delay, truth be told, I would marry him, because that would mean he was committed to spending the rest of his life with me.

12

LUXURY

My Brothers' Keeper

As soon as Desire said we were rushing, it made me slow down and think. She was right, but I knew it in my heart that we were made for one another. I didn't need a whole lot of time to seal the deal. Felt like I had thought long and hard enough about it. I had blurted the marriage shit out because I wanted to see if she was feeling what I was feeling.

Her reaction told me she wasn't ready for all that, so I wasn't going to push it. I knew she was in pain over losing Mina. I knew all about that pain, because the pain I had felt when I lost my brother had never left me. Life had gone on, though. I wanted her to shake that shit and live her life. Nothing was wrong with mourning, but at the end of the day, we had money on the table, and we couldn't just leave it there.

I sat on the couch in the hotel room after I finished rolling a blunt. I picked up my iPhone to take a picture of how she looked as she wrote in her new little journal. She liked writing her raps in there.

She looked up at me with a smile. “What you doing over there?”

“Takin’ pictures of you, with ya fine ass.”

“Thank you, baby. You’re so sweet.”

I swear, she didn’t have any flaws to me. She was more than perfect in my eyes. It was hard for me to be hard on her, because she was like this delicate flower, but I couldn’t be no soft-ass nigga. That just wasn’t me.

I looked over the photos I had taken of her as she walked over to me.

“Let me see,” she said.

I titled my screen toward her so she could see.

She nodded. “What you plan on doing with those?”

“Use one as my background and one for my lock screen.”

“That’s how you know it’s real. I get to be on your phone’s background,” she mused.

I scrolled through the photos, and a pic of Frill and De’Vonn popped up. I pushed the side button to turn the screen black.

“Wait,” she said. “Let me see that picture. Go back.”

I hesitated before I showed it to her.

“Hey, Frill and this nigga look identical. Y’all got another brother?” she said, looking confused.

“There was five Monnahan Boyz in total.”

“Really? I didn’t know that.”

“Yeah. That’s De’Vonn. He was Frill’s twin.”

“Oh. Why you say *was* like that? What happened to him?”

She was genuinely concerned. Since she wasn’t asking merely to be nosy, I felt comfortable enough to talk about it.

"De'Vonn was killed when he was only sixteen years old. The fucked-up part is that our own brother killed him. Travis is currently spending the next eighteen years in prison. So, you know, I know all about losing somebody close."

She wrapped her arms around me. "That's the craziest shit I've ever heard. I'm sorry to hear that, baby. You're pretty fuckin' strong. That's why you can be so strong for me."

"I don't know how else to be," I said. "You smoking this blunt with me?"

"Now, you know I don't smoke. We gotta head to the airport soon. You got your stuff packed?"

"Not yet. I'll get it all together once I finish this blunt. Cool?"

"Yup."

I watched her go back to her journal to write her rhymes. I stepped out on the balcony to smoke my blunt. Tears threatened to appear as I thought about De'Vonn. I shook the sadness away and put some fire to my blunt. If I could turn back the hands of time, I would've been there to stop my brothers from fighting. Travis never would've shot De'Vonn if I'd been there.

13

DESIRE

The Grind

We landed in Miami the next evening. It was peak hurricane season, and a category-three storm was threatening to make landfall somewhere in South Florida, though some computer models had it veering offshore. Since we didn't know where or if the hurricane would hit, we had to rush to get someplace safe. We had music to record, so Luxury suggested we stay at Lavish's, since that was where the studio was. As we drove, the wind was howling like in some scary-ass movie, and it was darker than dark. Lavish had invited Nia, Lala, and Egypt, along with some other people, to hang out at his place because it was pre-tour celebration time. They didn't give a fuck about the hurricane. They were acting like not everyone had been warned. Once everyone was inside the house, the winds grew stronger, so Luxury and Frill boarded up as many windows as they could.

Down in the studio, it was me, Lavish, and an Arabian sound engineer named Nuri Bank$. So far Luxury had popped in to check on me every half hour or so, but when he didn't come back after two hours, I got to wondering. *What the fuck is he doing?*

"Hey, can we go ahead and call it a night?" I asked through the headphones. "My vibe is not right."

Nuri and Lavish looked at one another and said a few words I couldn't hear.

"Yeah, but you already know Luxury wants this finished tonight," Lavish said.

"Fuck Luxury," I said. "I'm tired."

Lavish shook his head. "A'ight. We'll pick back up tomorrow."

I tossed off the headphones, rushed out of the booth and up the stairs. My heart was beating so fast that once I made it to the top, I was out of breath. I seriously needed to start working out. All this eating late and being booed up had me gaining a few pounds.

I made my way through the crowded kitchen, looking for Luxury. Panic was starting to rise inside me, as I thought that he might've left without telling me. The DJ had the music loud and bumping hard in the living room. The room started spinning around me, and I clutched my heart, because it felt like it was about to beat out of my chest.

Am I having a panic attack?

I drew in a few deep breaths to calm myself down. After looking for Luxury for what felt like forever, I finally found him engaged in a conversation near the staircase. I cringed, as women were all up on him, surrounding him.

"The fuck?" I said under my breath.

As I walked toward him, these bitches didn't seem to give two fucks about me. Their eyes were sparkling in fascination, and their fake-ass laughs sounded stupid.

One bitch had the nerve to stand in my way, so I couldn't get to him. I fluttered my eyelashes and looked at Luxury, but he wasn't looking at me. Matter of fact, he hadn't noticed I was there.

"Excuse me," I said, loud enough for everyone to hear me.

The aggressive bitch's lip curled into a snarl as she turned around to look at me, but still she didn't move.

"Move, bitch!" I shouted.

"Bitch? Who you callin' a bitch, bitch?" she asked, getting in my face.

Before I could snap back at her, Luxury barked, "Let her through."

The girl moved to the side, though she made it clear that she really didn't want to. "Are you his girl or somethin'?" she muttered.

"Bitch, you don't worry about who the fuck I am," I snarled.

Luxury grabbed my hand and pulled me toward him. He walked me away from the crowd, but I could hear the girl talking shit about me to the others. I tuned them out, mugging Luxury.

"You finished the recording?" he asked, staring me right back down.

"Yeah. I was at the same song for hours. You didn't even come back down there."

"Is it done, though?" He was looking at me like I had done something wrong.

"Not yet—" I said, trying to explain, but he interrupted me.

"So, don't you think you should be in there until it's done?"

Was this nigga trying to check me? He hadn't been the one in the studio, recording until he was hoarse. I was exhausted and ready to go to bed.

I blew air through my lips. "I'm tired, Luxury."

"A'ight. Take a break for a minute or two."

"I need sleep."

"We ain't got time to sleep . . . What's the real reason you came out here trippin'?"

"Why can't these broads take into consideration that you got a bitch?" I screamed, feeling frustrated. It was like he wasn't listening to anything I was saying.

He frowned, shaking his head at me. "Chill . . . You act like everybody doesn't know we're together."

"Everybody knows, but they clearly don't give a fuck. So, which one are you fuckin' or did you used to fuck?"

He chuckled. "You're delirious and delusional. I'm gonna let you excuse yourself. Hey, why don't you go upstairs, since you so sleepy?"

"I'm just tired of recording."

"How you gonna be a star and you tired of recording? You better get used to it." He stepped back and then nodded, as if a thought had come to him. "You can go to bed . . . but first, I gotta hear this song." He walked toward the basement door.

He was the one who wanted me to be a star, not me. He was acting like this was *my* dream. I hadn't asked for this shit. I had had crazy fun dancing at Queen's. Recording music in the studio was far from fun to me. It was boring, and half the time I felt stupid. Luxury wanted every song to be perfect. No one was perfect. He was asking me to do the impossible.

I followed him down the stairs to the studio. Nuri was still around. And Lavish and Frill were there with their dynamic trio, Egypt, Lala, and Nia, and were listening and bobbing to a new Monnahan Boyz track. These two hardly went anywhere or did anything without these three broads, because the trio was behind their style and everything professional.

I didn't fuck with them like that. Luxury had mentioned something about Lala and Nia working with me on my style and Egypt becoming my assistant, but I hadn't commented about it. I hardly spoke to them, and they barely talked to me, so I wasn't too thrilled about it.

"Aye, cut on the track Desire was just recording," Luxury commanded.

Nuri cut off Lav's track to put mine on. As soon as the beat came on, everyone's heads were bobbing hard except for Luxury's. His arms were folded across his chest, and he was staring straight at me. I crossed my arms over my breasts and looked right back at him. I dared him to check me in front of everybody. I could see that my music did not please him, as a hint of his temper crept into his expression.

Oh, God, he hates it, I thought to myself. I was nervous as fuck, afraid of what he was going to say, but I didn't show it.

The song played all the way through to the ending chorus. Luxury made a cutting motion at his throat for Nuri to stop it. Then he folded his arms across his chest again and rubbed his facial hair, which was growing into a perfectly lined beard.

"Surely, I'm not the only nigga in here who knows that shit is weak as fuck," he muttered.

"Nigga, you trippin'. That track is fye," Frill hollered. "You be straight spittin', Desire. You crazy for thinking otherwise, Luxury."

Luxury ignored Frill and said, “Start the track from the beginning.” He listened once more, a deep scowl on his face, and then he made the cutting motion at his throat again before the hook. “Less than perfection won’t be muthafuckin’ tolerated. I know you can come harder,” Luxury said roughly to me. “I don’t know what all this prissy shit is, but you need to get nasty on this shit. You don’t need no featured rappers on it, either. That’s just how hot it is, but I want Frill on the track. Frill, hop in the booth and let me see something.”

“You ain’t said nothin’ but a word, bruh.” Frill hopped into the booth and put on the earphones. “Let me do verse two and that chorus with her, so run that shit back from the top, so I can get in my groove.”

“Babe, I’m tired,” I whined, not feeling it.

“I’m not tryin’ to hear that shit right now,” Luxury replied, staring at me coldly. “We’re not going to bed until you get this shit right.”

I had heard about how ruthless Luxury could be when he was in the streets, and his demeanor now let me know not to fuck with him when he was serious. I started thinking of what to say to change up my lyrics. I grabbed the pad and pen I had earlier.

Frill was going hard on my track, so I was left with no other choice but to bring it to keep up with him.

As it turned out, that song—which we worked on all night, until it was right—shot to number one on the rap/hip-hop charts on iTunes as soon as it dropped. I hated to admit it, but Luxury knew what he was doing. That song changed our lives.

Luxury handed me my first "music" check while I was making a salad in the kitchen, and I couldn't believe what I was seeing. I had felt so mad at Luxury for forcing me to work on that song until he thought it was perfect, especially since he was doing way too much for nothing, but the money showed me that this rapping stuff yielded great rewards.

"One song and I get all these damn zeroes?" I said, incredulous.

"I told you I know what I'm doing, baby. I got you."

I hugged him and placed a kiss on his soft lips. For the first time, I was glad I had quit the strip club.

Then I realized something. "How am I supposed to cash this? I don't have a bank account."

"You don't? Why not?"

"I don't trust 'em. I usually keep all my money in a safe in my closet."

"Well, you ain't got a choice now. I got a credit union you can go to. I'll give you the address."

"You can't go with me?" I said.

"Nah. I got some business to handle with the label, but I'll meet you on time at the spot for your album-cover photo shoot."

He gave me the address for his credit union and left. I ate my salad, staring at the check the entire time. I recalled when I used to wonder what it would be like to have money like this, and what I would do with it. Now I had it, and I still didn't know what I would do with it. The check was no more than a rectangle of thin paper, and the digits weren't even aligned perfectly, but it was all mine. I couldn't finish my salad, because I was too anxious to deposit my check into an account.

I showered and dressed in a cute summer dress and sandals. Using Google Maps, I found my way to the address Luxury had given me. It was a branch of the Miami Federal Credit Union. I parallel parked along the curb, in an open spot right in front of the grand building. I walked straight into that bank, feeling like my shit didn't stink. I had new money, and my fine-ass man was making sure I was well taken care of. Nobody could wipe the smile off my face.

I wasn't quite sure where to start. As I looked around, a woman walked up to me in her professional business attire and said, "Good afternoon. How can I help you today?"

"Um, I would like to open up an account and deposit a check."

"Okay, no problem. Have a seat right over there, and a personal banker will be with you shortly. Would you like some coffee or water? You can help yourself at the station set up behind you."

I looked behind me. "No, but thank you."

I walked over to the soft chairs and sat in one. There was soft music and warm lighting. I stared at the posters of perfect-looking white people. They were all smiling, had perfect teeth, and were well dressed, like business professionals. I started feeling a little out of place, but I waited, anyway. After about five minutes, a personal banker smiled at me and invited me to sit at his desk.

"What brings you in today?" he asked once we were both seated.

I put the check on his desk. "I would like to open an account."

"Okay. Awesome. Let me gather your information. I'll take your ID and get started. Is your current address correct on your ID?"

I retrieved my license from my purse. "No, I moved. I live at thirty-four Tahiti Beach Island Road."

"What kind of work do you do?"

"I'm an entertainer . . . a rapper."

"Really? That's cool. I don't listen to rap much . . . Are you famous?"

"Almost, I guess," I replied with a shrug.

"Okay. Can you write your SSN on this piece of paper for me? I'll rip it up and toss it right after."

He handed me a Post-it Note, and I wrote down my Social Security number.

After I passed him the Post-it, he typed the information into the computer. "Go ahead and sign the back of the check."

I did that.

He picked up the check and said, "I'll be right back. I'll deposit your check, gather some paperwork for you, and then you'll be good to go."

While he went to the back, I noticed that a man across the room was staring at me. He was a tall, handsome light-skinned man with a nice fade and a shadow goatee. He was wearing that navy-blue suit and tie well. He was next in line at the teller. For a few minutes, I watched him conduct his transaction and put a fat stack of money in a briefcase. Before he left, we made eye contact briefly. Then he was on his way.

I waited patiently for the personal banker to return.

"All right, Miss Fernández, you're all set. Everything you need to know about your new account is right here," he said, handing me a folder with my account information and online banking directions. "Your ATM card will be coming in the mail. If you need to order checks, the paperwork explains how to do that. If you need to withdraw any money before your card comes, just come in and show your ID, and we will be more than happy to help you. Do you have any questions for me?"

"No, I'm all good. Thank you."

The banker walked me to the front door and opened it for me.

I walked to where my car was parked along the curb. I couldn't help but notice the man in the navy suit, his sunglasses on, leaning up against a white Porsche. He was parked behind my car, as if he knew the Benz was mine. I pretended my hardest to act like he wasn't standing there.

"You're gorgeous, you know that?" he said.

I looked at him and saw just how tall he was, as he had stood up straight.

I said, "You really should be careful about walkin' up out of that bank with all that money in your briefcase. People could be watching—"

"You were the only one watching me." He smiled sexily. Though his eyes were hidden, I could tell he was taking in all of me.

I pushed the door handle to open my car door.

"I can't get your name?" he asked, revealing the tattoo on his neck when he turned to the side to watch a few cars driving past.

"What's *your* name?" I asked, deflecting.

He removed his glasses to reveal his light hazel eyes. "I'm Nasim."

I opened my door and got in my car without giving him my name.

"Damn. Like that?" he called.

I started up the car and rolled down the window. "You're wasting your time. I'm in a relationship."

"You can't have friends? I'm new to Miami, and I don't know many people out here. Can I get your number?"

"No." I pulled out of the spot.

I drove off while shaking my head. Luckily, I was happy in my new relationship, or else I would have been all over that. I didn't need no new friends, especially not fine-ass ones like him.

"The shoot is going to start in about ten minutes," Luxury yelled as he breathed down the makeup artist's neck.

Terry, the makeup artist, was finishing the last few touches on my makeup, and I could tell he was irritated at how Luxury was yelling at him every five minutes. Nia had already installed and styled my weave, and Lala was steam pressing my outfit.

I stared at Luxury out of the corner of my eye. You would think he wouldn't be so antsy, since he was in the industry. He should've smoked a blunt or something, the way he was pacing. As my manager—a title he had given himself—he was a stickler about time, and nobody could be late. When he walked out of the dressing room, we all could breathe better.

"Is he your man or your manager?" Terry asked, prying.

"He's both," I replied, feeling my bad attitude rising.

The expression on Terry's face as he chewed on that gum had me looking at him like he had lost his mind.

"Please, don't frown. I don't want your makeup to get fucked up, boo," he told me.

"Why the fuck you looking at me like that?" I asked, gazing up into his eyes.

"Girl, how you deal with Luxury's baby mamas? That's what I want to know."

"Baby mamas?" I kept my face as straight as I could, but my voice was raised.

"Shhh," he said, going over my cheeks with the brush and lowering his voice so that Nia and Lala wouldn't hear him. "You don't know about his kids?"

"He don't have any kids, boo boo."

"Mmm, looks like somebody hasn't told you. He definitely got kids, boo boo," he replied and smacked his lips together.

"How many you heard he got?" I asked, trying my best not to frown, but it wasn't working.

"Two. The second one ain't here yet, because she's still pregnant, but she's due any day now. I'm shocked you ain't heard about it. Everybody's talking about it."

"Well, I don't know who you been listening to, but I live with him, and I haven't seen or heard anything about these bitches, so . . ."

"Wait . . . How long y'all been living together?"

"Nigga, finish my fuckin' makeup before we have a problem," I barked.

He pursed his lips while he continued his handiwork.

Terry seemed like the type who would be friends with one of the baby mamas and would run and tell all the business. I didn't know him, or who he was affiliated with, so I kept my mouth shut. As soon as he finished my makeup, I made my way over to Lala so she could put me in my first look.

"What was Terry's messy ass over there talking about?" Lala asked, fixing my pants at the bottom.

"Nothing," I replied. I didn't trust Lala, either.

She twisted her lips and rolled her eyes, as if she knew I was lying, but didn't press me.

When she was done, I walked out of the dressing room. Luxury was waiting right outside the door to escort me onto the set.

When we reached the set, the photographer was still testing the lighting and wasn't ready for me, so I stood there and looked over at Luxury. He was sending someone a text message.

"You got a baby on the way?" I heard myself ask.

He didn't look up from his phone as he said, "She says so, but I don't think it's mine."

"You don't *think*? When were you going to tell me?"

"When I found out for sure he's mine. No use in bringing it up if the baby is another nigga's."

"So, uh, what about the other secret kid somewhere?"

"Not mine. A blood test proved that, sweetheart." He took a good look at me. "That pussy-ass nigga was in your ear, I see. I told Lala and Nia I don't like that nigga, but they swear he's the fuckin' best. You believe everything everybody tells you?"

"I don't. That's why I asked you. I'd rather hear that kind of shit from you."

"If ya ain't heard it from me, then it ain't true, point-blank, period."

Before I could read him to determine if he was telling the truth or not, the photographer was walking our way.

"Desire, are you ready?" she asked. "You look glamorous, by the way."

"I'm ready. Thank you." I smiled.

I followed her over to the backdrop.

She took over a hundred shots of me, and I changed clothes two more times. When the shoot was over, she uploaded the photographs. Luxury stared at them on the computer screen and chose his favorites. I got to add my input too. I was impressed at the raw photos. Once the Photoshop editing was done, my album was going to be perfect.

Luxury said to the photographer, "I'll have our assistant, Egypt, look out for the final shots."

"It was a pleasure to work with you and Desire. She's gorgeous and looks good on camera."

"Thank you so much, again," I told her and smiled. Then I walked to the dressing room with Luxury.

"You did good, baby, but you almost pissed me off with that rumor shit," he said.

"I was thinking about it . . . I know this all happened before we got together, so . . . I'm not going to worry about it."

"You shouldn't worry about shit. Your man is handling it," he replied. "Now let's go have us some dinner. You hungry?"

I nodded. "I'm starving."

"Good, 'cause I am too. Get changed."

I walked into the dressing room, and Lala helped me get out of my clothes. I couldn't stop thinking about the fact that Luxury had kept his past dealings with other women a secret from me. *Why*? I wondered. I didn't care that the kids possibly were or weren't his, but I felt that I should've known from the jump that these allegations were swirling around.

When I walked out of the dressing room, Luxury was ending a call. He was breathing hard and gritting his teeth.

"Is everything okay?" I asked.

"Frill just got fuckin' arrested."

"What? For what?"

"Bullshit." He walked toward the exit.

I followed him. "Bullshit like what?"

He stopped walking and faced me. "Some dumb street shit."

"Street shit like what? Drugs?"

"Not using drugs, but . . ." The muscles in his masculine jawline danced while he gritted his teeth. "Now is not the time to explain or go into detail. I gotta get him out, or Mama will kill me."

"You got a lawyer?" I asked him.

"Of course. I have the best lawyers that money can buy, baby."

I observed him, stared intensely into his eyes. He wouldn't maintain eye contact with me.

This wasn't making sense to me. Why would Frill get arrested for street shit like selling drugs? He was making way too much money to be involved in the drug scene. That got me to thinking that all of them still had ties to the drug business.

"Are you still in the street shit too? You the plug?" I quizzed.

"Stop askin' all these fuckin' questions. You don't need to know everything. I don't want you to be into this if it gets ugly. Matter of fact, you don't know nothing. Follow me."

We walked outside and got in his car. As we rode, I turned up the music to help change my mood. Hearing that shit about his potential baby-mama drama had rattled me a little. I wanted Luxury to be up front and honest with me. I realized that if I wished to get honesty, I had to look into Luxury's eyes, because they were the windows to his soul. Everything I needed to know was written beyond those slanted deep brown eyes.

14

DESIRE

Saving Grace

Luxury bailed Frill out, but he wouldn't be released for a few hours, so Luxury wanted me to go get something to eat and head home without him, because he needed to talk to Frill about some things. At first, I was a little upset. I didn't like how Luxury was trying to kick this incident under the rug. If he wanted to marry me, how come I didn't know everything? This wasn't about me meddling in his business, either. This was about me knowing exactly who he was and what he was into.

It was times like these when I missed Mina so much. I wished I had other friends whom I could call up and kick it with. I wished I had clicked a bit with Egypt, Nia, and Lala, but I hadn't really tried.

Luxury drove me to my car, which was parked outside the spot where we had the photo shoot, and then he went on his way. I was hungry as hell and wanted some good soul food, so I headed to one of my favorite spots.

I drove with my new, unreleased album playing. My music was surreal to me. I wasn't sure if I could ever get used to hearing myself. The song I had written for Mina came on, and I cried a little as I listened to it. Living my life without her was hard, and at times, the pain was too much, but Luxury helped me keep myself together. After pulling up to the curb near the restaurant, I dried my tears and got out.

I walked into the restaurant and looked at the menu before I ordered three fried chicken wings, mac 'n' cheese, greens, yams, and corn-bread muffins. I paid for my food. As I waited for my order, I scrolled through Facebook to see what was going on, on my page. Ever since Luxury had told me to create a fan page, I had all these likes. People were telling me how much they loved the music. When my food was ready, I took the bag and walked out.

A bunch of niggas were hanging out outside the restaurant. They had their music turned up, and they were trying to talk over it. In the group was that man whom I had seen at the bank earlier. I walked toward my car, acting like I didn't recognize him.

"Why you walking so damn fast? Slow down," he said from behind me.

I turned to look at him, and I couldn't help but notice how fly he looked in his dark jeans and white button-up shirt. Baby was looking good. There was no doubt about that. I was irritated with Luxury, and there was no telling if he was being straight up about his baby mama issues. Other than Luxury, I didn't have any friends. I needed someone other than him in my corner.

"How long have you been living here?" I asked, remembering he had said he was new to the city.

"About a week," he replied, showing the gold grill on his bottom teeth.

"You got family out here or something?"

"Something like that."

"Where you from?" I asked.

"New York. Harlem."

"Interesting," I responded, taking note of his New York accent.

"How so?" he asked before he licked his lips and held his hands in front of his waist.

"I've never met anyone from New York before. So, um, what brings you to Miami?"

"The weather . . . I needed a change. I love the weather here. You from here?"

I didn't respond to that question, because I didn't want him to get the whole scoop that quickly. "Well, I don't want to be rude, but I'm hungry, and I need to get home."

He stared at my bag. "Eating alone tonight?"

"My man's at work, so yeah, most likely. Where's your better half?"

"My better half? Yo, I'm single, very single. Wait, I feel like I gotta introduce myself all over again, since I doubt you remember my name."

He was right. I didn't remember his name. I just knew that I needed someone I could talk to during the times Luxury was too busy for me. My best friend was dead, and I had no one. What would it hurt?

"I'm sorry. I don't."

"Nasim." He extended his hand. "My name is Nasim."

I shook his hand. "My name is . . ." I paused, debating whether I should give my stage name or my real name. "Desire."

"Is that what ya mama named you?"

"That's just what everyone calls me."

"Is that what you would like for me to call you?"

I nodded. "Yeah."

"A'ight. Well, it's nice to meet you, Desire. Here, take my number. I know you gotta get home to eat your food while it's still hot, so I won't keep you."

I took my phone out of my purse, and he gave me his number. I saved his number in my phone and called the contact N. Though I had a lock on my phone, I didn't know if Luxury was the type to spy.

"Well, it was good seeing you. I'll be in touch," I said.

"A'ight. Cool." He licked his lips and watched me get into my car.

I put my food on the passenger seat and drove off. My phone was ringing, and I didn't recognize the number, but I picked up, anyway.

"Hello?"

"Damn, big shot. You lightweight famous and you can't call your only brother?"

"Jav?" I asked. I couldn't believe my ears. I hadn't heard from my brother since I left home.

"Yeah, who else would it be? I got your number out of Papi's phone."

I was so happy to hear from him. "Oh my God. Brother, what's up? Where you been?"

"Home. You act like you don't know where that is. I've heard you all on the radio. I didn't think rap was your thing, but you're good at it."

I laughed. "Shut up. How's Papi? You know, I haven't heard from him in a while."

"Well, that's why I'm calling you. I know you don't need any news like this right now, especially since Mina passed. Papi is in the hospital and has been for a while. It's not looking too good. He's dying, Desi."

"Dying? Wait? What?"

"He's at the end stage of lung cancer. He's asking about you, saying he really wants to see you. Can you come up here, like, right now?"

My heart plummeted. Fear crept over me like an icy chill, numbing me. There was no question that I would be there. My mind could register only that I had to be at my dad's side in his last moments.

"I'm on my way. Where is he?"

I sped to the hospital as fast as I could. Thinking about my dad dying, I couldn't eat. With everything going on in my life recently, I hadn't called to check up on him, and I felt terrible about it. I felt as if I was living in hell on Earth, and it took everything in me to stay strong right now.

Javier met me in the lobby of the hospital, and we hugged and cried for a little while. I couldn't help but notice he looked a lot different than he had the last time I saw him. The obvious thing was that he had lost a lot of weight. He looked good in his fitted dark chinos that stopped at his ankles, his loafers without socks, and a mint-green button-up, which he had paired with a sports jacket that matched his chinos. His hair was slicked back into a ponytail, and his face was free of all facial hair.

"It's good to see you," he said when we finally wiped our tears.

It felt good to hear him say that, because all our lives, we had talked major shit to one another.

"It's nice to see you too," I said. "I need to see Papi."

Javier nodded.

I followed him to the elevator and then to Papi's room. At the door I paused, not sure if I was ready to go inside. I took a deep breath before Javier opened the door for me.

As I walked inside that hospital room, my heart felt like it had left my chest.

Mama was holding Papi's hand tightly, crying her eyes out. As soon as she saw me, she wiped her tears but wouldn't make eye contact. A look of disgust appeared on her face, but I ignored her. I thought about speaking to her, but the look on her face prevented me from saying even hello. She moved over so I could be at my dad's side. At least she did that.

I stared at my father. He was skin and bones, pale as a ghost. His face couldn't mask the ordeal going on inside his body. Cancer had taken his hair. He was almost unrecognizable.

"Oh, Papi," I let out, tears flowing down my face. I kissed him on the forehead.

He looked into my eyes with tears in his own, and I sensed that he was shocked to see me. His lips parted slightly, as if he was about to speak.

"My baby," he whispered. "Desirae."

I took his hand in mine and held it, feeling my heart crumble. "I love you, Papi."

"I love you more," he whispered back.

I looked over at Javier, who had stationed himself at the end of the bed. "Why didn't anyone call me sooner?" I asked him, crying hysterically.

"He didn't want anyone to know. You know Papi. So secretive."

"Papi . . . ," I cried, laying my cheek on his chest.

"I'm sorry," Papi said.

First Mina. Now Papi. This was too much. As I cried, it felt like I was being ripped apart from the inside out. From my mouth came a sound that a wounded animal might make.

"How long you gonna be here?" Mama asked with an attitude.

I stopped crying at that moment, but my chest was so tight that I couldn't breathe. How heartless could this bitch be? I wanted to be here for my dad, and she couldn't wait for me to leave. Instead of keeping her feelings to herself, she had voiced them, without a care in the world about my feelings.

"Papi, I'm here for you," I said, making sure she could hear me.

He nodded, and I felt him try to squeeze my hand, but he was weak. "Thank you, baby."

"Okay, he saw you. Now you can go," Mama uttered in the nastiest tone.

"Why do you hate me so much?" I asked her, tears cascading down my face.

She rolled her eyes and sucked her teeth. "Please, don't start with me."

"You're starting with me. Just let me have my time with my papi, please."

"I know you're a rapper, or whatever you call yourself these days, but don't forget who you're talking to."

"Enough," Papi said. He attempted to shout, but it came out as a whisper.

"Mama, let her have this time with Papi," Javier interjected.

She rolled her eyes and said, "Text me when she's gone. I don't care to share the same air." She stormed out of the room.

I closed my eyes, feeling the pain of my mother's cruel words, but then I let it all go and went back to looking at Papi's face.

"She loves you," Papi said.

“Oh, no, I don’t believe that.”

“She just has high—” Papi stopped to cough.

“Papi, please don’t try to talk. You can’t even breathe,” Javier said. “Give him a sip of that water, Desi.”

I picked up the cup and put the straw up to his lips. Papi took a sip and lay back, with his eyes closed.

“Now that she’s out of here, I got something to say to you, Desi,” Javier said.

“Me?” I asked, wiping my tears again. “What’s up?”

“Well, I don’t know if you noticed the change in me.”

I looked at him. “I have. You lost some weight, right?”

“Yes, I have.”

“You look amazing, Jav.”

“Thank you. I’m moving out of the house.”

“What? It’s about fuckin’ time. Where you moving to?”

“Orlando.” He paused before he added, “With my boyfriend.”

Boyfriend? I looked at him closely to see if I had heard him right. I had never suspected that Javier was gay. I mean, he had never had a girlfriend, but I had thought it was because he didn’t know how to talk to girls.

“That’s fabulous news, Jav. Are you happy?”

“Extremely,” he said, beaming.

“Congratulations. Does Mama know?”

He shook his head vigorously. “Uh, no, but I think she suspects. I came out to Papi a long time ago, and he said if I told Mama, it would break her heart, so I couldn’t. I just feel like I have to tell her, before someone else does.”

“I understand. I’m happy you get to go and do you. I love you, Jav.”

I reached for a hug. He hugged me tightly.

“I love you too, li’l sis. I’m the happiest I’ve ever been.”

“I can tell. Well, keep in touch with me. You’ll be far, but I’m only a phone call away.”

He smiled, but then his expression turned serious when he looked over at Papi. "I'm just glad he got to see you."

"I know. I'm glad too." More tears fell from my eyes.

We stayed right at Papi's side until he took his last breath early the next morning. To no surprise, my mother did not come back in the room until I was gone.

15

LUXURY

Drive Me Crazy

After bailing Frill out, I tried to call Desire to see if she wanted me to bring her anything to eat, but she wasn't answering. I kept calling. When her phone started sending me straight to voicemail, I figured either her phone had died or she'd turned her phone off because I was annoying her. Either way, I didn't play that shit. All she had to do was let me know what was up. I wasn't sure if she was mad off that baby rumor and these fake wannabe baby mamas or if she was mad because I couldn't take her along with me to bail Frill out of jail. Whatever it was that was bothering her, all she had to do was say it.

She couldn't go missing like this. She had a radio interview in the morning. Each time I called, anger boiled deeper in my system, and it wanted to flow out like fiery lava. My rage was churning within, and I felt I would self-destruct at any moment. The pressure I felt was about to force me to say some shit I didn't mean. I almost left a few crazy-ass texts and voicemails for her, but then I stopped myself. What if she had been in a car accident?

I went home, and I stayed up, checking the news. I searched through all the local accident reports and didn't see anything about Desire. I was relieved that she wasn't hurt, but I was still mad. Each time I dozed off, I would wake up and check the garage to see if she had come home. Once again, I refrained from texting some crazy shit, but I wanted to so bad.

As I poured a drink and rolled a blunt, I started thinking she wasn't coming back. I needed to relax, but then I thought of the worst. Like what if somebody had hurt my baby? What if she was lying out there in the street, bleeding to death? The shit with her best friend being executed like that had never sat well with me. What if whoever had killed her friend had wanted to do her in next? Hopefully, whatever that was about didn't have anything to do with Desire, or somebody was going to have to feel my wrath.

This love shit was new to me. Was I supposed to sweat her like this? Was she supposed to disappear for hours and not say anything? Usually, when I got this close to someone, I would push them away or say some dumb shit to make the chick fall out of love with me. This time, I wanted things to be different. I was older now, but I still had some learning to do. I mean, I did some dumb shit from time to time, but on everything I loved, I wanted Desire to spend the rest of her life with me.

After I took a few shots and smoked my weed, I lay on the couch and checked all her social media pages to see if she had posted anything. She didn't have any updates. I got distracted by some funny shit Mike Epps had posted on his Instagram. I laughed at that craziness and fell asleep.

I was jolted out of my sleep when my phone started ringing, and I jumped up. I saw it was my mom. Feeling disappointed, I answered, anyway, "Hey, Mama."

"Hey, Poo. How are you?"

"I'm straight. You?"

"I'm good. You got Jon-Jon out of jail?" she said.

"Yes, ma'am. He's with Lavish."

"What Spoodie up to?"

She never called us by our street names and hardly ever by our government names. She had said that no matter how famous we got, she would always call us by the nicknames she had given us. I was the oldest, and my birth name was Tyriq, but she called me Poo. Lavish's real name was Levante, but she called him Spoodie. Frill was named De'Jonn at birth, but she called him Jon-Jon. De'Vonn was Frill's identical twin, but she called him Man-Man. Travis was the baby, born only a year after the twins, but she called him Dinky. We were her Monnahan Clan.

"Nothing much. What's up?" I said.

"I'm just calling to make sure you got Jon-Jon out of jail, since he didn't come home. That's no place for him to be, especially with me dealing with Dinky being in prison. I need you to make sure Jon-Jon stays his ass out of jail. I don't want another son spending the rest of his life in no cage."

"I know. You ain't try to call him?"

"I did, but he didn't answer."

"He might be in the studio at Spoodie's house, working on the new album."

"Okay." She paused for a moment before she said, "I heard you got another baby on the way. How you feel about that?"

I shook my head. This rumor was irritating me. Now my mother wanted to believe it too. "Mama, I took a paternity test, and that first baby ain't mine, so don't say *another baby*, as if it is mine. I'm sure this one ain't mine, either. You shouldn't listen to everything you hear."

She grunted, "So, this is how you gonna keep doing things, huh? If you wear a condom, you wouldn't have to get no kids tested."

"Mama, not right now. I got a lot going on."

"Jon-Jon say you got a new girlfriend. I'm just wondering when I'm gonna meet her."

"Soon," I replied, hoping Desire was still my woman. If she didn't come home with a good reason as to why she hadn't answered my calls, we were going to have a problem.

"Well, come to see me sometime, Poo. Damn. Y'all done put me in this big house but don't come to visit. Jon-Jon doesn't ever come home. I don't want to have to call to chase after any of you. I'm getting ready to call Spoodie and see if he picks up."

"Okay. I love you."

"I love you too."

I waited for her to hang up first, just in case there was something else she wanted to say.

Thinking about Desire made my stomach hurt. I hopped up from the couch and poured another drink while I called her again. Straight to voicemail. Where the fuck was she at?

16

DESIRE

Death Is Too Unkind

After kissing Papi one last time, I went home. I was overwhelmed with grief and heartache. I couldn't stop thinking about how many years I had stayed away from home. I could've at least checked on my papi more often. He had had cancer for the past two years, and I had had no idea. Never once during our lunch dates had he mentioned it. The reality that the two people who loved me the most were no longer on this earth was devastating.

Death was mean. It didn't care about nothing or nobody. It had snatched up the most important people in my life, people who had been far too good to me. Death didn't pretend to care about my feelings. It had ripped away the most significant part of me, my papi. My heart was turning cold, and I felt empty.

When I entered the house, I found Luxury sitting in the living room, looking at the TV. He looked like he hadn't slept much at all.

He jumped to his feet. "What the fuck, Desire?"

“I know . . . I know,” I said, not knowing what else to say.

“You couldn’t call me to let me know you were all right? Where the fuck were you?”

I paused. My phone had died, and I hadn’t had a charger with me. I hadn’t been concerned about it, because I had been focused on being there for my papi.

“I was at the hospital. My papi . . . I watched him take his last breath . . . I’m sorry.”

He searched my eyes for the truth, wondering if I would be so heartless as to lie about my dad dying. When he saw my tears, he softened. “Come here, baby.”

I went over to him and cried in his arms.

“I was worried and, man, I didn’t know. You got a radio interview this morning, remember?”

I hadn’t been able to think about anything but Papi dying in my arms. I had completely forgot about the interview. I was sure Egypt had called me to remind me.

“Can we reschedule? I . . . just need some time.”

Luxury let go of me and looked confused, and for a split second, it looked like he wanted to cuss me out.

“What?” I scowled.

“You gotta find a way to work through your pain. I know it’s hard, but you have to.”

“That’s what I’ve been doing. Workin’ nonstop. I didn’t even have time to mourn my best friend, and now my papi is dead. I feel like what’s left of me has died, and I’m supposed to just keep going like nothing has happened?”

“I’m not about to get into it with you right now. Your first album drops in less than a month. We don’t have time for any setbacks. You don’t show up for scheduled interviews, you’ll get a bad name before anybody has time to know who you are.”

I wasn't feeling what Luxury was talking about. He didn't understand where I was coming from. I hadn't said I didn't want to do it. I just needed a little time to myself. Could I bury myself in bed just once? All I needed was a few days alone.

"Maybe we need a break or something. I just feel like I need to breathe," I said.

His chest was heaving up and down. "You can't breathe with me around?"

My bottom lip was trembling, and my tears were building back up. "It's just all this . . . It's too much. My papi was the one person left in this world who loved me unconditionally."

"Baby," he said. "Listen to me. I love you. You got me. I know I'm hard on you, and that's only because you're almost there. You have a hit record and an album that's about to drop. Do this for your papi and for Mina. They wouldn't want you to quit because they're gone."

My chest was hurting, and I felt like giving up, but he was right. I was almost there. I was in too deep to quit.

"I promise, you can have some alone time soon," he said. "I'll make sure of it."

He allowed me to cry in his arms for a little while longer.

17

LUXURY

Time to Shine

When I woke up and realized we were late for Desire's radio interview, I started cursing. I hadn't meant to fall asleep, but as soon as we'd sat on the couch, we'd both dozed off. I grabbed my phone, and I had about a dozen missed calls from Egypt.

"Fuck, fuck, fuck," I groaned.

Desire woke up. "What's wrong?" She stretched and yawned.

"We're late, baby. We gotta get showered and dressed fast. We don't have time for hair and makeup and all that shit. So you gonna have to improvise."

She got off the couch and took a ten-minute shower. I hopped in after her. She put on some ripped jeans, a black shirt, and some jewelry. I wore a long-sleeved white shirt, black jeans, and black Air Jordan 5 Retros. I grabbed my keys and jogged down the stairs to the garage. We got in my car and headed out. My phone was blowing up, and I kept sending the callers to voicemail. As soon as we stepped into the radio station, Egypt began glaring at us.

"You're almost an hour late," she said.

Egypt was always on point, always and forever. We went back to childhood, project days. We went to the same elementary school, junior high, and high school. And she and her cousins, Nia and Lala, were still around. Egypt was cool with my mama. She wasn't on some scandalous shit, and she was about her business. Shit, Egypt had even flushed my dope down the toilet when the cops were coming one time. I trusted her with my life. That was why she had the job. Nowadays her main job was to assist Desire. Desire had never said much to her, so I wasn't sure if she liked Egypt, but it didn't matter if she liked her or not. Egypt had a job to do, and that was to stay on top of Desire and handle all her bookings.

"Rough night?" Egypt asked, inspecting us from head to toe.

"Very rough night," I said.

"Good thing they know how artists are never on time. Don't make this a habit, though," she said. "I'll let them know you're here. You can wait in the guest area. Follow me."

Desire and I followed Egypt to the guest waiting area before she walked down the hallway.

"I have to go pee," Desire said to me.

"All right," I said. "I think I saw the bathrooms down the hall."

"Okay," she replied and excused herself.

After a few seconds, Egypt walked into the waiting area. "Where did she go?"

"To the bathroom. She'll be right back."

"Okay, cool. They said in about fifteen minutes, she'll be on. You are more than welcome to sit in with her."

"Oh, she wasn't going in there without me," I stated.

"You're so protective of her," Egypt said, looking at me strangely.

"I gotta be. Too many vultures in this business."

"Mixing business with pleasure is dangerous," Egypt warned.

"Not really," I countered, staring her down. If she didn't watch her mouth, she would be looking for a new job. I didn't care how far we went back.

She cleared her throat and shut right on up. She knew me better than that. She had never seen me in love before, so this was all new.

I paid attention to the way she was looking at a nigga. Egypt wasn't ugly at all, and I had told her she was cute once in high school. Plus, I could've fucked Egypt, but my excuse had been that I didn't want to mix business with pleasure. She could now see that I could combine business with pleasure, and she didn't like that too much.

"Some chick came up here right before you got here," she said. "Asking and looking for you." She handed me an envelope.

"What's this?"

She shrugged. "I don't know. She said she wanted me to give this to you."

I took the envelope from her and opened it. I pulled out two sheets of paper and read them in a hurry. The paragraph at the bottom of the first page said that there was a 99.9 percent probability that I was the father of a baby boy named Tyriq Letrell Monnahan Jr.

"Shit," I said, folding the papers back.

I guessed Charity hadn't lied when she said she was having my baby. She had given birth to a boy, and he was mine. I had mixed emotions about this. I was pissed, but I couldn't show I was pissed. It had been irresponsible of me to have sex unprotected with a bitch I didn't even like. Charity wasn't a bad person; she just wasn't what I had in mind when it came to someone I would have to spend the next eighteen years in contact with.

"Do they have something to drink here, like Henny or something?" I asked Egypt, feeling like I needed something to deal with this harsh news.

"Yeah, they have a few bottles of something. Let me get it for you."

"Get a shot for Desire too," I told her.

She frowned at first, then nodded and left the waiting area. How was I going to tell Desire this shit?

18

DESIRE

Unexpected Stranger

I used the bathroom, washed my hands, and took a few deep breaths to calm my nerves. When Luxury had told me Egypt would be my assistant, I hadn't tripped, because that meant I could watch her sneaky ass. When we'd met up with her here at the station, I hadn't been feeling her at all. I mean, I always side-eyed her whenever she was around Luxury, because she acted like she had a crush on him and couldn't stand looking at me. I wasn't stupid or blind. I didn't have to ask him if they had fucked, because I could tell they never had. She was too thirsty for his attention all the time.

When I came out of the bathroom, I couldn't believe who was coming down the hall toward me. His handsome face wasn't paying attention to where he was going, because he was all into his phone. Finally, he looked up, and he smiled when he saw me.

"Are you stalking me, Nasim?" I asked.

He chuckled at the thought. "Nah, not at all. My boy works here. We about to go have a few beers in a little bit."

"He's a radio host?"

"Nah. He's a DJ. You sure you ain't the one stalking me?"

"Not at all . . . So, you mean to tell me that I see you at the bank, then at the soul-food joint, and now here, at the radio station? Does this sound like a coincidence to you?"

"That's what it is. What you doing here?"

"I have an interview with Big Joe."

"You . . . ? You're the artist Desire?"

I nodded. "That's me."

"Damn, I didn't know. I didn't even put two and two together. Hey, I like your style. I bump yo' shit."

"That's what's up. I'm glad you didn't know who I was at first. Well, I gotta get in here and do this interview."

"A'ight. Hey, it's mad cool to text me sometimes, you know. You got the number."

Before I could respond, he went into the men's bathroom. My nerves were even more all over the place now. I would be crazy not to admit I was attracted to Nasim, but I couldn't go there. I pushed him out of my mind and walked back to the waiting area.

Luxury handed me a shot of Henny. "Here. This should calm your nerves."

"I haven't eaten anything yet. I don't want to get sick."

He pointed to the tray of croissants, muffins, and fruits. "Egypt got that for you."

I tried not to roll my eyes as I forced myself to smile at Egypt. She smiled back at me. I went over to the table and picked up a croissant. I took a few bites before downing the shot. That was exactly what I needed, because my anxiety calmed all the way down.

"They're ready for you, Miss Desire," Egypt said.

I took a deep breath and followed her into the room. Luxury and I sat down.

"Welcome to the show," Big Joe said.

"Thank you for having me," I told him.

"We're about to go live in a bit here. You nervous?" he said with a smile.

"A little," I admitted, feeling my hands starting to shake.

"This your first interview?"

"Yeah, something like that."

"Wow. I feel blessed to have you give me your first exclusive interview."

"No problem. Anytime."

"A'ight. How you doing, Luxury?"

"I'm good," Luxury replied. "It's been a while."

"I know. I see the label is doing good for you. Got the Monnahan Boyz and now Desire. You're on fire right now, bro."

"Yes indeed. You know how I do it."

"Indeed. A'ight, we're about to go live . . . in five, four, three, two, one . . . You're listening to Big Joe in the morning. Sitting in with me this morning is the lovely and talented hot new rapper on the scene, Desire. Welcome to the show, Desire."

"Thank you," I said into the mic. "It's a pleasure to be here."

"So, tell me how you got started with rap. Was this something you always wanted to do?"

"Honestly, I was just messing around in the studio with the Monnahan Boyz, and they liked the way the track sounded. The rest is history."

"Right, right. Well, your flow is hot. I know you hear that a lot, but you got bars."

"Thank you."

"Tell me about what it's like working with the Monnahan Boyz. They've been on the scene in Miami for years, and now they are platinum-selling artists."

"You know, they're like my brothers. This whole experience has been, like, mind blowing."

"I bet. You seem to be keeping your relationship on a good foot too," he said.

"Yeah, me and Luxury, we good."

"Luxury is in the building, sitting right here. I must say, y'all don't seem too affected by the baby-mama drama that hit the Net."

"Nah, it is what it is," I responded. "That was before me, you know. Luxury keeps it real with me. We're good."

I kept answering Big Joe's questions. Luxury spoke up from time to time, when he knew I was stuck. I felt myself sweating. I probably sounded like a hot mess.

After the interview was over, I felt so relieved. I hadn't wanted to speak about Luxury's baby mama or any rumors. It had seemed to me like Big Joe wanted to collect some dirt and be the first to get the exclusive story. The shit had bothered me.

"You need to sound more confident," Luxury told me once we were back in the lobby with Egypt. "I get it that this was your first interview, but you gotta know they will ask some tricky-ass shit to get you caught up."

I frowned. "Yeah, I see that. I don't think it's anybody's business what goes on in our personal lives, though. I don't get it."

"That shit is going to happen. All we can do is answer the way we did. I'm proud of you, baby. Thank you for being strong right now. I know it's tough, with your dad passing last night and everything."

He embraced me and placed the deepest kiss on my lips.

"It's hard, but like you said, the show must go on, you know," I said when we broke our embrace.

"That's right. We got this, right?"

"Yeah," I replied.

Out the corner of my eye, I could see Egypt pretending that she wasn't staring at us with envy.

19

LUXURY

Downhill

Two weeks later . . .

Lights were flashing, bottles were popping, and Desire's music was blaring throughout the club, where the hottest celebrities and other important people had turned up for Desire's album-release party. The crowd was going crazy.

"Wassup wit y'all, Miami?" the DJ yelled over the mic. "Y'all deep in this bitch tonight. DJ Triton in the building. The moment y'all been waiting fa is here. Give it up for *Desire*."

Desire grabbed the mic and said, "I want to thank everyone for coming out to show me love. I've worked hard on this album. Thanks to my niggas, the Monnahan Boyz, for treating me like a li'l sis. Those are my brothers for life. To my baby, Luxury, for being my boo and making this rap shit happen for me. This has been a crazy year, but I'm pushing strong." She paused, and the crowd howled and clapped. "I hope y'all enjoy the album."

I nodded my head at her. I had yet to tell her the paternity news, but I figured that shit could wait until the right time. I had made sure to make the child-support situation cool with the baby mama, Charity.

I took down another gulp of the thick purple liquid that Lavish had poured into my cup. I wasn't big on Lean, but this shit had me feeling right. I dizzily checked my phone and saw that Charity had thanked me for the money. I didn't respond.

"Luxury, baby, you might want to slow down on that shit," Desire whispered in my ear, trying to take the red cup out of my hand.

"I'm cool. Stop." I pulled the cup away, stumbling back.

"You're high as fuck. Maybe we should go home." She grabbed my wrist and pulled to try to get me to sit down.

"Hold up, baby. Tonight's your night. This is your album-release party. I ain't going nowhere. All these people are here for you."

The club was packed now, and the loud trap music was blaring through the speakers. The song that was playing sounded too damn good.

Desire gave me the cutest little worried look. I pulled her into my arms and whispered in her ear, "You know I love the fuck out of you, right?"

"I know that. I love you too."

My baby meant the world to me. A second later, my phone was buzzing, and so was hers. She pulled out her phone and stared at her Twitter. I looked at mine. I kept seeing all these tweets about my baby mama and how I had a baby I wasn't claiming. *Fuck.* I looked up and gazed at Desire's face, hoping her phone wasn't going off for the same reason.

"What the fuck! What is this, Luxury?" she shouted.

"Baby, I can explain."

"You *know* about this? Did you take a paternity test?"

I nodded. "I got the results two weeks ago."

"Two weeks ago? Oh, wow." She stormed out of the VIP area.

Frill scowled at me. "What's up with Desire?"

I didn't respond as I tried my best to follow her. I was so fucked up, I could hardly steady my steps. I felt someone grab my arm. I turned and saw that it was Egypt. She had her phone in her hand.

"Do you know what this is going to do to her album sales?" she yelled over the music. "Controversy sells more records, Luxury, but you gotta make it right with her."

I snatched my arm away from her. I could fix this shit. It wasn't like I was in a relationship with Charity.

I saw Desire leave the club, but by the time I got outside, I didn't see her anywhere. With her father's funeral only a few days behind us, I didn't know if this would be her breaking point. I prayed it wouldn't be. I staggered back into the club and sent her an "I'm sorry" text and waited for her reply.

20

DESIRE

Fresh Air

Album-release party or not, I got the fuck up outta there. I was gonna go the fuck off if I didn't get out of that stuffy-ass club. I hopped in my car, with tears flowing. This nigga had lied. What else had he lied about? If he had lied about a baby, what else was he hiding? I was too fragile to deal with this. My papi's body hadn't been in the ground a whole week, and now I had to deal with this shit? If I couldn't trust Luxury, who could I trust? I was so angry. I felt this tightness in my chest, like I couldn't breathe.

I had nowhere to go except home, and I didn't want to go there. If only Mina were still alive, I would go to her house. I just needed somewhere to go to cool off. I didn't want to hear anything from Luxury until I was calm enough to ask him about his secrets.

Nasim came to mind because I just needed to get away, and he was the only person I could call. I called him, and to my surprise, he picked up.

"Yo, you finally decided to hit me up?" he said, with his New York accent on thick.

"I know, right? What you doing right now?"

"Well, I'm about to go somewhere to drop something off. What up with you? Don't you have an album-release party tonight?"

"Yeah, but I just found out some crazy shit, and I need to get away. Mind if I roll with you?"

"I don't mind, but you sure?"

"If you ask me again, I might say no, so don't make me change my mind."

"Come on. I'll shoot the address."

I ended the call. He sent me his address, and I drove over there.

From the outside, Nasim's house looked so small, but inside, it was a lovely three-bedroom and was beautifully decorated for a bachelor pad. He didn't have much furniture, but what he had was so nice. I really needed to get away from Luxury's drama, and this was a breath of fresh air.

My phone was going crazy, so I put it on silent. I didn't want to read another tweet or blog related to Luxury.

He gave me a hug as he held a duffel bag in his right hand. "You've been crying?"

"A little. Just going through some shit right now. I don't want to talk about it, either, so don't fuckin' ask."

"A'ight. You don't have to. Let's go."

I followed him outside to his car. He opened the front passenger door for me, and once I was in, he closed it. He put the duffel bag on the backseat before getting in the driver's seat. We rode in silence for a little while.

He seemed to be lost in thought about something, and I couldn't stop thinking about Luxury having a baby. Was I supposed to be this baby's stepmother? I didn't know shit about that life.

"You straight?" he asked.

"I'll be fine."

He pulled up to this high-rise building downtown and said, "You can come inside with me."

I got out of the car and followed him after he grabbed the duffel. I was starting to regret my decision to roll with him, because I had no idea what kind of business he had to handle. We walked in the building, headed down a hallway, and entered a large office with an open floor plan. Nasim pointed at a lounge chair and invited me to sit. The space was full of professional black people dressed in business attire. This event looked much like a business mixer or something. Nasim walked to the back, and I saw that he was talking to someone. I looked around and noticed that everybody was staring at me.

A tall woman approached. "Aren't you the rapper Desire?" she asked.

"Yeah, that's me."

Like a reporter, she walked even closer to me. "Is it true that Luxury got some girl pregnant? I read it on the Shade Room website."

I stood up and rolled my neck. Just then Nasim walked over. I was sure he had heard the woman's comment.

"I'm done. Let's go," he said. He left the office, and as we walked out of the building, he wrapped an arm around me.

"I'm so glad you appeared at that moment, because I was about to cuss that ho out," I told him.

"So, I guess it's true about him having a baby on you, huh?"

"No, he didn't have the baby on me. She was already pregnant when we got together. He didn't know it was his until this paternity test."

"Is that why you called me?"

We got into his car, and he pulled away from the curb.

I sighed. "No. Well . . ."

He chuckled. "It's mad cool. I'm not tripping. I just want to make sure you a'ight."

"I'll be fine."

I was quiet for the rest of the ride back to his house. This whole ordeal with Luxury and his baby mama was something that wasn't going to go away. I was just so hurt that he hadn't just told me and kept it real with me. Nasim parked his car and turned it off. Before getting out, he looked over at me.

"You've been too quiet. You sure you straight?"

"Look, Nasim, I said I don't want to talk about the shit. What don't you get, nigga?"

He put his hands up. "Whoa. Damn. I won't ask anymore, with yo' spicy ass. You coming inside or what?"

Before I could reply, some woman walked up to the car and knocked on his window, looking like she was ready to get high. Her hair was in a messy ponytail. She had on short-ass shorts and a red shirt with holes in it. He glanced at her through the window and stepped out of the car. I decided to stay in the car, because I wasn't trying to be recognized.

"Hey," she said dryly, forcing a smile to the edge of her cracked lips.

"What's really good with you?" he muttered.

"I need some money," I heard her mumble.

I tried to mind my business, but it was hard to block them out.

"I just gave you money yesterday. You remember how much that was?"

"About six hundred, but I need five more. Then I'll be set for the week."

"The week?" he blurted out. "The fuck you think I am? An ATM?"

"Nah. I just need some help with my rent for the kids." She sucked her teeth, sounding like a fiend.

"You got about six muthafuckas running in and out of ya crib. None of them niggas can't help you? Yo, you already owe me, and I'm waiting for you to pay me back, but I know you ain't got it."

"Why you so concerned about who comin' in and out of my house?"

I watched Nasim reach into his pocket, pull out some bills, and hand her the money. Then she went on her way and disappeared around the corner.

I got out of the car and said, "No offense, but why'd you give that bitch all that money when you just gave her some the other day?"

"She needs it. She got five babies. I guess you can say I got a soft spot when it comes to kids."

"I'm not trying to be all up in your business, but she looks like she's on drugs. She's probably about to go get high right now."

"Nah, she's not on drugs."

"Let me guess. One of those kids is yours? Or do you not pay attention?"

"She's my sister. The only reason I'm out here is to look after her and my nieces and nephews."

"Oh," I said, feeling silly. This was their family business, so I was going to stay out of it.

"You still coming in?" he asked.

I thought about it. I needed to go home, and whenever Luxury arrived, I would deal with him. I couldn't wait to get home, take a shower, collapse in my bed, and run my legs along my silk sheets before going to sleep.

"Nah, I'm gonna get home. Thanks for letting me ride with you."

"No problem. anytime. Be careful on your way home. Hit me to let me know you made it safe."

He walked over to me and gave me a big, soft hug. It felt like I melted in his arms. I backed away and walked to my car.

By the time I made it home, Luxury wasn't there. I looked at my phone and noticed I had one text from Luxury, saying he was sorry. I also had another from Egypt, saying that if I needed someone to talk to, she was available. Her text seemed genuine. I didn't know why I had pushed her away so much. She was close to Luxury, but she didn't treat me funny. Whether it was business or personal, her checking on me was nice of her.

I called her.

Egypt picked up after a few rings. "Hey. Are you okay? You missed the cake we got for you."

I took a deep breath and exhaled. "I'm sorry. I guess I gotta be okay with this. It's not like we've been together that long. I just hoped he would tell me the truth . . . I asked him about this a few weeks ago, when the makeup artist at the album photo shoot brought it up. He brushed it off like it was nothing."

"Look, Luxury loves you. That chick doesn't mean nothing, but he gotta support that baby, whether he likes it or not. I understand you're mad, but if you love him, you'll ride this out."

"I *am* riding it out. You're acting like I said I was leaving him. I just needed some air."

"Okay, good. PR will call you in the morning to make sure things will be smoothed out with the press. Okay?"

"Okay."

"I'm driving him home, since he's too intoxicated to drive himself, and I'll be pulling up soon."

"Thank you, Egypt."

"Don't worry about it. Have a good night."

I ended the call and headed upstairs to take my shower. I allowed the hot water to cascade down on me. I knew that I loved Luxury so much and that we could get through this. He needed my support right now, and I was going to support him.

I stepped out of the shower and turned around to see Luxury standing in the bathroom doorway, looking fine as hell in Versace pajama pants but with no shirt on. I dried off and wrapped the towel around myself, waiting to see what he had to say.

He pulled me to him and attached his lips to mine instantly. Between kisses, he said, "I'm sorry, baby. I didn't mean for any of this to hurt you."

"I know. You want to tell me about her."

He took a deep breath. "For starters, my baby mama's name is Charity. We've never been in a relationship. We fucked around, and she got pregnant. I didn't think the baby was mine, because I had another bitch lie about this shit before. I got the DNA results when we were at the radio station. I tried to find a way to say it, but it was like it still wasn't real to me. I started giving her money as soon as I found out, so I didn't think she would go to the blogs and Twitter and shit."

"It's okay. Thank you for telling me all of that."

"I know you just left the club a few hours ago, but I missed you. A few hours without you is a long time, Mama." He kissed my neck as his hands rested on my ass. "I want you to marry me. Will you marry me?"

"That depends."

He dropped his hands and licked his lips. "Depends on what? I'm not fuckin' with nobody else, if that's what you're worried about."

"If you want to get married, Luxury, you'll have to stop being so secretive about everything. I need transparency."

"I told you I didn't know if the baby was mine or not, and that was the truth."

He was missing my point. I wasn't in the mood to explain what I meant. "Look, it doesn't matter."

"Fuck you mean, it doesn't matter? Of course shit like this matters. I want you to be able to trust me, which means you gotta give me the benefit of the doubt. I don't like arguing with my woman, all right?"

"That's cool and all, but you got me out here looking stupid. I don't wanna be out here looking stupid." I wrapped my arms around his neck and pressed my lips against his. "You really want to marry me? I'm saying, like, Seriously, is that what you want?"

"Yeah, I want to be your husband."

"You got a ring?"

"Of course I do." His hands moved to rest on my ass again. "Will you marry me or not?"

We hadn't been together for even three months, and we were ready to get married. I wanted more than anything to be his wife. This was the second time he had brought up marriage, so he wasn't playing with me, and I didn't want to imagine my life without him.

"Yes, I'll marry you," I said, and then I gave him the deepest tongue kiss. We both moaned together.

Pulling away, he said, "Put your clothes on. Let's go."

"Let's go where? It's almost one o'clock in the morning."

"We going to Vegas."

"You want to get married right now?"

"Right now."

That was how it was with Luxury. He was always a "right here, right now" kind of nigga. Though we had had some bumps along our trail, I was still down for the ride.

21

LUXURY

Marry Me

We took a five-hour flight to Vegas in a private jet. We got some sleep on the way and landed at 6:00 a.m. I put a nice six-carat, teardrop-shaped diamond ring on her finger, which she loved, as we got eloped in a wedding chapel on the Strip. Straight after that, we had to wait until the courthouse opened so that we could get our marriage certificate. As soon as we checked into the biggest suite at Paris Las Vegas Hotel, we made love. We slept for a few hours. I woke up before her at around one o'clock in the afternoon and called Mama, Lavish, Frill, Egypt, Nia, and Lala and told them that I had married Desire.

The only person who said something negative was Egypt, which didn't surprise me, because she had always been protective when it came to me.

"I married Desire," I told her.

"Why?" she asked.

"What you mean, why, E?"

"I know you say you love her, but why the rush?"

"Why not? You either for me or against me, and if my own mama didn't have shit to say against us getting married, why do you?"

She was silent for a long moment before she replied, "You're right. I'm sorry. Congratulations, Luxury."

"Thank you. Now, pack your bags and get to Vegas, so we can celebrate. Check your email. I booked everyone on the same flight, first class."

"Okay."

I planned to have everyone, including Desire's brother and mama, come to Vegas to celebrate with us. As much as Desire had said she didn't get along with her mother, I wanted to surprise her. I made some calls to set up the suite for a celebration.

Once Desire finally woke up around two o'clock, I went to the side of the bed and said, "Good afternoon, Mrs. Monnahan."

"Good afternoon, Mr. Monnahan. I still can't believe we got married this morning."

"Believe it, baby. You weren't dreaming. After we eat a little somethin', I want you to get dressed, because I have something special planned. It's a surprise." I planted a kiss on her lips.

"Okay. You want to order room service?"

"Yeah, that works."

We had a relaxed lunch, we showered, and then we headed out to go shopping for what we would wear for my surprise. We even did a little gambling and drinking for a few hours. When we got back to the suite, I looked at my watch and saw that it was close to seven o'clock. Everyone should be arriving soon.

"Get changed into your new dress and get dolled up for me," I said.

"I wish I knew what you had up your sleeve, but I'll do what you say. I can't wait to see this surprise."

"You'll love it."

While she got ready in the bathroom, I put on my new black jeans, black button-up, watch, and chain. I texted Egypt, and she let me know they would be pulling up to the hotel soon.

I walked into the bathroom, where Desire was putting on her makeup. "You look beautiful, wifey."

"Thank you, hubby."

I put my hand on her stomach. "I could put a couple babies in you. Give you a mini me and a mini you. What you think?"

"One day . . . Don't distract me." She messed with her eyebrows with some powder and a brush. "Okay, I'm done. How I look?"

"You look beautiful, as always." I licked my lips, pulling her to me. "Man, you got me ready to say, 'Fuck this dinner,' so I can get back up in them panties."

She laughed. "You nasty."

I palmed her juicy ass and squeezed hard.

"Stop, or else we ain't gonna make it for your surprise," she said.

"Nah, we got to. I got something fly in the works."

"You always got something fly in the works."

"You're one hundred percent mine now, baby, and you got to realize that this is what I do." I checked my phone and saw that Egypt had texted that they were waiting for me to let them into the suite.

"I'll be right back," I said.

"'Kay."

I walked out of the bathroom and to the front door. When I opened the door, I put my finger up to my lips to let everyone know to keep it down, because I didn't want to ruin the surprise.

"Go chill in the dining area, and I'll bring her out."

Mama hugged me, and I kissed her on the forehead. My brothers gave me a hug as they walked in. I shook Javier's hand, as this was my first time meeting him.

"Mom couldn't make it," he whispered.

"Oh, man. A'ight. How is she?"

"She's good, but you know she doesn't get along with Desirae, right?"

I nodded. "Yeah. I was just hoping, you know."

He patted me on the back. "I know. It's better this way."

Nia, Egypt, and Lala walked in after Javier, and I hugged them all.

"Keep y'all voices down. I'll go get her," I whispered.

I walked back into the master bathroom. "You ready?" I asked her.

"After I slip into this dress. Give me five more minutes."

I walked out of the bathroom to give her time to finish getting ready. Just when I was going to check on her again, because she had already taken longer than five minutes, she came out of the bathroom. I paused. She was flawless, and her skin was glowing. Her inner beauty lit her eyes and softened her features. When she smiled, I couldn't help but smile. When I was with her, I always felt like a king.

"I'm ready," she said.

"You look so good, baby. I swear, I'm lucky as shit."

"Thank ya, boo. I'm pretty lucky too."

I took her hand in mine and led her to the dining area. She heard the voices before she saw everyone, and she frowned.

"Who is . . . ?"

"Hey!" Frill said. "The married couple."

My mom, Lavish, Frill, Egypt, Nia, Lala, and Javier were gathered around the table, with glasses of champagne in their hands.

Desire put her hand over her heart. She started crying as soon as she saw her brother. He came over and put his arms around her.

"Don't mess up your makeup," he said. "Congrats, Mrs. Monnahan."

"Thank you." She laughed through her tears.

"This is so nice, Poo," Mama said as I hugged her again.

"Mama, this is Desirae, but everyone calls her Desire."

Desire extended her hand, but my mom pulled her in for a hug. "I give hugs, sweetie. Welcome to the family. You're so beautiful. Luxury didn't tell me you were so gorgeous. Look at you."

"Thank you. It's so nice to meet you. You're beautiful yourself."

"Thank you." My mama blushed as she grinned. I could tell she liked Desire.

While my mama and Desire got acquainted, Frill approached me. "Damn, bruh," he said, looking around. "This suite is huge as hell. King shit right here, boy. You weren't lying when you said you got the biggest suite they had."

"You know I had to do it."

Lavish pulled me to the side. "So, you went and married her, huh? You feel that guilty about the baby?"

"Nah, dumbass. I love her. Period."

Frill patted me on the back. "We know you love her. That rock on her finger is serious. Congrats, bruh."

Lavish nodded. "I dig it. Married is a good look for you. Mo' hoes for me."

I laughed and shook my head. "You can have them hoes. I'm officially off the fucking market."

Lavish said, "I'm proud of you. Big bro is all grown up. One day I want to be just like you."

Egypt handed me and Desire a glass of champagne. "I'd like to make a toast to the most adorable couple I know. It's a pleasure to work as Desire's assistant, and I know the love you two have will supersede all things. Congrats to the bride and groom."

I looked at Egypt, surprised that she would make a nice toast, knowing she had doubts. I nodded my head at her, and she smiled at me. Behind her eyes were tears, but she wiped them away quickly.

"To the bride and groom," everyone said, lifting their glasses.

"Dinner will be served in a bit," I said. "Everyone can sit at the table."

I sat at the head of the table, and Desire sat on the right side of me.

"So, what's next for you two?" Mama asked. "Do I get to meet my grandson, li'l Tyriq, next?"

I tried not to get irritated that she had brought this up at this moment. "Yes, ma'am. You'll meet him soon. We'll talk about that later."

Desire seemed unbothered as she took a sip of her champagne, but I knew her well. The mention of my son was a sore spot.

"Desire," Mama said, "where's your mother? I thought I was going to meet her tonight."

Desire gazed at me with a confused look on her face. "I didn't know she was supposed to be here. I actually didn't know any of you were coming."

"I wanted to surprise her. Her mother didn't feel too good, so she couldn't make it," I lied.

Javier nodded his head, as if that were the truth.

"Can I speak to you for a second, Luxury?" Desire said, getting up from the table.

"Yeah." I got up from the table and followed her into the living-room area of the suite.

"Why didn't you tell me you invited my mom?" she asked.

"Because I wanted to surprise you."

"I already told you that I don't get along with her. She hates me. That bullshit about her being sick is just . . . She can't stand to see me happy. If she had come, she would've been so fuckin' disrespectful. You know, she couldn't even look me in the eye at my papi's funeral. She acted like I wasn't even there." She started to cry.

I pulled her to me. I didn't like seeing her hurt and feeling bad. "Baby, come on . . . Let's just forget about her. I'm sorry. I didn't realize how fucked up things were between you. Let's just celebrate our moment."

She nodded and wiped her eyes.

"I can't keep watching my woman cry like this. This shit is fuckin' breaking my heart."

She nodded again and dried her tears. "I'm sorry."

"It's okay. I apologize for trying to repair your broken relationship. I was out of line. Forgive me."

"I forgive you."

After she fixed her makeup, we went back to the dinner table and enjoyed the meal. Everybody was laughing and talking. At the end of the meal, Lavish, Frill, and I stepped out on the patio to smoke a blunt.

"You said Desire got a few shows overseas?" Lavish asked.

"Yeah," I answered.

"You going with her?"

I shrugged. "I don't know yet."

"What you think she gonna say when she finds out you don't fly over water?" Lavish chuckled.

I shrugged again. I hadn't thought about it. I hadn't conquered my fear of flying over water, and I didn't plan on confronting it anytime soon. I just knew that Desire going overseas to promote her new album was the perfect opportunity for her.

"She'll be fine without me," I answered. "It's only a few weeks. I gotta let her do her thing without suffocating her, you know? We both gotta accept that this is part of the business."

"True, but she'll be so far away, bruh," Frill said. "Y'all just got married. You think you want to be away from her that long?"

Lavish nodded, as if echoing Frill's words.

I brushed them off. "Y'all overthinking it. She'll be fine."

"We ain't worried about *her*. We worried about *you*. You were tripping when she was gone that night when her dad died. How you think you gone handle not seeing her for days on end?" Lavish commented.

Frill passed me the blunt, and I took a few pulls. They were seriously thinking too hard about this. We were going to be fine.

"I got this," I assured them.

22

DESIRE

Overseas Life

I was officially Mrs. Monnahan, and it was all over the news and tabloids, the blogs and social media. That story overshadowed Luxury's paternity test news. Egypt had said she'd leaked the marriage to the press for that reason. Our wedding also boosted the hell out of my album sales. I was already certified platinum. Everything was happening so fast, and Luxury didn't want me to slow down, not even for a minute. The person I used to be no longer existed, because I had no control over anything I did. Everything had to be approved by Luxury. What I wore, what I drank, what I ate, and what I said in public all had to approved by my husband.

I rehearsed my ass off for these shows I had to do in Paris, Barcelona, and a few spots in the United Kingdom. Days and nights felt like they were mixed together. I couldn't tell you what the date was without looking at my calendar. After a couple of weeks of constant practice, we got ready to go to Paris. That was when Luxury hit me with the news that he wouldn't be at my first show. He said he had some executive business to take care of.

The label was blowing up now that he had two platinum-selling acts. The Monnahan Boyz had almost finished their second major album, and I was catapulted to the top of the charts with every single I dropped. I should've been happy about it, but I was still grieving my father's death. I missed him so much.

My first flight overseas was cool. There was hardly any turbulence, and I felt like a boss in first class. Egypt and I laughed and got to know one another along the way. I killed my first sold-out show in Paris. I felt on top of the world. I just wished Luxury was with me.

After the show, I retreated to my hotel room, and Egypt brought me a pint of praline ice cream because I was craving something sweet and creamy.

"Oh my God. You're a lifesaver," I said as I took the pint. Somehow ice cream made me feel a little bit better about missing my dad.

"I got your back, girl," she said.

Egypt could never be Mina, but it felt good to have a friend who was a girl again.

Before leaving my suite, she said, "Hit me up if you need anything else."

"Okay. I will."

As soon as I had the top of the ice cream container off and I had dug into it, my phone rang. It was Luxury on FaceTime. I answered and put the spoon in my mouth, then sucked it clean, feeling excited to see my husband's face, "Hey, baby."

"Don't be sucking that spoon like that," he teased.

"You jealous?"

"Nah, 'cause you suck my dick way better. I miss them pretty-ass lips, though. What you doing, Mrs. Monnahan?"

"Missing you. Missing my dad, but, anyway, E just brought me some ice cream. I'm chilling now. What you doing?"

"Just got home. I took the baby to see Mom today."

"Oh. How'd that go?" I felt my heart drop. I still wasn't used to him having a baby. It was like my heart wouldn't let me.

"Good. He's lookin' so much like me, it's ridiculous. Anyway, I'm sure E spoke with you about the itinerary for your shows."

I nodded. "Yeah, she did. Everything is happening so fast that I hardly have time to myself. When are you coming? I feel like I'm gonna die without you."

"I'll be there soon. I miss you."

"I miss you so much."

"I heard you killed your first show." He paused and looked away from the camera when someone said something to him in his background. He looked back at me. "I gotta go to this studio session with my brothers right now, but I'll hit you up before I go to bed. I know with the time-zone difference, you'll be asleep."

Feeling a little disappointed because he had to go, I said, "I might be awake, so hit me."

"Gimme a kiss."

I kissed the phone, and he did the same.

"I love you," I said, fighting back my tears.

"I love you, and don't you forget it," he replied and ended the FaceTime.

Tears running down my cheeks, I sighed and took a huge spoonful of ice cream. I wiped my tears, put the top back on the ice cream container, and put it in the small freezer by the minibar. I needed a drink or a shot of something. I took the cap off the bottle of Patrón on top of the minibar and swallowed a big gulp, spilling some on my chest. I wiped it off. I wished I could go back to the carefree days when Mina and I were dancing and enjoying our lives. God, I missed her too.

I picked up my phone and decided to go live on my Facebook. I looked at myself to make sure my hair and face looked cool before I sat on the bed. I hit the GO LIVE button and spoke into the camera.

"Hey, everybody. It's ya girl Desire. As you can see, I am almost ready for bed. I just got done performing in Paris. This city is seriously so beautiful. I can see the fuckin' Eiffel Tower from my window. The show was amazing. Bananas. What's going on with y'all?" I looked at the screen and saw people saying hello. Somebody asked me where Luxury was.

"Luxury is back home, working on some things with the Monnahan Boyz. He'll be here soon. Can't wait to see my babe. Anyway, I just wanted to hop on here real quick to say hey and to thank y'all for rocking with me. I fuckin' love y'all. Real shit. I am so tired, y'all, but the fans, y'all make everything worth it. I'm just chilling in my room, sipping some Patrón."

A phone call was coming through, so I wrapped up my live video.

"A'ight. I'm about to go to bed. Callin' it a night. Bye."

I pressed END, looked down at my phone, and saw that Nasim was the caller. I hadn't heard from him since the night before I got married. I hadn't texted him, and he hadn't bothered me at all. But right now I really could use someone to talk to, I decided.

"Hey, you. How are you?" I said when I answered. I didn't mean to say it sexy like that. It just slipped out.

"I'm good. You?"

"Good. You just interrupted my live video."

"Oh shit. My fault. I'll call you back," he said.

"Nah, I ended it. What you doing?"

"I just saw your show tonight. Dope as fuck."

"What? Are you serious? You're here in Paris?"

"Yeah, I'm in Paris. I wanted to catch a show, and you were sold out in all the US cities, so I was like, 'Fuck it. I'll go to Paris.'"

"That's what's up. I'm glad you enjoyed it. Where you staying? We should catch up."

"We should. I'm at a Novotel Hotel right now. The Paris Centre one," he said.

"I have no clue where that is, but I'll figure it out. Is it cool to come your way? I'm bored as hell."

"That's cool with me. Let's have some drinks. You hungry?"

"Not really, but drinks sound cool. We should probably stay in your suite. I wouldn't want anyone taking pictures. You know how that is. I wouldn't want Luxury to assume the worst."

"I understand. I'm on the fifth floor. I'll text the room number. See you in a bit."

I ended the call and sent Egypt a text informing her that I would be out sightseeing. She texted back for me to be careful. She was going to get some sleep because she was exhausted. I took a couple more gulps of tequila and got dressed. I called an Uber, grabbed my bottle of Patrón and my purse, and headed down to the lobby. I brought my bodyguard, Meek, with me for protection, in case someone recognized me.

Meek stood outside the door as I walked into Nasim's hotel suite. Jazz music was playing, and I could smell his cologne. I didn't know why that gave me the chills, but it did. The tequila had me feeling sexy as fuck. When I took a good look at Nasim, I realized that he looked a little different. He had decided to grow a beard, which had becoming popular with men ever since Rick Ross and James Harden had started rocking one. I loved Luxury's, and Nasim's beard looked just as sexy.

"You like jazz?" I asked, with a slight frown on my face. I was so used to trap music playing all the time that jazz sounded foreign to me.

"Yeah, I do." He reached out for a hug. I went into his arms so smoothly. When he squeezed me, I felt like I was melting into him. "It's mad good to see you."

"It's good to see you too," I replied, feeling hot as we parted.

"You want something to drink?" he asked but then laughed when he saw the bottle of Patrón sitting in my purse.

"I brought what I was drinking already. You want some?" I took the bottle out of my purse.

"I'll have a few shots with you," he said with a smile.

"Hell yeah."

He walked over to the wet bar and retrieved two plastic cups that were wrapped individually. He took them out of the wrappers and held them out to me. I set my purse down on the couch and poured a little Patrón into each cup.

"Cheers to a great show," he said, holding up his cup.

"Cheers," I replied, allowing my cup to touch his.

We tossed back our shots.

After he swallowed, he made a face, as if the tequila was nasty. "No chaser?" he asked. "Whew."

"Nope. I never have chasers with Patrón. Ice would be nice, though."

"I can go get some," he said, then paused because I was staring at him while biting my lower lip.

He looked me up and down as I admired his new fade and his sexy new beard. There had been high sexual tension between us from the moment I walked through that door. I cleared my throat, because I could feel myself blushing, and my panties were getting wet by just looking at him. The expression on his face let me know that he felt exactly what I was feeling. We were both feeling the same thing. He reached for my hand to pull me back to him, but I stepped back a little.

His eyes were still on me. He stared at me as if I was the dopest chick he'd ever seen. It could've been the Patrón that had me so turned on or the fact that I was ready to escape from the pressure Luxury always put on me to be perfect. I didn't know for sure. Luxury had been driving me to do music without giving me any real time to grieve Mina or my father. He hadn't even given me enough time to get used to our rushed marriage. I was in one of the most romantic cities of the world without him, and I was alone with a very sexy man to whom I was sexually attracted.

Nasim seized the moment and kissed me. With his lips on mine, I opened my mouth, eager to feel his tongue. I indulged in his kiss for a little while before I moved my hands to the back of his neck. The passion between us was so intense, I didn't want to part. His tongue teased my tongue, and I sucked his bottom lip. We kissed just that way, sucking each other's mouths, making our tongues twirl. He was such a good kisser that he took Luxury out of my thoughts.

Eventually, we pulled away from one another and tried to catch our breaths. However, his hands remained around me. As he bit his lower lip and stared down at me, I could feel his hands sliding up my dress.

"Wait," I started to protest. "I don't want you to think this is why I came to your hotel room."

"Of course I don't think that. You came to catch up, didn't you?"

I nodded and tugged his beard for him to kiss me again. He lifted my dress over my head. With Luxury in the farthest place of my mind, I allowed Nasim to carry me to the couch. Without hesitation, he kissed and licked my inner thighs and made a trail up to my neck. He stopped to take off his clothes, leaving on his boxers. I was amazed at how good his body looked naked, all lean and sculptured. I was waiting for him to drop his boxers so I could see what he was working with.

"You got a condom?" I asked, feeling excitement fill me.

I was finally doing something without Luxury's say in the matter. For a brief moment, I wanted to feel independent again, even if that meant cheating on my husband.

He nodded his head. "I got one in my wallet." He bent down and picked up his pants. He took his wallet out of a back pocket, opened it, and revealed a gold wrapper. I knew what a Magnum meant. I hoped he wasn't the type to walk around with Magnums in his pocket even though they didn't fit him.

I bit my lower lip while I waited for him to put it on. As soon as he dropped his boxers, I got to see that he was more than qualified to wear the condom. Once it was on, he wasted no time giving me the deepest kisses. Right there on that couch, he twisted my body in ways I didn't know it could be bent. Every time he entered me, I felt as if I was going to scream. All my pent-up aggression was released, and he felt more than good. He felt amazing.

I woke up to Nasim's light-skinned arm lying across my breasts. Our night together came crashing down like a tidal wave. I sat up, removed his arm, careful not to wake him. He was on his stomach, sleeping peacefully.

Bitch, you just cheated on your nigga, I shouted in my head. *You cheated.*

Luxury was good to me, so what did I do? I felt guilty, but there was something between Nasim and me that was undeniable and special, one of a kind.

My head was throbbing. It felt like a balloon being inflated slowly. The hangover from the Patrón had me squinting at him. Nasim was handsome, and I could see myself being with someone like him. Well, that was if I were single.

I groaned, and the guilt of letting him do all those naughty things to my body consumed me. This thing with Nasim had happened so fast, and he had fucked me too good. If I had to compare him and Luxury, I would have to say Luxury fucked like a beast and Nasim made love like he was a vampire, sucking my soul dry. I shook my head, trying to shake the sexy images out of my throbbing head, but it didn't work.

You're such a fucking ho. Bitch, get the fuck out of here.

I eased out of his bed and quietly gathered my panties, dress, and shoes. I almost tripped while trying to put my panties back on and fell on the bed.

"You just gone dip without saying bye?" he asked.

I looked over my shoulder, and he was sitting up in the bed, looking so motherfucking fine.

"Um . . ." I exhaled. "I figured I would leave since Egypt is probably worried about me. I left Meek at the door."

He frowned and got out of the bed, naked. He took my dress and shoes out of my hands and tossed them back on the floor. Pulling me toward the bed, he stared into my eyes. "Don't feel bad about this. I know y'all got married, and that's mad cool, but how do you really feel about being out here without him?"

"I'm fine. Luxury has business to take care of with the label. Stuff has been just skyrocketing."

"I get that, but it ain't shit that he can't do from a virtual office, and that will allow him to travel with you. I'm just saying. If you were my wife, you wouldn't be nowhere without me. Ain't he the boss? I don't know any bosses who can't call their own shots. Feel me?"

"So, what you saying? You think he's cheating? What you hear?"

"Nothing. I don't check for Luxury. Trust. I just know men 'cause I'm a man. He's in the industry. Tell me you don't have doubts."

I shrugged. Nasim was hitting the nail on the head, and I was almost mad at him, but I knew why he was saying it. He didn't want me to feel guilty about anything.

"Nasim, I had a good time with you last night, but we can't do this again."

"I know. That's why I'm trying to hold on to you for as long as I can. I know you gotta go. I won't make this harder for you than it already is. Just promise me you won't let him dog you out."

I nodded. "I won't."

He licked his lips before he planted the deepest kiss on mine. I felt like kissing him for the rest of the day, but

I couldn't. I was already convincing myself that I could never see Nasim again.

When I walked out of the hotel room, I started to apologize to Meek, but then I realized he had gone. I didn't blame him, because I wouldn't wait outside no door overnight like that.

"Shit," I said underneath my breath, because I was sure he had to tell Egypt or Luxury about leaving me.

I caught an Uber back to my hotel. As soon as I reached my door, Egypt came out of her room across the hall.

"I've been calling and texting you. Meek said he left you at the Novotel Hotel with some dude. Tell me you're not fucking around on Luxury."

"I'm not fucking around on Luxury." I left it at that. "I'm back now, so we're good." I walked inside my room, and she walked in behind me before the door could close.

"Glad you're safe. We got a flight to catch, and we don't have a lot of time. Promise me you won't ever do that again. I was worried. I must always know who you are with. Who is this guy you went to see?"

"Don't trip, Egypt. I'm fine. I had a few drinks and passed out."

She nodded slowly and said, "Okay. Okay. I'll be back in thirty so we can check out. We're flying to Spain. Oh, and call your husband. I didn't answer his calls, because I didn't know what to tell him. You know he's mean as hell sometimes."

She walked out of my room, and I sat on the bed, sighing. I should've called Luxury back, but I was thinking about being up under Nasim all night. My emotions took over, and it felt like my mind was transporting me to a place I shouldn't go back to.

23

LUXURY

Overcoming Fear

Three days later . . .

I still couldn't believe I had got on a plane to fly to Barcelona. The flight felt like it was the longest nine hours of my life. I did everything I could to take my mind off the possibility of the plane crashing into the sea. I couldn't wait to get off that plane.

Egypt had told me to get my ass there to be with Desire as soon as possible, because my girl needed me. I was willing to put my fear to the test because that was how much I loved her. Although fear traveled through my veins as I sat in that airplane seat, no one around me could tell, because I played it so cool. As soon as I was off that plane, I felt relieved. I had made it. I felt like kissing the ground.

I had to do what I had to do to see my baby. I missed her too much. All that FaceTime shit wasn't going to cut it. I should've never let her travel without me, but I hadn't wanted her to see me scared like this. Air travel was the one thing in life that scared me. I had made Egypt promise not to tell Desire that I was coming to see her, in case my fear stopped me from getting on the plane.

The limo pulled up to the restaurant where Egypt said they would be dining. I hopped out with my backpack. I hadn't traveled with a huge piece of luggage, because I couldn't stay long in Europe due to a few shows my brothers had to do. But it was better to spend a little time with Desire than no time.

"Do you need a table, or do you have a reservation?" asked the young woman at the front.

"Neither. My wife and a friend are here."

"Oh, yes. They're right this way. Follow me."

I followed her to the back of the restaurant, to a table near the wall-length aquarium. Desire had her back to me and was sipping hot tea, but Egypt saw me walking up. She didn't say a word, and she pretended not to see me.

"I'm homesick already, and I don't know how I'm going to make it for three long weeks," Desire said to Egypt. "These shows are good money, but it's like, 'Damn, I need a fucking break.' Plus, when is Luxury coming? I feel like he's giving me the runaround. I'm sick of his shit."

"You sure you sick of my shit?" I asked.

She turned around, her eyes wide with surprise. She stood up and leaned into my arms, and I embraced her. Her fragrance sent chills down my spine. I was glad to be there. This moment made that painful flight worth it.

"I missed you so much," I mumbled into her neck.

"I missed you too, baby." She caressed my neck and then the waves in my hair.

I took a good look at her. She looked like she had some heavy shit on her mind, like she wanted to spill her thoughts to me. I sat in her seat, then pulled her down to sit on my lap.

"What's good, baby?" I asked her. "You either about to tell me some bad shit or you got some good shit. Spit it out."

"Why you assume I got something to tell you? I'm simply happy to see you," she said.

"Because, first, I know my wife. Something is up, so tell me."

She smiled before she kissed me. Her hands trailed down my chest slowly. She knew that drove me crazy. "I'm just missing you, is all. It's been so long."

"Three days is long?" I asked with a chuckle.

"That's too long."

We kissed again.

Egypt cleared her throat. "Excuse me, lovebirds. I hope y'all not about to have sex right here. There are rooms for that."

"Is the hotel nearby?" I asked.

"Right across the street," Desire whispered in my ear.

"What we waiting for?"

She stood up and pulled me by my hand out of the restaurant, leaving Egypt to eat alone.

We nearly broke the bed with our rough sex. Desire put it on me, and I had to give it to her. The sex was so good, I felt we should do this distance thing again. Afterward, she fell fast asleep, snoring and all. She had seemed exhausted earlier. About an hour later, her phone, on silent, started vibrating. I wasn't the type to go through phones, so I wasn't about to start now. I went into my backpack and pulled my weed from a secret compartment. I needed a blunt before going to sleep.

My cell rang just then, and it was Egypt.

"What's up, E?" I asked when I picked up.

"Is Desire sleeping?"

"Yeah, she's knocked out."

"Okay, I was just calling to tell her that her promo shoot was pushed back until later tomorrow, so she can rest. I know she needs it."

"A'ight, I'll tell her," I said. "Hey, Nia and Lala will be here in the morning."

"Yeah, Nia called me. You sure you don't need them for the boys' shows?"

"Nah, they're good. Desire needs more of y'all to keep her company."

"Okay."

I ended the call.

Desire stirred in bed and groaned. "Egypt keeps calling. I can't get no kinds of rest."

"She said your shoot got pushed back until later tomorrow."

"Yesss."

"Nia and Lala will be here in the morning."

"I heard. That's cool."

I went to the bed and cupped her face in my hands. I pressed my lips against hers. As our kiss deepened, she pulled me down on the bed.

"Babe, we just had sex," I said, pulling away. "I need to smoke."

"And I want to do it again. Round two. What you wanna do?" Her hands were untying the string of my sweats.

"You missed this dick, huh?"

"Shut up. You gotta make up for the time we lost."

I smacked her ass hard on each cheek. My phone rang again. I started to answer it.

"No, don't answer it," she whined.

I pulled away from her, in case it was Charity calling about my son or my mama, anybody. I saw that it was indeed Charity, so I answered. "Hello?"

"Li'l Tyriq needs diapers and some formula," Charity said.

"What happened to the money I just gave you?" I asked.

"What you mean? I had to get my hair and nails done, and I needed some clothes. That li'l-ass piece of change wasn't enough."

The pit of my stomach instantly started burning. "Bitch, what the fuck you say? You spent my son's money on yourself and then gone ask me for some more money for diapers?"

"Don't come at me like that, Luxury! You don't know how hard it is to have a baby by yourself. Shit, I needed to do something nice for myself for a change. You gone give me the dough or not?"

I gritted my teeth. "I'll be back tomorrow, so I'll drop it off then." I hung up.

"You leaving tomorrow?" Desire asked with a frown.

"Tonight actually."

"Wait, so you came here to fuck me and leave?"

"It's not like that. I have business to handle. Don't get upset. I'd rather see you when I can than not at all."

"The fuck? You know this is hard for me, being alone. I don't have nobody but you, Luxury. Nobody. Baby, look, all I'm saying is that you make me feel loved, and when you're gone, I feel so alone."

"Baby, you're not alone. We're married now. I ain't goin' nowhere. This is all a part of the industry. You don't think there are days when Jay and Bey can't be by one another's side? This shit is gonna be tough, and you gotta be strong if this is what you want to do."

"What if I don't want to rap anymore?"

"Don't say that. You're doing the damn thing right now."

"You got enough money to take care of us. I don't need this shit."

"I do have enough, but it's always good to have your own shine, baby. Now, as soon as I'm done smoking this blunt, let's go eat."

She rolled her eyes at me. "This is a no smoking room, so you gotta take that shit outside." She got out of the bed and went into the bathroom, then slammed the door behind her.

I already knew she would be mad at me for leaving so soon, but in the end, this would all pay off.

Desirae made sure that I wound up missing my late-night flight. I had to catch one early the next morning, after arguing with her about leaving. The trip back was horrible. The turbulence made me feel like I would never, ever fly overseas again. I didn't care. I wasn't going back to Europe. As soon as I got home in Miami, I went straight to Charity's apartment to drop off the money.

She opened the door with a smile on her face. "Come in."

The smell of kush hit me in the face. I didn't like her smoking in front of my son, but she was a grown-ass woman, so I couldn't chew her out about it.

"Where's my son?" I asked, looking around.

"Down for a nap. Where the cash at, nigga?"

I rolled my eyes and handed her a wad of money. "That should hold you and my son for a while. Don't say shit about no lights getting cut off, or I'm cutting back, straight up. You know, I'm still mad at you for that Twitter shit."

"Come on. That was, like, two months ago. Get over it."

"Don't fucking tell me what to do."

"Well, we're even. You embarrassed the fuck out of me, curbin' me for that fuckin' stripper-ho bitch. Yeah, she thinks she the shit now, 'cause you took her up outta the strip club and made her a wife, but she still a ho if you ask me."

"Man, you was fucking around with another nigga the entire time you were fucking me, Charity, so watch who you callin' a ho."

"Whatever." She counted the money. "I don't even need all this. I rather you just spend time with your son." She was complaining, but she didn't hand a nigga any of the bills back.

"I'll do that. I got business, though, so chill with all that public shit."

"Hey, I'm not trying break up your relationship, 'cause she bringin' in that money. What's good for you is good for my son, so I'm cool on your li'l wife. She'll fuck it up enough on her own. I'm sure you'll find out she's been fuckin' around Miami with some big-time D-boy named Nas."

"What the fuck you say?" I asked, tensing up.

She laughed, as if it was funny. "Calm down. I'm just letting you know. I can't have you out here looking stupid. You are my child's father, and I do care about you.

Keep ya eyes open, playa. That's all I'm sayin'. Ya wife got her a li'l boyfriend."

"Fuckin' liar." I stomped to the front door. "Kiss my son for me. I'm out."

She slammed the door behind me once I was outside. *The nerve of that bitch.* Desire didn't have no time to fuck around. Shit, if she knew what was good for her, she wouldn't try me.

24

DESIRE

Alone

"He was here for maybe eight hours, and then he got back on the plane to go home," I complained to Egypt, Nia, and Lala while we chilled in my room right after my photo shoot.

Luxury was supposed to stay so I could forget about Nasim, but with him leaving like that, it made me think only about how Nasim hadn't wanted me to leave his hotel room.

Nia shook her head, as if she felt sad for me. "I can only imagine how you feel."

Lala said, "The good thing is that we know Luxury had to get home to take care of business. With the rise of you and the Monnahan Boyz, the label seriously needs him, as the CEO, to be more hands on in the office. Well, at least until he selects a president who can fill that role. I hope that makes sense."

It did, but it didn't. My husband was supposed to be on my tour with me. That alone feeling had its grip on my heart and was squeezing the life out of it. It was killing me more each day. If this was how things were going to be, I didn't know if I was cut out for it.

"I hear you," I said. "I can't wait to get back to the States."

"Girl, fuck the States," Nia said. "Shit, you got to see Paris for a few days, and now Spain for a week. People would kill to go to these places."

"I think you'll like the United Kingdom," Egypt said. "I love London."

"Do you think Luxury will come back before the tour is over?" I asked.

Nia and Lala looked at one another uneasily. I could tell that Egypt was thinking of how to answer me.

"So, that means no?" I asked, feeling crazy that these bitches knew before I did that my husband wouldn't be joining my tour.

Egypt said, "The Monnahan Boyz will be in Baltimore, New York, and Dallas during the last week of your tour, and you'll be in the UK, so he's going with them."

I wanted to cry, but I just couldn't bring myself to mope around, not when I had to be so hyped up for these shows. Just when I was about to start feeling depressed, my phone rang.

It was Nasim, so I stepped out in the hallway to take the call.

"Hello," I said, feeling my heart skip a beat.

"What's up, gorgeous?"

"Nothing much. Just left a shoot."

"Nice. Where you at now?"

"Barcelona."

"Spain. That's mad dope, yo. I saw your Snap with Luxury. I know you're glad that he could finally make it to be with you."

I sighed. "He was here, but then he left. Looks like I'll be in Spain for a week and the UK for another week without him."

"You playin'?"

"No, I'm not playing."

"What? That's lame as fuck to me. Not dissing your husband but seems to me he only put a ring on your finger to make sure you wouldn't fuck around."

"Don't seem like that worked too well, did it?" I said, feeling butterflies fluttering in my tummy.

"How you feel about him not being there?"

"How you think I feel about it?"

I was so mad at Luxury for not sticking around for my shows. Then he dumped Nia and Lala on me, as if that would take the sting off the wound. I still wasn't all that cool with them like that. They were friendly and all, but if he thought any one of them could replace Mina, he thought wrong. Nobody could replace Mina.

"What if I was there? Would that cheer you up?" Nasim said.

That sounded good, but I already knew what that would lead to. "We already talked about this. We can't kick it like that."

"Shit, we don't have to have sex. You act like all I'm trying to do is smash. We can talk and do whatever you want to do. Plus, I need a little two-week vacation."

"Uh-huh. I doubt that you want to come all the way to Spain and the UK to do Netflix and chill. What you doing right now?"

"I'm shopping for a new Rolex."

"Nice." I got to thinking. I had a nigga who wanted to see me and be with me. My own husband didn't. "Hey, so why don't I pay for your flight, 'cause I don't really want you flying all the way over to Spain on your dime. And I'll get you a room to my liking. How does that sound?"

"That sounds cool, but I can pay my own way. You know how I roll."

"I do, but let me do something nice for you, since you want to do something nice for me, like spend a week in another country to keep me company."

"Okay, I'll roll with it this one time. Just let me know. What else is going on with you?"

"I don't want to bore you with my boring-ass life. Being a so-called celebrity is not what it's all cracked up to be. I work so much that I don't have time to enjoy shit. All work and no muhfuckin' play."

"You can talk to me about anything."

"It will take hours," I sighed.

"I got hours."

"Well, I don't really know what to do with my relationship right now. I love Luxury, but I can't help but feel like this nigga is hiding something."

"You try talking to him?" he asked.

"It's like I don't know what to say."

"From the outside looking in, I know you love him. He must love you too. How can he not? But he gotta figure out how to balance work and married life, you know? If you're feeling any kind of way, you should talk to him. You gotta learn to communicate a whole lot better. Feel me?"

"I hear you," I said, not trying to hear that. Luxury was supposed to know what I was feeling. Who would want to be halfway around the world without their new husband?

"I'm just keeping it real. I'm your friend, Desire."

Egypt peeked her head out the door, and I held up my finger. She went back inside the room.

"Hey, I gotta go. I'll call you later. Send me your email so I can shoot you the itinerary for your flight. Okay?"

"Yeah. Talk to you soon."

I went inside the room, and Egypt said, "I didn't mean to interrupt, but we going to the bar. You coming?"

I shook my head. "Nah, I'm going to get some rest."

Egypt nodded. "Okay. Good night."

"Night," Lala and Nia said as they followed Egypt out of my room.

"Night, ladies."

As soon as they left, I jumped on my MacBook to book the flights and the hotel for Nasim. It was expensive, but it wasn't like I didn't have the money. I made sure to put him in hotels in Spain and the United Kingdom that were near mine. If Luxury wasn't going to be here for two weeks, I was making sure I had my own company.

Luxury confirmed that he would be with his brothers for the next two weeks, and he made it clear that he would not be joining me for the rest of my tour. I didn't understand this sense of abandonment I felt. Of course, I had lost my best friend and my father, and Luxury was supposed to fill the void for me. But I used to be so strong, I used to be able to stand on my own two feet. I supposed that the deaths in my life had taken a toll on my self-esteem.

Why did Luxury need to be with his brothers and not with me? I wondered. Something felt fishy, and I wasn't feeling this at all. I needed Luxury more every day. I was used to him dressing me, telling me what to do every minute of the day, and now he wanted me to be without him. We argued about it for the next two days, and he apologized and sent flowers and candy to my hotel room, but I was still mad.

The only thing that cheered me up was the fact that Nasim was on his way. As soon as Nasim touched down and arrived at the hotel I had booked for him, I told Egypt I was going to bed really early because I was exhausted, and didn't want to be disturbed. She didn't seem to mind, since she and the girls were out sightseeing. I gave Meek the night off, which he was happy about.

Before I could head out, Luxury decided to FaceTime me.

"Shit," I exclaimed. Exhaling, I tossed my purse down and lay in the bed, just in case Egypt had told him I was going to bed early.

"Hey," I said after the camera loaded.

"Hey, baby," he said, staring all dreamy eyed into the camera. "What you doing?"

"Trying to get some much-needed rest."

"Damn, you must be tired, 'cause you ain't even took off your makeup yet."

"I know. I miss you," I said to deflect from the fact that I had fresh makeup on my face to go see Nasim.

"I miss you too. I just wanted to jump on here and see your face real quick."

"You look nice," I said, noting how handsome and fresh he looked.

"Thank you. Pray for me before I get on this plane. A nigga hates flying, for real."

I paused. He had never told me that he hated to fly. When we'd jumped on that private jet to Vegas, he'd been cool as ever. "Luxury, you have a fear of flying?"

"Well, kind of. Quick flights are cool, but I prefer the bus kind of touring."

I thought about it. Flights overseas were the longest. "Tell me that's not the fuckin' reason you ain't here right now."

He hesitated before he said, "Look, I know it sounds fucked up, but . . . Okay, I don't like flying over water. I know you're safe and you got Egypt, Lala, and Nia to keep you company. It took a lot for me get on the plane the last time. I don't want to sound or look like no bitch around you."

"What? Are you serious? I can't believe you. Why didn't you just fuckin' say that, nigga?" I said, spazzing.

"I didn't want to sound like no pussy-ass nigga."

"That's the dumbest shit I've ever heard. Look, I'm not about to do this with you. I'm tired and ready to go to bed. I gotta go."

"Baby, don't get off the phone like this. Just try to understand."

"Bye, Luxury." I ended FaceTime.

I waited for a little while to compose myself before leaving my room. I took the stairs so I wouldn't run into the girls in case they were on the elevator. I didn't want to have to try to come up with a lie. I walked to the hotel where Nasim was staying, as it was only a block away.

25

LUXURY

Monnahan Boyz

I made Desire so mad that she wouldn't even pick up FaceTime for me after she hung up. I had managed to guide her to stardom, but now she didn't know what to do with herself when I wasn't around. I had thought this tour would be a good opportunity for her to get that foreign money and forget about the pain of not having Mina and her pops, but the distance was causing a major problem in our relationship. She had every right to be upset and feel a little lost, but I could tell she was hiding something from me. No matter how tired she was, she never went to bed with her makeup on. Never. That was the first red flag. I had to call Egypt on FaceTime to see what was good.

Egypt picked up, and it looked and sounded like she was out somewhere. She put in her earpiece and said, "Hey, Luxury."

"Hey, E. Where y'all at?"

"Me, Lala, and Nia found us a little bar, and we're having some drinks. Desire didn't want to come, because she's tired. She's back at the room."

"I know. I just got off FaceTime with her. How she been?"

"She's been a mess. When she's not onstage, she's crying and in a screaming rage. I mean, she misses you like crazy. Why are you torturing her like this?"

"I'm not trying to. Does she seem a little depressed?"

"She's close to it, but I figure it's because she's out here without you."

"Yeah? Well, she knows I'm afraid of flying over water now. She hung up on a nigga after it slipped out."

"Damn. Give her some time. Once she gets home, she'll be fine."

"A'ight, E. I gotta get over to Lav's, so we can get to this airport. I'll call back once I make it to B-more."

"Okay."

I ended the call and grabbed my suitcase. I turned off the lights as I walked through the house. Then I drove to Lavish's, with heavy thoughts on my mind. During the short drive over to his place, I tried not to be mad at myself for slipping up and telling Desire about my dumb fear. She was going to find out sooner or later. I just hoped she wasn't too mad at a nigga.

I got out of the car after pulling up in Lavish's driveway. I knocked on the door and rang the doorbell. There was no answer. I pulled out my cell and called him, but the call went straight to voicemail. I hit Frill's line to see if he would answer.

He answered, sounding like he was still asleep. "Hello?"

"Nigga, answer the muhfuckin' door. I'm outside."

I stood there for another minute before Frill opened the door.

"The fuck? Y'all niggas still asleep?" I shouted.

This was typical Lavish and Frill bullshit. They always partied all fucking night when I said that we had to catch a flight the next morning. I walked down the hallway toward Lavish's bedroom.

"Please tell me you're up, Lav," I hollered when I reached his closed bedroom door.

Now I was frustrated. We had thirty minutes to get to the airport, and that was pushing it. I should've known I had to get here earlier, because this was their typical bullshit. I opened the door to Lavish's bedroom, and I shook my head. Girls were sprawled out all over his bedroom, and they were all sleeping. Some were half naked. Some were completely naked. Blond girls. Dark-haired girls. White. Black. Latin. Lavish was wildin'. I didn't see him, but I could hear the shower running in his bathroom. I went to the bathroom door, so I could let him know it was time to go.

"Lavish, nigga, we gotta go," I called through the door.

The door was opened by a woman who was dripping wet. It looked like she had just jumped out of the shower. Her slim but curvy chocolate body greeted me. "He'll be out in a minute," she said with a smile as steam escaped into the bedroom.

I shouldn't have stared at her for so long, but she was fine as fuck and that body . . . I turned away quickly.

Lavish said, "Baby, can you hand me a towel from the linen closet?"

She turned away from the door and walked over to the closet. She grabbed a thick towel and walked back to the shower. He reached his hand out to get the towel.

"Lav, why are you just now getting out of the fuckin' shower? I told y'all to be ready when I got here," I shouted.

"Why you always bitchin' 'bout us being late? Ain't nothin' new. You bitch at Desire this same way?"

"Fuck you, muhfucka. Don't worry about my wife and me. Hurry up and get yo' ass dressed."

The dark-skinned beauty arched her eyebrow, giving Lavish an intrigued look.

"What's up, baby? You lookin' like you need something," Lavish said to her as he stepped forward. He grabbed her by the hips and pulled her into him.

"We ain't got time for all that. Hurry the fuck up!" I yelled, and then I walked out of his bedroom. I made my way quickly through the house to find Frill.

He was in the hall bathroom, brushing his teeth.

"Y'all know how I am about time. Y'all keep playing with my time," I groused.

"Chill, big bro. We gone make it on time." Frill tossed his dreads out of his face so he could spit in the sink.

I sighed loudly and paced the hallway, looking at my watch. I instantly felt like I had made the biggest mistake in choosing to stay here with these niggas. I should've just faced my fear and stayed at Desire's side.

26

DESIRE

Doing Me

Fuck Luxury with his lying ass. Why wouldn't he want to tell me the reason he wasn't with me on this international tour? That was the stupidest shit I had ever heard. I was his wife, and although our relationship had moved at the speed of light, his fear was something I should've known off the top.

Then I thought about it. This nigga was full of shit. He wasn't afraid of flying over water. That was an excuse so he wouldn't have to be here. I bet if Lavish and Frill were on an international tour, his ass would be right there with them. He acted like he was their fucking babysitter, anyway. I was more than pissed off, and Nasim was precisely what I needed to take my mind off Luxury's bullshit.

After opening the door for me, Nasim sat down on the couch, leaned back, and flipped through the channels to see if anything interesting was on. "I'm looking for a good movie," he said. "What you want to watch?"

I stared at him until he looked up at me.

“What’s up, Desire?” he asked, looking at me with those piercing hazel eyes.

“I really hate bringing this nigga up. Like, you know, I am happy you accepted my invitation to join me.” I walked over to him and straddled his lap. “But this nigga said he has a fear of flying over water. He didn’t mean to tell me, but he did.”

“So, that’s his excuse for not being here?”

“Yup. Crazy.”

“Yo, he might really have a fear. Well, I’m glad you invited me,” he said while grazing his juicy lips against the crease of my neck.

I moaned and leaned into Nasim’s kisses. “Mmm.”

He grunted softly to let me know that he was enjoying my lips just as much as I was enjoying his. His tongue became entangled with mine, and it felt like we were two longtime lovers. I slid my hands down his chest, feeling the muscles there. My hands stopped when I reached his joggers.

“Take what you want, shawty,” he demanded assertively.

My hands eased their way inside his joggers and took hold of him. My hands moved up and down, feeling him get harder.

“You see what you do to me?” he asked in the sexiest voice ever.

“Yeah,” I said, losing my breath from the excitement of stroking him.

He lifted me up from the couch and turned me over, unbuttoned my jeans, and took them off. His hands roamed all over my thighs. After grabbing my hips, he pulled me close, and his dick poked against my lace panties.

"Why are you so fine?" he asked.

I moved my panties to the side so he could get inside me. This thing with Nasim had just evolved into whatever it was we were doing. He didn't care about Luxury, and at that moment, I didn't, either. This was about pleasure and comfort, and I was glad he could be there for me.

Suddenly, there was a knock on the door. We froze. Who was at the door?

"You brought your bodyguard?" he asked.

"No. I gave him the night off," I replied, feeling puzzled. I prayed I hadn't been followed.

He walked to the door, his stiff dick leading the way. "Who is it?" he asked once he had his ear up to the door.

"Room service."

"Damn. I forgot I ordered us some food," Nasim said. "Toss me my pants."

I picked up his joggers and threw them at him. He caught them in midair and put them on fast before opening the door. The room-service man tried to wheel the cart inside the room, but Nasim took it from him.

"Thanks, man. I got it." Nasim pushed the cart inside before tipping the man and closing the door.

"What you get?"

"Just some buffalo wings and cheese fries. Nothing fancy."

"That sounds good. I am hungry."

"Hold up," he said with a naughty grin on his face. "You see how hard I am right now? That food can wait."

He came over to where I was sitting on the couch, lifted me up, and carried me to the bed. Nothing could stop this attraction. Like flies drawn to a barbecue picnic, we couldn't deny what we felt for each other. Without a condom, the pleasure I felt was unreal. In the back of my mind, I made a mental note to get Plan B first thing in the morning.

After our steamy romp, he caressed my arm as we lay in bed. “How do I make you feel, Desire?” he asked, staring deeply into my eyes. “I can’t seem to get enough of you.”

“The feeling is very mutual. I wish we’d met sooner.”

“Yeah?”

“I wish I had met you before I got with him,” I confessed.

“Things happened the way they were supposed to. You love him?”

“I love him, but I don’t know what’s going on with us. Everything was good before I came out here. This distance is killing what we have.”

He gave my lips a good kiss. When our lips parted, he said, “Yet distance has lit a fire under what we have . . . I’m trying to keep my feelings at bay. Let’s just enjoy the rest of the week, and then, after that, let’s see how things go between you two. I’m not going anywhere. No matter if you stay with him, I’ll always be here.”

“I appreciate that. Ever since my best friend was murdered, I’ve felt so alone, you know.”

“Your best friend was murdered? What happened, if you don’t mind me asking?”

I sat up and looked into his eyes. “She and I used to dance at the Queen of Diamonds. Her and her nigga were into all kinds of shit, so I don’t really know all the details, but they were gunned down right in front of the club. It was really fucked up.” I paused to stop myself from choking up. Just thinking about it had me ready to cry.

He frowned. “Wait . . . That was your best friend?”

"Yeah, we grew up together. My only friend in the world."

He closed his eyes and groaned. "Yo, um . . ."

"What?"

Sitting up, he rubbed the top of his head. "This is crazy."

"Why?"

He thought for a moment and then said, "I'm sorry. Yo, I heard about it on the news."

"I think it's fucked up that nobody knows who did it. I hope they find the muthafucka before I do."

"I hear you. Look, I can only imagine the pain you're in. That's even more reason for Luxury to be here for you right now."

"Exactly. I used to be so carefree and independent. I never needed a man to do anything for me. Luxury is demanding, and I can't even pick out what to wear without him changing it. Since my best friend died, I feel like a part of me went with her."

He put his arm around me, and we rested against the headboard.

His voice was calm as he said, "When you're with me, you don't have to worry about anything. With me, you can relax your mind and be free."

I was so comfortable in his arms that I fell asleep.

27

LUXURY

Stuck

We wound up missing our flight because Lavish and Frill could not get their shit together on time. By the time we touched down in Baltimore, the promoter had decided to pull the shows and refund the tickets. Since we were so late, they hit us with a fine. So not only did we not get paid, but we also lost more money. Lavish and Frill didn't seem to care. They wound up finding a party to go to and taking as many bitches they could back to the hotel. Meanwhile, I was blowing my baby's phone up, and she wasn't answering.

After partying and drinking and popping a few smackers, I fell asleep. I awoke the next morning and looked at my phone. Desire still hadn't hit me up. This was getting old. I called her repeatedly, until she finally answered.

"Hello?" she said, sounding irritated.

"I've been calling you," I said carefully, because I really felt like cussing her ass out.

"I know."

I was feeling annoyed by her blasé attitude. "So, you weren't going to answer or at least call me back?"

"I have nothing to say to you, Luxury. I don't want to hear your lies."

"Fuck. Just stop this nonsense. Your little tour is ending in a few days, and I don't want you comin' home all mad. I'm sorry I hurt you, but you gotta talk to me. You can't be going hours without answering."

"I'll see you when I get home. You got some serious making up to do for not coming on tour with me."

"I got you, baby. You already know my wheels are turning. I'm about to roll up a fat blunt and then take a shower."

"Well, I gotta get some rest. I'm tired. I'll call you when I get up," Desire said.

"A'ight. I love you."

She hesitated a little before she finally replied, "I love you."

It was taking everything in me not to jump on a plane and get to her. But the thought of crashing into the ocean had me shaking my head. Man, I was just going to have to wait to see her when she got home.

28

EGYPT

If I Was His Girlfriend

Wrapping up the tour for Desire was like seeing the light after getting lost in a dark cave. Working for Desire wasn't no easy thing to do. She was moody as hell, and most of the time, I wanted to slap the hell out of her. She could be a sweetheart one minute and a straight-up bitch the next.

With her disappearing acts, me and the girls were suspicious. I had had to pump Meek for some info, and he'd mentioned that back in Paris, he waited for her outside some hotel room and then left before she came out. He'd told me he was certain she stayed the night. When he'd said that he saw a nigga answer the door, I'd been stunned. What the hell was Desire thinking?

After she'd kept curbing him and giving him nights off, he'd been under the impression that she was still seeing this dude. I wasn't the type to snitch, but I oversaw all of Desire's personal affairs, and I had noticed that her financial activity was unusual of late. She had some unexplained credit card transactions. If Desire didn't slow her roll, I was going to have to let my boy Luxury know. At the end of the day, he was my friend first.

I really hated how crazy this job was becoming, and if it weren't for my cousins, Lala and Nia, I would've gone mad by now. I was feeling more like a reporter for Luxury these days. Luxury was continually calling, wondering what was going on with Desire. Half the time, I didn't even think she wanted this lifestyle. Seemed to me like her ass wanted to go back to what she was used to, taking her clothes off for a dollar. I couldn't even wrap my mind around what he was thinking by trying to turn her into a household name. True, the fans enjoyed her music, but in my eyes, she would always be a gold-digging ho.

I spent the final day of the international tour preparing for Desire's last appearance at a local nightclub. I had to call the club owner to make sure they would have everything Desire needed. Nia and Lala wanted to go shopping since it was our last day in the United Kingdom, but I wasn't feeling it. They went without me, and I finished a couple of things for Desire.

About an hour after my cousins left the hotel, there was a knock on my hotel door, so I got up and opened it.

Desire walked in with shades on her eyes, looking like she had just crawled out of bed.

"What's up?" I asked her.

"Nothing much. Bored out of my fucking mind. I can't wait to get back to the States," she said.

"Bored?" I scowled. Her ass wasn't bored. I was sure she was just trying to lay it on thick so I wouldn't be suspicious of her whereabouts. "Well, tonight is the last show, so it will all be over soon, and you can get back to your husband."

She didn't respond.

I ran my fingers through my hair, then pushed a section behind my ear. I took a good look at her and noticed a big red mark on her neck. Was that a hickey? This bitch had no tact. How was she going to hide *that* when we were back in the States in twenty-four hours?

"What?" she asked, noticing the way I was staring at her. She tried to pull the collar of her Puma zip-up jacket over the hickey.

"You fuckin' bitch," I let out.

Suddenly, she pulled her shades off and squinted at me while looking me up and down. "What the fuck you just call me?"

"You heard me. You walk up in here after being gone all fucking night. Matter of fact, you've been gone every night since we got here. You got a hickey on your neck? What's wrong with you? Luxury is gonna kill you."

"You really should mind your own business." She kept trying her best to hide the hickey with her jacket.

"Oh no, don't try to hide it now. Who is he? Is he the nigga you hooked up with in Paris? He must be important, because suddenly, you got substantial amounts of money flowing out of your bank account for plane tickets, hotels, and room service. You better tell me right now."

Desire smacked her lips, looking guilty as hell. "Calm down. It ain't all that serious."

I took a deep breath and tried to rationalize with her. She was miles away from her man, and he wasn't here for her. I had to put myself in her shoes to try to understand. Maybe if I was here for her now, I could learn everything there was to know, so that when it was time to expose her ass, I would have all the evidence I needed. She didn't know what to do with a man like Luxury. I, on the other hand, had always wanted Luxury. That man was so fucking sexy. How could she cheat on him? He was loyal.

"Okay . . . look, I don't mean to come at you foul. As your personal assistant, you shouldn't try to hide shit like this from me because if it were to get out to the press, we'd have to do damage control. If you're having an affair, that's on you, but just know that I am a woman too, and I have needs, so I understand. You don't think I'm lonely out here?"

"Yeah? You got a man?"

"I don't, but that's beside the point. My point is, you're doing what you gotta do. You have needs."

Desire looked at me as if she couldn't believe I had just switched up, but she said, "It's not what it looks like. Well, Luxury lies a lot. If he had just said that he had a fear of flying over water, I would've been able to handle that. I have a friend. That's all we are, friends. He's a nice guy, doesn't mean any harm. Things just got carried away between us, but he understands that I'm married. We have an understanding. No need to worry."

"Can I ask you something? Why'd you marry Luxury so fast?"

"I do what Luxury wants me to do. Since my best friend was murdered, and my father died of cancer within a month, I felt lost. It was still hard to deal with that, and Luxury was there for me. He showed me a new world and a life I could never dream of."

"I get it," I said, but I didn't get it. "Does Luxury know your guy friend?"

"Nope, and I expect this conversation to stay between us. You don't say a word, and you get to keep your job." Desire threw her shades back on and walked out of my hotel room.

I took a deep breath and exhaled. If only the bitch knew that I could end her career if I wanted to. I was going to keep her secret about her lover to myself, but she had better hope the media didn't get a hold of this news, or else she would have some explaining to do. Luxury was the wrong one to fuck around on. If he were mine, he wouldn't have to worry about anything.

29

DESIRE

Back on Track

I was home, sweet home. Being home felt like heaven, but I was so nervous. As I walked up to the front door, my stomach was twisting into knots. I had to face Luxury. What if he could see my guilt? I felt stupid for sharing what I had with Egypt. What if she told him? When I had talked to him before my flight, he'd acted a little funny. He'd kept giving me short answers, as if he was irritated with me.

Though I should've been more cautious, I'd wound up spending the last night in London with Nasim. We'd made a promise that the time we'd spent in Paris, Spain, and the United Kingdom would be our secret. Once we touched down on US soil, we would go about our lives, pretending as if it had never happened.

I opened the front door and stepped inside. "Luxury?" I shouted, dropping my luggage at the door.

The house was so quiet. No TV. No music. He wasn't there, to my surprise. In his last text message, he had said he would be on the plane from New York while my plane was still in the air, but he should've made it back home by now. He should've beaten me by hours. I checked my phone to see if he had messaged me. Nothing. I texted him, but he didn't respond. That made me even more nervous.

I would kill Egypt if she had told him my secret. A part of me wanted so badly to quit this rapping shit and take my ass back to the strip club. I even considered leaving Luxury so I could do me. This lonely life wasn't what I had signed up for. Then I started thinking. Was he messing around with his baby mama? Everything lately had been "his baby this and his baby that." If he was messing around, it was cool, because I surely was doing what I wanted to do.

I headed upstairs, and when I didn't find him in any of the bedrooms, I got ready to take a shower. Before I hopped in, I inspected every nook and cranny of our bedroom and my closet to make sure he hadn't had the next bitch up in here while I was gone. Then I went to the mini fridge and pulled out the bottle of Henny. I took a few sips and sent a text to Nasim.

Me: I made it home.

N: I'm almost home. I had to stop for some business.

Me: Okay.

N: When can I see you again? You should come by.

I shook my head. I had told him we wouldn't be able to kick it anymore, unless we were in public.

Me: If I have some free time, let's go to a bar or something.

N: Just hit me up.

I smiled and locked my phone. Taking off my clothes, I let the warm feeling of the liquor consume me. I got in the shower, humming to myself. While I showered, I kept thinking about the way Nasim's hands felt on my skin. I got so lost in his hazel eyes whenever I was around him. There in the shower, I entered a beautiful world, which held all my best memories of our time together in the UK. He had told me everything about himself and how he'd grown up. I, in turn, had told him about my childhood. I had told him all about Mina and how much I missed her. Through our vulnerable moments, I had learned that his faults were his perfections. His choice of words always made me feel good, I realized. I felt tingly all over as I reminisced about our moments with each other.

Wait. Am I falling in love with Nasim?

It was like my feelings for Luxury were dying, and my feelings for Nasim were thriving. My eyes fell closed, and I immersed my head in the water, as if I was standing in a continuous waterfall. As the images of Nasim kept playing like a movie in my mind, the water poured down, dripping at my sides. The sensation of the steamy water was calming. I shook my head, telling myself to make these memories fade. I was going to have to pretend that what we did had never happened.

I quickly finished my shower, dried off, put some lotion on, and threw on a Givenchy tank top and shorts.

I heard a noise from downstairs, so I walked out of the bedroom.

"Luxury?" I called.

I walked down to the living room, but nobody was there. I went into the kitchen and still nobody, but I saw his car keys on the counter. Then I heard something move on the balcony. I walked to the glass sliding door and pushed it open. A thick puff of smoke greeted me.

Luxury was sitting on a patio lounge chair, his shirt unbuttoned and open above his black jean shorts and some Gucci slides. Just the sight of him made me feel weak. In my heart, I started to regret all the dreadful things I had done. I felt like I didn't deserve him.

He gave me a half smile before blowing out another cloud of smoke. I tried to read his eyes to pick up on any hints that Egypt had thrown me under the bus. He seemed a little disoriented as he motioned for me to sit on his lap.

I straddled him and put my head on his chest. Closing my eyes, I felt my heart beating hard. I had missed the way he smelled. I had missed the way I felt in his arms. I swallowed the hard lump that was forming in my throat. I was home now, and that was all that mattered.

"Hey," I said.

He didn't respond, just kept smoking. His silence was uncomfortable, and it was killing me, because I couldn't read him. I was even more nervous now. Right when I was going to ask what was up with him, he put his blunt in the ashtray and wrapped both his arms around me. He stroked my back before planting a kiss on my forehead. It felt so good to be in his arms. Memories of the first time I saw him came crashing down. I wanted to get back to that feeling.

"Did you miss me?" he asked with glassy eyes.

He asked me that question as if he had doubts. That really put me on edge. Given all the arguing and shouting we had done while I was away, he should've known that I missed him.

"You know I missed you, Luxury. Did you miss me?"

"Of course I did," he said as he stroked my hair.

"Why you acting like you didn't, then?"

He didn't respond, just kept caressing my hair. He was not helping my insecurities. My palms started getting sweaty. Though there was fear in my chest, I didn't show it. I was cautious, because if he didn't know about Nasim, there was no need to bust myself out.

"What's the matter with you?" I asked.

"Nothing."

His eyes told me different. Something was bothering him. Luxury's eyes were always honest, though his words weren't. At that moment, I realized that lying to me was something that came too easy to him.

"Hmmm. Well, I texted you to let you know I was home."

"I know," he said quietly.

Why was he giving me short-ass answers and staring at me as if I were a stranger? I hoped I was just paranoid. What if Egypt had told him something crazy, and he was just waiting for me to say it?

"What you mean, you know, Luxury?" I scowled, trying to keep myself on track.

He picked up his lighter and blunt. He lit what was left of the blunt, drew in smoke, and swallowed it before he blew it back out. "I was busy."

"So, you get at me with an attitude if I don't answer, and if I said I was busy, you would have a fuckin' fit. You were too busy to tell me you were busy?" My eyes started to water.

He inhaled more smoke as he stared into my eyes, searching me. The longer he was silent, the harder my heart was beating.

"So, you're not going to say shit?" I questioned, almost feeling fed up.

A fat ring of smoke hit me in the face. That was his answer.

With a deep scowl, I started to get up, but he roughly grabbed my wrist.

"Where you going?" he said.

I rolled my eyes, trying to snatch my arm away from him, but he was stronger.

"What, Luxury? I come home to you having an attitude. Would you like it if I hadn't come back?"

His grip loosened up completely. "Today is the anniversary of my brother's murder . . . It's always hard for me on this day, so I'm sorry. I'm a li'l fucked up right now. I've been drinking all day."

My heart sank. I had had no idea it was the anniversary of his brother's passing. It had been so easy to assume that his attitude had something to do with my wrongdoings.

"Baby, I'm sorry. Is there anything I can do?" I said sincerely.

"Nah, you're good. I popped a Xan to chill me out. This day is never good for me."

I nodded. "I'll probably feel that way around Mina's and Papi's too."

"Let's not talk about it. I'm happy we're home, baby. You know, not being able to see you, touch you, kiss you . . . I couldn't handle it. I thought I could, but I couldn't. I will never leave your side for that long again."

I placed both hands on his face as I pressed my lips against his. When we kissed, he took my breath away. I was so stupid to have betrayed him. This was the man I had wished for, and now that I had him, I did him this way?

When our lips parted, he looked into my eyes, and his hands were right back in my hair again. I didn't want to argue or fight with him. I just wanted to stay like this.

"Do you really love me, Luxury?" I asked.

He was staring so deeply into my eyes that it felt like he was staring into my soul. "You don't have to ask, Desire. Do you love me?"

"And you don't have to ask me. Fuck, yeah, I do."

That was the truth. I loved Luxury with all my heart. I didn't have a real excuse for cheating on him. What I had done was unacceptable.

His tongue traced my lips before it entered my mouth, as if he wanted to taste my words.

Nodding his head, he said, "Good, 'cause I love the fuck outta you."

"Good."

"Hey, I got some news. You and the boys were offered to do a li'l mini tour."

"In the States, right? Since you have a fear of flying over water."

He smacked his lips. "Yeah, in the States. Like, only fifteen cities. We got Los Angeles, Miami, New York, you know. I gotta get on these niggas, because they been dumb and unprofessional lately. Late to shit and canceled in B-more for missing our flight."

"What? You didn't tell me that."

"I didn't want you to worry. That's they shit. Anyway, you gotta get back in the studio, 'cause I got some hot collaborations happening."

"All right. Sounds good. Now, let's go up to the room. I gotta show you just how much I missed you."

"You know a nigga with that shit." He put out the end of his blunt.

After taking his hand in mine, I pulled him all the way to our bedroom.

Over the next few days, Luxury had me recording and rehearsing like a maniac for this new tour with the Monnahan Boyz. As always, he kept me busy day and night. In between the times when I wasn't recording, we had sex. Sex with Luxury was good, and it seemed like it had gotten better since I got home. The time we'd spent apart had been much needed.

Nasim was becoming a problem. He had been hitting me up, but I hadn't called him back. There was no point in talking to him when I knew what talking would lead to. The best thing I could do was keep what we did on the low. The last thing I wanted was for Luxury to catch wind that Nasim even existed.

One afternoon Luxury walked into the studio as I was wrapping up this song I was doing with the pop singer Roxx. She wasn't in the studio, because our schedules wouldn't line up. Her part was already prerecorded, and I just had to do my part. Luxury nodded his head and motioned for me to come out of the booth.

"Hey, boo," I said, walking out of the booth.

"Hey. That's a hot song," he said. "You done?"

"Almost."

"Where's Egypt?" he asked, looking around.

"She texted me and said she has the flu and wouldn't be down here tonight. I told her I hope she feels better," I replied, sitting on the couch.

"I'll check on her later."

The studio door opened, and some short, light-skinned chick walked in and smiled at Luxury.

"What you doing here?" Luxury scowled. "How you even find me?"

She rolled her eyes at him. "You shouldn't tag your whole life on social media, nigga. Everybody knows where to find you. You got to do mo' betta."

Who the fuck is this rat-faced bitch? I rose to my feet from the couch and put my hands on my hips.

She took one look at me, turned up her nose, and faced Luxury. "I came because you ain't been answering my calls about your son. He needs new clothes. He's growing fast. So I came to collect."

"This your baby mama?" I asked, feeling my skin crawl.

I looked her up and down. She had a cute shape, and she was dressed fly—I couldn't deny her that—but she was ugly in the face. I never would've thought he would fuck around with anybody that looked like Master Splinter's daughter.

"Well, hello to you too," she said, finally making eye contact with me. "Since you're my son's stepmama, wouldn't you like to meet him soon?"

"Let me talk to you for a minute, Charity," Luxury said, roughly grabbing her arm to take her outside the room.

After snatching her arm away from him, she pointed her long nail in his face. "Take yo' fuckin' hands off me, nigga. Just give me the dough, and I'm up outta here."

"Why can't you hand her the fuckin' money right here in front of me?" I asked, feeling some kind of way. This secretive transaction shit between them was on my last nerve.

"Chill, Desire," Luxury stated.

"First of all, ho, this doesn't even concern you," Charity snarled, rolling her eyes at me. "Why don't you go back to recording with your weak ass?"

"Chill, Charity," Luxury muttered.

"Who you callin' weak, bitch? You better watch how you talk to me. You might regret it," I yelled.

"Please, the only thing I'm regretting is not beating yo' ass right up in this studio, ho. Don't get embarrassed in front of your husband."

I stepped closer to her, and Luxury wedged himself between us.

"Chill, Desire. Charity, chill. Aye, let me handle my business with Charity, and I'll be right back. Don't make me repeat this shit." Luxury was doing his best not to lose his cool.

"You better listen to your *husband* and chill," she taunted.

I lunged at her and swung, but Luxury wouldn't let me get to her.

"Move out of the way, Luxury. You gone let her disrespect me like this?" I barked.

"The only person you're disrespecting is yourself, ho. Fucking around with Nas. Yeah, you think nobody knows about that shit, huh?"

I froze, and my mouth nearly dropped open, but I came back with, "Who the fuck is Nas?"

"Yeah, bitch, you know *Nasim*. Don't front. You should be more careful who you creep around with, triflin'-ass ho. Don't ever get at me crazy again," she stated. Before she walked out of the studio, she said over her shoulder, "Now, what's up?"

Luxury gave me this look that said he would get to me later about it. I blew air from my lips, feeling ready to beat her down. How did she know about Nasim and me? Was he friends with her? I felt like calling him up to find out if he was running his mouth like a bitch. While

Luxury was out there talking to Charity, I hit Nasim with a text.

Me: So why Luxury's baby mama just brought you up in front of Luxury? Do you know her?

It didn't take long before Nasim replied. N: Who his baby mama?

Me: Some bitch named Charity. The one who likes to run to the media to talk shit.

N: I don't know nobody named Charity.

Me: Well, you been talking to somebody, because, for some reason, she knows about us.

N: I don't know how. When can I see you, beautiful?

Me: Things have been better with Luxury, so I don't know.

N: When you get some time, let's do lunch or dinner.

I sighed. I didn't know why it was so hard just to tell Nasim no. I cared about him and his feelings, and it was wrong for me to string him along and use him in times when I felt lonely. This thing about Charity knowing about what we had done had me a little stressed out. What if she had proof? What would Luxury do?

Me: I'll hit you up.

I erased our messages and got back in the booth to finish the song.

"Run that shit back to the bridge," I said to the producer.

"I got you," he said.

30

LUXURY

Show Some Respect

"Charity, you can't be saying shit like that to my wife. Any business about our son is our business, so you gotta leave her the fuck out of it."

"She started it. So, um . . ." She smacked her lips. "Why hasn't she met our baby yet, Luxury?"

"Chill. In time. Let's get to why you're here. How much you need this time?" I took cash out of my pocket and handed her all I had. "That's all I got right now. I can come by tomorrow, after I go to the bank. We're about to hit the road again, so I'll be gone for a little while."

She quickly counted the bills and rolled her eyes. "This will do for now. I don't mean to keep bringing this up, but my homegirl swears that Nas and Desire kicked it all while she was in Spain, or wherever she was. I think you should look into that."

"Man, why do you keep going with this bullshit?"

"My girl said that he told her that he's been fucking with her all up throughout the world. And get this, she covered his first-class flights, shopping sprees, hotel suites, all his expenses, Luxury."

My heart was pounding, but I couldn't take her seriously. This shit sounded like some reality TV scripted bullshit. Charity had to be lying. I felt like she was trying to sabotage my relationship, because she couldn't stand to see me with anybody but her.

"Shut the fuck up. That's bullshit, and you know it."

"Nigga, what?" Her face was frowning all up.

"I don't fucking believe you." The fire in my eyes could scorch her.

She backed up a little, paying close attention to my body language. "I know we ain't all that cool at times, but trust me when I say that I am not a hater. I just don't want to see you out here looking dumb as fuck. I wouldn't lie to you about something like this. She's a ho, Luxury. Plain and simple. You picked her up from the strip club, so now drop her ass back off there. That's where she belongs."

"You're really jealous, Charity. It's okay to be jealous, baby. You ain't gotta lie, though. She would never fuck around on me. You know who the fuck I am."

"*I'm* jealous? Me? Of who? That ho?"

"Yeah, you're jealous. You think by telling me this that I'm gone get rid of her. News flash, she ain't going nowhere. She's my wife, so deal with it, with yo' thirsty ass."

"*Thirsty*? Nigga, you got me all the way fucked up. You need to wake the fuck up and realize your wife is a ho. While she was overseas, suckin' and fuckin' the next nigga, she got you over here thinking she's top-notch when she's just herself, a stank-ass ho. You're dumber than I thought."

"So, what does that make you, then? Getting pregnant by a nigga who doesn't want you."

"Fuck you, Luxury. Don't come crying to me when you find out the real."

I gave her the middle finger before walking back into the studio. She had me hot. I was the wrong nigga. I didn't believe anything that came out of her mouth. Desire didn't have time to be fucking no niggas other than me. I knew where she was always. Now, if I heard this shit from Frill or Lavish, I'd consider it and check it out, but coming from my baby mama, that was out.

Desire was ending her song when I walked in. I bobbed my head with approval. This was a certified number one hit.

"That shit is hot, baby," I said, clapping my hands.

She twisted her lips to the side in disbelief. "You didn't even hear it, talking about it's hot."

"I did hear it. I could hear it outside the door. Aye, come here for a minute. Let me holler at you."

She walked over to me, looking a little sad. I had a feeling the shit Charity said had got to her.

"Hey, don't trip off Charity. I'm sorry she got at you like that. Don't worry about shit she's talking about. She's just jealous, baby." I embraced her and placed kisses all over her face before kissing her lips.

"She better watch what she say, before people start believing her," she said.

"Hey, as long as we know the truth, we got nothing to worry about."

"That's right, baby. I'm glad you don't believe rumors."

"You already know how I feel about rumors. You ready to get up out of here?"

She nodded. "Yeah, I'm done for the night."

We wrapped up the session and left. On our way to the house, I received a call from Egypt.

"Who is that?" Desire asked, peering down at my phone.

"Egypt. Answer it for me. I didn't link the Bluetooth."

She picked up my phone and answered. "Hello?"

"Put it on speakerphone," I said.

She did what she was told, and Egypt's voice came through. "Oh, hey, Desire. Is Luxury around?"

"I'm here on speakerphone," I said. "I'm driving. What's up? How you feeling? I hear you sick and shit."

"I got the damn flu or something. Anyway, I don't have good news."

I frowned. "I don't like unwelcome news, E."

"I know that, but I have to let you know. So the guy you had that booked this fifteen-city tour fucked up. There is no tour."

"What you mean, there is no tour?"

"He took the money, but I can't confirm one single venue. I was trying to get Desire's calendar together, and the nigga's phone is disconnected. I called a couple of the venues to make sure this nigga wasn't a fraud, and lo and behold, nothing has been booked. They never even heard of the nigga."

"That nigga is supposed to be a promoter. He's booked shit for us before," I said.

"Yeah. I don't know what happened, but you won't be seeing a return on that money. I think you should go ahead and add the Monnahan Boyz to my list. I can handle their scheduling. That way, I can make sure their asses are on time."

"You sure you can handle them and Desire?"

"I got this," she assured me.

"Okay, let's give it a trial run. Try to get another American cities tour going. We gonna have the Monnahan Boyz with Desire, and our artist Lael will open for them."

"Sounds good to me. Any cities you don't want to hit?"

"Nah. Just no overseas right now," I told her.

"Got it. Well, you guys enjoy your night. Desire, I'll see you in about a week."

"A'ight," Desire said.

"Bye." Egypt hung up.

I tried not to seem pissed that this nigga had got over on me. I was the wrong one to fuck over. Trust I was going to find this dude.

"Babe, you okay?" Desire asked.

"I'm good. I'll feel even better when I find this cat. I don't like thieves."

"That is pretty fucked up. You going to meet up with your baby mama in the morning?"

"Nah, fuck that bitch."

"What's her problem with me?" she asked.

"She's just bitter. Don't trip off her. My son is taken care of. She's lucky I didn't beat her ass for that shit."

"You don't have to put your hands on her. I'm sure she just wants us to break up."

"If she keeps fuckin' with me, she'll leave me no fuckin' choice."

Desire was staring at me all crazy. I shook my head. I wasn't a woman beater, but I didn't like nobody getting over on me.

"Babe, I'm just talkin' shit," I said. "Putting my hands on a woman ain't my thing. I'm a lover, not a fighter, baby."

"Okay. I don't care what she does to you. I don't want you hitting on her. She's the mother of your child, so you gotta show some respect."

"That bitch knows nothing about respect. Why should I respect her if she don't respect me? I'm just some money to her. Having that baby was about money. There's no love there at all. Shit, it feels more like she's a bill collector. I can't wait for my son to get older. Then we will be able to bond more."

"I hear you. So when do you want me to meet him?"

"Whenever you're ready. I know it's a lot to handle."

She nodded. "I'll let you know."

I looked over at her with a grin. I really loved Desire. She didn't have to worry about me believing no damned rumors. If I didn't hear the shit from her or see it with my own eyes, I wasn't taking nobody's word as truth.

The days I didn't have anything to do, I just chilled in the house and watched TV. I was trying to get caught up on the show *Snowfall*. Everybody kept saying how good it was, and I wanted to binge watch it. Luckily, Desire didn't have anything to do, either. It was rare when we both had hardly anything to do at the same time. I was enjoying every moment.

"Baby, I'm thinking about making us dinner tonight," she said. "I haven't cooked in so long. It feels good just to be able to say I'm making dinner. I gotta go to the store. You need some more Henny?"

I pressed PAUSE on the TV remote. "You do realize that you may be recognized at the store, right? I'll call E and see if she can go to the grocery store for us. That's her job."

She rolled her eyes. "I know what her title is, but she doesn't have to do everything for me."

"She actually does. I'll call her for you. What you need?"

"I want to make baked chicken, asparagus, and twice-baked potatoes with shrimp."

"That sounds good," I said, picking up my phone. "You need all the ingredients?"

"Yeah, so just tell her I'll text the list." She disappeared into the kitchen.

I called Egypt, and she answered after three rings. "Hello?"

"E, what you doing?"

"A few things. What's up?"

"Desire needs some stuff from the grocery store. You think you got time to handle that? She's texting you the list."

"Okay, cool. I gotta go to the store too, so that's perfect."

"Thank you."

"No problem."

I ended the call, and my cell rang no sooner than I had set it down. My mom's picture was displayed on my screen. I placed her on speaker and answered, "Hello?"

"I'm so glad you answered for your mama, Poo. Spoodie nor Jon-Jon ever answer for me. I know they be seeing me callin'."

"They may be busy recording."

"I guess. I'm going to see Dinky tomorrow."

Why did she always feel the need to tell me every time she went to see that nigga? I had already told her that I wanted nothing to do with him.

"Mama, I really don't—"

"Just listen to me. I understand how you feel. Regardless of the situation, he's still your brother and my baby. No use in holding hatred in your heart. He's sorry about what he did. He needs a package, and I ain't got no money. I was trying to ask Spoodie and Jon-Jon, because I hate to ask you."

I looked up at the ceiling. "Mama, I told you I wasn't going to give him a dime, and I meant that. I'll see if they want to contribute, though, okay?"

"Okay. Thank you. When will I get to see you? I haven't seen you since you got married."

"Soon. I'll probably swing by in a few days."

"You gonna bring my grandson?"

"I might, depending on how Charity is acting."

"Bring your wife too. Would be good to see her again."

"Yeah, I'll bring her."

"All right, son. I love you."

"I love you too."

"Bye."

"Bye." I ended the call.

Desire came out of the kitchen and stared at me.

"What?" I asked.

"Your mom wants to see me and your son at the same time?"

I shrugged my shoulders. "Something like that, but I don't know how you would feel about that after what just went down between you and Charity."

She nodded and sighed. "Well, I just sent my list to Egypt. She said it will take a few hours. Once she brings the stuff I need, I'll start dinner."

"A'ight. You want to go get one of those fruity things you like so much from South Beach? It's been a long time. By the time we come back, E should be on her way."

"Yesss." She grinned from ear to ear, rolling her hips like a belly dancer.

We both put on our shoes.

31

DESIRE

Too Many Bitches

After getting a batido, my favorite treat, in South Beach, we decided to take a walk, with the bodyguard behind us. It felt weird strolling the strip with protection and with people snapping pictures of us. A few people asked to take photos with us. We stopped and posed for a few pictures, and I signed autographs.

"You ever want to move away from Miami?" I asked.

"No. This is home. I love Miami," Luxury answered.

"That's how I feel too."

I thought about the conversation he had had with his mother about his son visiting her at the same time as me. I was his wife, so I was going to have to get this over with. The sooner the better.

"Baby, I'll meet your son. I'm ready. If your mom wants us to come over there, we should go before our schedules get hectic again. I think Egypt was saying something about doing a late-night show in Los Angeles next week."

"Yeah. A'ight. I'll make the arrangements."

My cell phone chimed. I pulled it out of my pocket and saw that I had a text from Nasim. I opened it while Luxury was looking at the parade of lowriders cruising by.

N: I see you, walking like the happy couple. Glad that things are back on track, but when can I see you?

My breath nearly caught in my throat. I looked around to see if I could see Nasim. There were too many people out for me to spot him. He could be anywhere.

Me: I told you I would hit you.

N: I'll be waiting.

I hurried and erased the messages.

"Who is that?" Luxury asked, with one eyebrow raised.

"Just my brother," I lied. "He wants to link up before he moves."

"Oh yeah, he did say he was leaving Miami. We should throw him a going-away party."

"That would be nice."

Suddenly, we heard a feminine voice yelling, "Luxury. *Luxury*."

I turned to see who was calling my man like that. Some blond-haired bitch looking like a black Barbie was walking briskly toward us.

"Luxury, I know you hear me calling you," she said.

"Who the fuck is that?" I laughed at the sight of her.

"Nobody," he answered.

The bodyguard blocked the woman's path so she couldn't get to Luxury.

"I'm nobody?" she asked. "Tuh. I see you wasted no time marrying this li'l so-and-so. So that's how this works, huh? No phone call or nothing? You promised you wouldn't do no shit like that to me after all I've been through."

I was watching closely as I sipped my batido. Something was off about her. I knew Luxury had had bitches before we got together, but these random chicks popping up here and there made me wonder if he was still fucking around. I should've known he had some loose ends, but this was crazy.

Luxury didn't say a word as he pushed me toward the car.

"You trying to replace me with this bitch? You and I both know that no bitch can ever replace me. I'm the best you ever had, or do you not remember saying that, either?" the blonde screeched.

I shrugged, with a laugh. "Who the fuck is that?"

"Girl, don't think you the shit because you got hits or whatnot. Don't nobody like yo' whack-ass music. You can't even rap, ho. I hear you shake ya ass for cash better than you rap. Maybe you should go back to doing that." She laughed her ass off.

I got close enough to pour my batido on top of her head. My shake was now running down her face, and it was all over her ugly-ass yellow spandex outfit. She was trying to come after me now, but the bodyguard wouldn't allow it.

"Stupid-ass bitch! Fuck with me if you want to!" she screamed. "Luxury. Luxury! Don't do this to me."

Luxury grabbed me hard and pushed me into the car.

"Ouch," I said, pulling away from him. He slammed my car door shut.

As soon as he was behind the wheel and had closed his door, he said, "You gotta learn how not to react to these bitches."

"What is going on, Luxury? Was that a—"

Before I could finish, he interrupted. “Man, hell nah. End of story. There’s no need to start assuming shit.”

The woman was so extra, and her choice of clothing was interesting. I prayed to God Luxury was not into some crazy shit. I pushed the thought out of my mind quickly, because like he had said, there was no need to start assuming shit.

I stared at him. “Let me ask you something . . . You still fuckin’ around? Ain’t no way these bitches keep coming out of the woodwork over some dick they ain’t seen or touched in months. That’s probably the real reason you didn’t come overseas with me.”

“You don’t be listening, I swear. I don’t even know that lady. I don’t know how you figure I’m fucking around. You say the dumbest shit.”

“Oh really? I threw my batido at Miss Thing. Now I don’t have my shake. Ugh. How many bitches have you fucked, Luxury? How many others will try to come for me?”

He shrugged, as if it were no big deal. “I got this under control. You should know I won’t let anyone fuck with you.”

“You think I like hearing that some bitch done fucked and sucked my nigga?”

“You think a nigga want to hear the same shit about you?”

I paused before I replied, “Ain’t no nigga coming at you about shit, so it’s not the same.”

“You sure about that?” he asked in the oddest tone of voice.

“What’s that supposed to mean? I know you not talking about what Charity said to you. I thought you didn’t believe her lying ass.”

"I don't believe her, but you acting bogus as fuck right now. Look, you said you not fucking nobody, and I'm telling you I'm not, either. If you believe me, then I believe you."

I crossed my arms over my chest and looked out the window. The sad part was I knew all about my dirt. There was no way Luxury's ass wasn't out there still fucking around with other bitches. I mean, how else could he go weeks without no pussy from me? If he wasn't getting it from me, he was getting it from someone else. I chilled and made it seem like I believed him, but in the back of my mind, I had made up my own mind. I couldn't trust the nigga.

When we got back to the house, Egypt was pulling up. Perfect timing, but now I wasn't in the mood to cook shit. I stormed past Egypt and went into the house without a word to her. As I was heading upstairs, I got a text from Nasim.

N: I'm here if you need me.

I didn't respond as I lay on the bed. As much as I wanted to run into his arms, I wasn't about to fall into that trap. I closed my eyes to stop my head from pounding. I nearly fell asleep.

Luxury barged into the room, shouting, "Hey."

I smacked my lips. "What?"

"I don't know why you're tripping."

Taking a deep breath, I got out of bed. "Do me a favor and shut the fuck up," I snapped, then stalked toward the bathroom.

He yanked my arm before I could get into the bathroom. "You better check yo' fuckin' attitude and watch yo' mouth. You really ain't got no reason to be trippin' like this."

"Don't be yanking on me. How am I trippin'? I just want to go to sleep."

He wouldn't let my wrist go and held it firmly. "It's not even six o'clock, and you ready to go to bed? I thought you were cooking dinner?"

"You better take yo' fuckin' hands off me, nigga, before I really act a fuckin' fool."

He put his hands up. "You know what? Fuck dinner. I'm out. I'll go get my own dinner."

"Shit. That's fine with me." I went into the bathroom to pee.

As I sat on the toilet, he stood in the doorframe. "Why are you really actin' like this? You blowin' this shit all out of proportion."

"I'm not acting like anything, Luxury."

"Yeah you are. You care about that bitch we ran into?"

"Nigga, nobody gives two fucks about that bitch. Maybe you're the one who cares about the bitch, since you bringing her up."

"Man, I swear, girl. You need to stop acting so muh-fuckin' insecure. You shouldn't be worried about no bitch taking your place. This is the last time I'm saying that shit." He walked out of the doorway, and I heard him grab his keys.

I finished peeing and flushed the toilet quickly. I rushed out of the bathroom. "Where you think you going?"

"I told you, I'm out."

Before I could respond, he was down the stairs and out the door. I took a deep breath and exhaled. I knew I had cheated on Luxury, and if he was doing it, it would make me feel a little better, as I would be able to justify my own actions, even though it would piss me off. The sun was going down, and I was hungry. I decided to cook dinner.

I started feeling bad about the way I had acted, so I cooked enough for him. I put the food in a warm oven to keep it hot. Then I got in the shower, dried off, and changed into some black lingerie and a matching robe. I grabbed a bottle of champagne out of the fridge. Right when I was pouring a glass, he walked through the front door.

A smirk appeared on his face when he noticed my attire. As he sat a Tiffany & Co. bag on the counter, he said, "What you doing up in here?"

"Just a little something to say that I'm sorry for the way I acted today."

He rubbed his hands together and nodded. "I'm sorry, baby. You shouldn't have to deal with women from my past. I got you a peace offering gift."

"Ooh, what is it?" I sipped the champagne.

"Open it and see." He handed me the bag.

Inside the bag was a box. I took the top off the box and found an eighteen-karat gold wrap necklace.

"Babe, this is beautiful. Thank you." I placed my arms around his neck. "You're so good to me. I keep treating you bad."

"We're good, Mama." He kissed me. "I smell dinner. I didn't get nothing to eat."

"Good. So wash your hands and sit down."

He smacked my ass as I bent over to open the oven.

I fixed our plates as he washed his hands and sat at the table. I poured him a glass of champagne and turned on the R & B station on Spotify. I sat next to him at the table and put my feet in his lap while we ate.

"Where do you see us in five years?" he asked.

"Um . . ." I chewed and swallowed. "We're already married, so . . . You know, I love this house, but I still want my penthouse overlooking South Beach and my white-on-white Range Rover. Hopefully, we'll have a baby."

"You don't need to wait five years for any of those things. Shit, we can make all of that happen ASAP."

"Not the baby . . . yet, anyway . . . We'll have time for that. I gotta meet li'l man and see if I'll even be a good mama."

"You'll be a good mama. I know it."

I shrugged. "Not so sure. I mean, I don't have a good example."

"You'll know what not to do based on your relationship with your mom."

I nodded. "What about you?"

"I see us happy in a more trusting relationship, with millions and millions of dollars. I already have everything else that I could want."

Smiling, I leaned over to give him a kiss. I enjoyed being home with him more than performing and being onstage. A part of me wanted my life to go back to being simple like this.

Luxury's phone rang.

He answered, "Hello?" He listened before he put the call on speakerphone. "Say that again, E."

Egypt's voice said, "Roxx's song with Desire is number one on the Billboard charts, and we just dropped it the other day. There are talks of a Grammy nomination."

"What?" I shouted in disbelief.

Luxury bragged, "My baby got a Billboard number one."

"Congratulations, Desire," Egypt said.

"Thank you."

Egypt went on. "Roxx wants to shoot the video tomorrow. Sorry for the short notice, but her people said it was spur of the moment. We gotta go to Los Angeles tonight. We still gotta do the late-night show out there next week too. We will be back and forth in between to take care of these other things that are lining up for you. You might as well get your seat belt fastened, because we're about to be on one fast-ass ride."

"A'ight, E. We'll get our bags packed now," Luxury said.

I jumped up to wash the dishes. I hated leaving the house a mess.

Luxury ended the call. "Wait, baby, stop. Leave that here. I'll have someone come and clean up. Let's just get our stuff packed to get to LA."

My heart was beating so fast as I rushed up the stairs. Just when I had thought about quitting, my career had taken a turn for the better.

32

DESIRE

Dream Car

Going through LAX was crazy. It was like there were paparazzi everywhere, asking questions about my collabo with Roxx and taking pictures. We rushed out of the terminal and hopped into an SUV. I took a little nap while we drove to the hotel.

We checked in and got only a couple of hours of sleep before Nia had to rush to do my hair and makeup. The video shoot was the best experience of my life. We didn't get to see much of LA, because after the shoot, we had to be whisked to New York for an interview. Like Egypt had said, it was like my life was in fast-forward. Next thing I knew, makeup, hair, and wardrobe folks and a bunch of new people were around all the time. Everyone around the world now knew who Desire was, and it had taken only five months. It seemed as if my life wasn't about to slow down anytime soon. I didn't mind, since Luxury was at my side the whole time, keeping the new folks in check.

Before we knew it, we were back in LA to do a late-night show. After taping, we went to the hotel. Up in the room, Luxury received a call from his baby mama. She was fussing and cussing about him not showing up to drop off that money. She was threatening to put him on child support.

"I told you I'm out of town. I'll wire the money, so kill that noise," he barked into the phone. A second later he hung up in her face. "I gotta go wire some money to Charity, so she can leave me the fuck alone."

I rolled my eyes. "Okay. Is this how it's gonna be with her? Maybe it would be better to pay her once a month instead of on demand."

"Yeah, I'll have to work that out." He placed a kiss on my forehead and walked out of the room.

I went over to the window and stared out. LA was pretty at night. I sat on the bed and started scrolling through Instagram. I smiled as I looked at Luxury's posts with us backstage at the late-night show. I imagined I was an outsider looking in. All his posts showed nothing but love for me, but then I noticed something strange. He had his comments turned off. Usually, his comments were turned on. People could say some of the craziest shit, but those haters didn't matter to me. Something must've happened that had made him turn it off. I decided I would ask him about it when he got back.

I left his page and went down my newsfeed. I stopped at Nasim's latest post. It was a picture of him looking all fly. He was wearing all white and was resting against a white Range Rover. My heart stopped because that was my dream car. The caption said, "All white everything. #rover water splash emoji."

I had told him that the Range Rover was my dream car. What the fuck was up with that?

I pulled up his number and called him. He didn't answer.

I texted: You wrong for flossin' my dream car.

The door to the hotel room opened right at that moment, so I quickly made my screen go black. Luxury walked in, huffing and puffing.

"What's wrong with you?" I quizzed.

He didn't say anything, just went out on the balcony and rested his hands on the rail.

I followed him out. "You not gonna tell me what's wrong?"

"I don't want to talk about it right now."

I smacked my lips and walked back inside, but then I turned around because I wanted to know why he had turned his Instagram comments off.

"Hey, why your comments off on your Instagram?"

"I don't want to hear shit nobody has to say, that's why," he barked.

"Did somebody say something in particular that pissed you off?"

"They always talking shit, callin' my wife a stripper ho, talkin' about my son. I want to post my pics without the negative."

It wasn't like I hadn't seen the stripper comments before. I was used to shutting them out, but it felt different from them attacking him for choosing me.

"I get it," I replied.

My phone started ringing. It was Nasim calling me back. I sent him to voicemail. He called again. I sent him to voicemail again. While Luxury was on the balcony, I sent Nasim a quick text.

Me: Can't talk right now.

N: Okay. When are you coming to pick up your car?

I double blinked at the screen. *My car?* Wait, so he had bought that Range for me?

Me: Are you crazy? I can't take that car from you. What will I tell my husband?

N: He doesn't have to know I bought it. It's my thank-you for my li'l tour with you.

Me: Wow. Thank you. I'm in LA now, but I'll be back in Miami tomorrow. I'll TTYL.

I erased our messages and sat on the bed. I went back to Nasim's Instagram. My eyes grew heavy as I stared at Nasim in my car.

Luxury stayed out on the balcony, smoked a blunt, and scrolled through his social media accounts. I didn't bother him or twist his arm to find out what was going on. I fell asleep before he came to bed.

33

LUXURY

Played

I stood on the balcony, smoking and scrolling through my phone, all while trying to process what Egypt had just told me. I went back into the room, and then I headed out to go wire Charity some money at the Western Union nearby. When I stepped into the hallway, Egypt was coming out of her room. When she saw me, she waited until I reached her side. She had this look on her face that unnerved me.

"What up, E?" I asked.

"I just got a call from Charity, asking me if I know anything about this dude named Nas. She's threatening to go to the blogs about your wife cheating on you with this dude."

"Man, is she still on that shit? Look, don't believe the shit she told you. She's a bona fide liar, E."

"Where's Desire?"

"In the room. Hey, I don't mean to cut you off, but I gotta wire Charity some money. Once she gets it, she'll shut the fuck up. There's this Western Union about two blocks from here. I'll be right back."

"Mind if I come with you?"

"Nah. Come on."

We walked to the elevator. When we stepped inside, she said, "Meek saw Desire go into some nigga's hotel suite in Paris. I know she was fucking with somebody while in the UK. I got receipts to prove that."

I glared at her. "Oh yeah?"

"Yeah. Me, Nia, and Lala had our own suspicions, because she was acting so strange, like she was hiding something. I know I should've told you this sooner . . . That's not all. Desire had a hickey on her neck right before we left the tour. I talked to her about it, and she admitted to me that he was just a friend. I didn't say anything to you, because I didn't want to cause problems . . . But now with Charity talking about going to the blogs, I feel like I have to give it to you straight."

I gritted my teeth, thinking about everything Egypt had laid on me. "You know for sure? You saw the nigga?"

"No, but talk to Meek. He saw him for sure, and he said Desire didn't come out of that dude's room until morning."

"His name is Nas for sure, or you just guessing?"

She frowned as we stepped off the elevator. "I don't know his name."

"So, how you know it's the same nigga Charity's talking about? Could be a whole different nigga."

"Unless Desire is fucking around with multiple niggas, I'm just putting two and two together. Talk to Meek."

I shrugged, feeling like this was all some bullshit, but I was feeling my anger rise. I wasn't the type to believe rumors and shit. I had to have hard, concrete facts, and none of this was backed up with proof. If Meek could confirm it, then that would make three people who were saying the same shit. If they had reasons to believe she was cheating on me, then it had to be true.

"Look, I know how you are, Luxury. You're loyal and solid. I'm just saying to keep your eyes open. You don't gotta believe me, Meek, or Charity, because the truth will come to light regardless."

I didn't respond.

She fell back and turned to go back to the elevator.

I kept walking to the Western Union. Before I went inside, I called Charity. I couldn't believe I was going to have to ask her about this stupid shit. I hated that what she had been telling me all along was right.

She answered all hostile-like. "What you want, nigga?"

"Listen, you gotta chill with going to the blogs. I'm wiring you some money right now. Let's get on a monthly schedule. I'm gonna send enough to keep you straight until next month. Every month will be the same amount. Cool?"

"Yup."

"Do not go to the blogs with that story about this Nas or whoever. Tell me everything you know about this nigga and where I can find him. I got some questions of my own."

She paused. "You not gonna do nothing crazy, are you?"

"Nah. I just want the fuckin' truth."

"Did you ask her about him?"

"No. I'm not bringing this to her until I have facts. I need some muhfuckin' receipts, ya dig?"

"I hear you. Everybody calls him Nas. He's from Harlem, but he's new to Miami. He's connected with Fat Man Bo. I heard he's Fat Man Bo's new hitter. He got a crackhead sister he takes care of. He's known in these streets now."

"Why I haven't heard of him, then?" I said.

"You not in the streets anymore. Youse a Hollywood nigga now."

I shook my head. "I still should know or at least have heard of this nigga. Look, I'll call you back. I'm walking into the spot now to send the money. Kiss my son for me."

"I got you."

I ended the call and walked into the Western Union. My mind was running, and I was trying to think of any times that had seemed off with Desire. She was sneaky as fuck. She had the nerve to think I was fucking around on her, when she was fucking around on me? Not to mention, she was fucking with a nigga who was rocking with the muthafucka who had had her best friend killed. If he was Fat Man Bo's hitter, then he probably was the one who had pulled the trigger.

After I wired the money, I walked back to the hotel, feeling like I wanted to bust in that room and shake Desire up. I didn't know how to bring the shit to her. Would she come clean if I asked? My whole relationship was on the line.

When I reached my room, Meek was standing at the door, guarding it, as he was supposed to do.

As I took my key card out of my pocket, I said, "Hey, what happened in Paris? E said you saw Desire fucking around."

He looked behind him, as if Desire was at the door. I didn't care if she was there or not; I wanted to know everything.

"Spit the shit out, nigga," I barked.

"She had me go with her to Novotel Hotel in Paris. Some light-skinned dude came to the door. She went inside and stayed all night. I got tired of waiting and went back to our hotel."

"So, you left her there?"

"I was getting tired, and at least she could've told me what time to be back. You know what I'm saying?"

"You overhear a name or anything?"

"Nah, she was pretty sneaky about it. She even gave me a few nights off once we got to London. That was what really had me weirded out."

My heart split in two. This bitch thought she was slick, thought she had tricked me. She had a nigga all the way fucked up.

"Next fuckin' time, don't leave her, no matter what. I don't give a fuck if ya ass sleeps at the door. I pay you to protect my bitch, nigga."

He nodded. "I got it, boss. It won't happen again."

"Bet." I put the key card in the slot, opened the door, and walked into the room.

I was prepared to go the fuck off. I was going to let her ass have it, but as soon as I saw her beautiful face, I didn't know what to say to her. I felt disgusted and played. The way she quickly made her screen dark on her phone had me wondering if she was messaging the nigga. That was my opportunity to go in.

"What's wrong with you?" she asked, staring at my face.

I didn't say anything. I walked over to the sliding door and pulled it open. I went out on the balcony and rested my hands on the rail. I took a deep breath and exhaled. It was taking everything in me not to blow up.

She followed me out. "You not gonna tell me what's wrong?"

"I don't want to talk about it right now," I heard myself say. I could feel the steam leaving my ears. I felt hot all over.

She smacked her lips and walked back inside, but then she turned around and asked, "Hey, why your comments off on your Instagram?"

"I don't want to hear shit nobody has to say, that's why," I yelled.

That was the truth. The higher she rose in popularity because of her music, the more vicious my comments got about her. There were some good ones, but there was a ton of shade about her past.

"Did somebody say something in particular that pissed you off?"

It was then that I should've asked about this Nas. I should've asked if she was fucking him.

I replied instead, "They always talking shit, callin' my wife a stripper ho, talkin' about my son. I want to post my pics without the negative."

"I get it," she replied.

Her phone started ringing. She sent the person to voicemail. Someone called again. She sent that person to voicemail again. Then she disappeared inside to text someone.

I took a pre-rolled blunt out of my pocket. I needed something to calm me down, because I felt like snapping her little neck. I lit it and smoked. I had been nothing but faithful, and she had been playing my ass bad. I decided to go to her Instagram to see if someone named Nas or Nasim was following her.

I found some nigga named Nas2Real. I went on his page and saw that she was following him. His last post was a pic of an all-white Range, my baby's dream car. I smoked and studied the rest of his pics. He had been in Paris and London, judging by his pics. None of them hinted that he had been with her, but the fact that he had been overseas at the same time was all the proof I needed.

I smoked and processed. I started to send the nigga a message, but then I stopped. I would be damned if another nigga took my wife. I blamed myself for not being there on tour with her. For now, I was going to give her ass the silent treatment for a little while, until I figured out how I was going to address this problem.

34

LUXURY

She Created a Beast

We left LA and went home. For two days, I didn't say shit to her. My mama had always said that if I didn't have nothing nice to say, I should say nothing at all. It got to the point where she didn't say anything to me, either. No "Good morning." No "What's the matter?" Nothing. She had an attitude, and so did I. I knew everything was coming to a head, but I had no idea how big this pop was about to be.

As soon as we got home, she left and came back with that all-white Range Rover, claiming she had bought it as a gift for herself. She thought a nigga was stupid. She lied so effortlessly, as if my feelings didn't mean shit to her anymore. I could've easily exposed her, but I held it all inside.

E called a little later and said that Desire had an appearance at Square Eights that night. Desire hadn't even told me. Did she not want me to go? As she got dressed, I spoke up.

"You wasn't going to tell me you had an appearance tonight? I had to hear it from E?"

She fluttered her eyelashes at me. "You haven't been speaking to me, so I didn't think you cared."

"I'm going. You riding with me."

She rolled her eyes but replied, "Fine. Whatever."

I bit my lower lip to stop myself from going crazy on her. There was no way I was going to let my wife go to an appearance in my city without me. I took a shower, got dressed, and we rolled out together. She was decked out in her mink coat.

"Hey, I gotta stop by Lav's first real quick," I told her as we drove.

She blew air from her lips and rolled her eyes.

"Hey, lose the attitude. I'm not trying to fuck up your night, so don't try to fuck up mine."

Desire didn't respond as she scrolled through her Snapchat.

When I pulled up to Lavish's house, I parked in the driveway. I left her in my car and rang the doorbell.

Lavish opened the door with a frown. As soon as I walked in, he knew something was up.

"Hey, bruh. What's good with you?" he asked.

"Ain't shit good, bruh. My girl is fuckin' around on me."

"What? How you know?"

"First, Charity told me. Then E, and she had me confirm some shit with Meek. It's like I don't even know what to do about it. I want to kill her."

"Bruh, don't snap. Like, I can see that look in your eyes. You need to walk away and be done if it's really what everybody says," he said.

"I hear you. You got some more smackers? I need to get on tonight." I needed something to mellow me out. Ecstasy pills weren't something I liked to take all the time, but they got me in party mode.

"I got one," Lavish said, taking it out of his pocket. "I planned to pop it later, but you can have it."

"Cool. Good lookin'. Y'all coming to the club tonight?"

He shook his head. "Nah, we got to lay a few tracks. Frill down there right now. You know we stay working."

"Always." I nodded as I walked out the front door. "A'ight. Get at me later."

"Be cool, my nigga. Remember what I said."

I threw up the deuces, popped the pill, and hopped in the car.

Desire continued her silent treatment as we headed to the club. As soon as we were out of the car and walking up to the front of the line, people were screaming for Desire. Everybody was here to see her.

I scoffed at her to myself. She wouldn't have any of this shit if it weren't for me. Here she was, shitting on the only nigga who loved her. She didn't have nobody but me. I glared at her while she smiled and waved.

We were guided to our VIP section, where the DJ announced she was there. She waved to her fans, removed her mink coat and laid it on the couch, and sat down.

"You want some Henny?" she asked me as we got settled in VIP.

"Yeah."

She ordered a bottle, and as soon as it came, I took a few shots fast.

She stared at me. "You turnin' up hard. So are we squashing this invisible beef or what, Luxury? We need to do something, 'cause this 'ignoring me' shit is whack. I can't keep ignoring you back, waiting for you to talk to me."

I shrugged my shoulders. "I'll talk when you're ready to confess."

She gave me an odd look but then waved her hand at me. "Boy, bye. What are you talking about?"

I sat back, with a smirk on my face.

She rolled her eyes, stood up, and began dancing to the music, drifting away from me.

As the night wore on, I kept the drinks coming. At one point, I stood up and scanned the room until my eyes rested on this thick model chick who was standing there with her friends. I gave her a head nod. She came right over to me, walking like she was on a runway.

I licked my lips and smiled at her.

"Wow. You have the deepest dimples I've ever seen," she commented.

"Thank you," I said, staring down at her cleavage. "Damn, you bad," I said in her ear.

She giggled, placing her hand on mine. "Thank you." She was feeling a nigga.

I flirted right back. "Yeah, you got me ready to leave the club with you right now."

She licked her glossy lips but then looked to the right. "Isn't that your girl over there?"

I shrugged. "Why you worried about her, though?"

"Because I don't want any drama."

"Don't worry about her. That's over with. What you doing after this?" I said.

"Shit, I'll do anything with you."

"Anything? Don't play with me, girl."

"I wouldn't play with you."

"You ready to go?"

"I can't leave my girls." She looked back at them. "Can they come?" she asked.

"Depends."

Desire was getting pissed by the second. She had never seen me entertain no other bitches in her face like this. I wasn't myself that night. And I wanted her to feel the pain I was feeling.

Desire stomped over to us. "I'm gone give you two seconds to take your hands off my man," she yelled.

I grabbed the woman by the hand gently and said, "Let's get out of here."

Desire looked at me as if I had lost my mind, but I didn't care.

She snatched her mink coat from the couch and bolted out of the club. I rushed after her.

Where the fuck is she going?

Once she was outside, she put on her coat, then stood in front of my car and shouted, "I'm done. I can't take this shit anymore, disrespectful-ass nigga! I'm gone."

She was leaving me? To do what? Be with Nas? If anything, I should've been leaving her ass. I had never felt so much rage until that moment. Was I just some carpet she could walk all over? I had done nothing but love her, and she wanted to leave me?

She turned to walk away, with her phone in her hands.

Who is she calling? Nas?

I snatched her ass up so quick that her cell phone crashed against the concrete. My hands were gripping the collar of her coat as I shouted, "Bitch, you ain't nothin' without me. I made you. You hear me, bitch? I said you ain't shit without *me*!" Blame the liquor and the drugs for the way I reacted, or blame my suppressed emotions. I wasn't about to let her get away with disrespecting me.

"Luxury," she breathed, and her breath turned into fog. Her eyes were welling with tears as she pleaded, "Please, let me go."

I smirked. "Hell nah, bitch! I ain't lettin' you go. Get yo' ass in the car right now. You out here playin'."

There was no way I was going to lose to some fuck boy. That nigga had no respect for the fact that she was a married woman.

She squirmed, trying to break free of my grasp, but I had the tightest grip on her neck and was choking her. She tried to scream to get people to intervene, so I backhanded her.

"Bitch, you think I'm playin' with you? Get yo' ass in the car! You ain't goin' no fuckin' where. Don't make me say it again."

The more she fought to get out of my reach, the madder I got. All I could do was think about her running into that nigga's arms. I would make sure she wouldn't run. All I could see in my mind was her fucking this nigga. This nigga kissing her. That motherfucking Range Rover. I was beyond hurt. I didn't deserve love like this. No matter what people said about her, I loved her. I still loved her. I pushed her to the ground.

"I poured everything into you! Now you wanna up and leave? Muthafucka, it don't work like that," I shouted. "You think I don't know Nasim bought that Range for you? I'll be damned if I lose you to this bitch-ass nigga."

My eyesight became blurred from the tears that had welled up. Everything was starting to become fuzzy; then I saw nothing at all as my rage took over my body. I felt as if I was floating through an empty space filled with thick static. My heartbeat was pounding loudly, echoing in my ears, alongside Desire's fading pleas for help. I was no longer me, and I didn't remember how many kicks or punches I landed.

Desire was out cold, and as I looked down at her, I realized what I had done. A crowd had formed, and I panicked. So I picked her up and put her in the car as fast as I could. On the way to the hospital, I prayed she wouldn't die.

35

DESIRE

Nightmare

I heard voices. I woke up, confused, my eyes wide. Then I realized that I had been unconscious, but I didn't know for how long. My dreams had not been a figment of my imagination. I was interpreting the feedback my senses were giving my brain as I wiggled my toes. Aside from my own breath, I could hear voices and the beeps from machines. I lifted my arm that was hooked to an IV and saw bruises along it. It wasn't clear to me what had happened, not yet at least.

"Miss?" A woman police officer approached the side of the bed. "Miss? My name is Rebekah. I'm with the Miami Police Department. We need to figure out what happened to you."

I didn't know what to say other than, "Where's Luxury?"

"Is that your husband? The one who assaulted you?"

Everything seemed to have moved too fast for my brain to put the pieces together. I started crying, as if I were back in that parking lot of the club, with Luxury kicking my ass. I felt heavy, helpless, and alone. My mind left the room, and I repeatedly felt his kicks and punches all over again. It came to me like a nightmare. The beating felt like it lasted forever . . . until I felt nothing else.

"Miss. Miss, you must calm down. No one is going to hurt you. You're in the hospital, and he is in our custody. We want to know if you'd like to press charges."

Breathing in deeply, I looked at the woman. Her green eyes were so warm, so concerned. I didn't say anything, didn't even try to talk.

"Do you remember what happened before the assault happened?" she asked quietly.

"I don't remember," I heard myself say. I wasn't going to say anything to hurt Luxury any more than I already had.

He knew that I had been unfaithful. His words about Nasim and the Range as he was beating me senseless had let me know that my little secret wasn't so secret anymore. I had fucked up, but did that mean I had deserved to get beaten down? Hell no. Yet I wanted to protect Luxury. I blamed myself for not being real with him, sneaking behind his back, showing the next nigga attention.

The officer asked, "What do you remember?"

"I just told you. I don't remember shit." Tears were filling my eyes, making it hard for me to breathe. My throat was tightening, and I started hyperventilating, as if on the verge of a panic attack.

The nurse rushed to my side and gave me an oxygen mask. "Take in deep breaths. That's it."

The officer said, "I'll come back later. Hopefully, you'll remember something then."

As she left the room, I focused on breathing. After a minute or so, I took off the mask and asked the nurse, "Did my husband bring me here?"

"Yes. He did."

"Where is he now?"

"He's in police custody."

Tears cascaded down my face. "Will I be okay?"

She nodded. "Yeah, no major injuries. Just some scrapes and bruises. You and your baby will be fine. The doctor will be in to see you soon."

I nodded, but then I realized she had said, "You and your baby." "Wait, did you just say *baby*?"

Staring at me oddly, she answered, "You didn't know that you're pregnant?"

I shook my head slowly. I tried to recall if I had missed a period. I had been so busy that I did not realize until now that I had missed two periods.

"How many weeks?" I asked.

"We did an ultrasound, and you're six weeks. I'll be right back with some ice water, okay?"

I nodded slowly again. After she left me alone in that hospital room, I placed my hand on my stomach. With all my heart, I wished I could retract all the negative things I had ever done and said to Luxury. I couldn't believe he was in jail. I hoped to fix this between us, but truth be told, we had gone too far. I wished I could erase everything and go back to the days when everything felt brand new. I wanted to make amends. I was learning now who and what really mattered in my life, but was it too late?

36

EGYPT

Delusional Mind

The fight between Luxury and Desire was all over the news. I still couldn't believe that he had hit her like that. For as long as I'd known Luxury, he had never put his hands on a woman. Never. The blogs were having a field day, calling him a monster. It was straight bullshit. I blamed that bitch, and she had got what she deserved. Desire's affair with Nas was something that had broken Luxury down. He loved Desire so much, but I hadn't thought he was this crazy in love.

The news reported that he had turned himself in, so I gathered money from Frill and Lavish to post his bail. It didn't matter what his bond was set at; we were going to pay it if they said we could. The process took forever, but by the next morning, I received a text from Lavish saying Luxury was getting out of jail. I let Lavish know that I would be right there to pick Luxury up.

While I waited in the car for Luxury to walk out of jail, Nia called me.

"Hey, cuzzo," I answered.

"Cuzzo, you get him yet?"

"I'm waiting on him now."

"Okay. Hold on." She took her ear away from the phone to talk to someone. "Lavish, E said she's still waiting on him." She put her ear back to the phone before she said, "E, have Luxury call Lavish as soon as possible."

"Okay. What y'all up to?"

"We chillin', doin' what we do."

I hummed, "Uh-huh. Y'all some freaks."

Lavish and Nia had been messing around since we were teenagers, but Lavish didn't want to settle down with anyone. Nia was okay with him fucking other bitches, because half the time she was fucking with those bitches right along with him. I didn't see why they couldn't make it official. They were around one another all the time.

She laughed. "Well, call me if you want me to meet up with you later."

"I will. Bye."

"Bye," she said.

As I ended the call, Luxury walked out of jail, looking like shit. His face looked sunken in, and those deep dimples I loved when he smiled were nowhere to be found. All joy seemed to have vanished from his eyes. I got out of the car and waved to let him know I was there.

He looked up, but then he put his head down. He strolled to the car and got in. Once inside, he kept his head down. I stared down at what he was looking at. He was staring at his busted knuckles. I had seen Luxury look this defeated only once, and that was when De'Vonn was murdered.

"What happened?" I asked.

He shook his head. "I really don't want to talk about it. It's like . . . I don't know what the fuck happened. I was drunk out of my mind and high as fuck. I was so gone. That shit with Desire and that nigga Nasim, or whatever the fuck his name is, got to me. That's no excuse, though. I fucked up, E. I took her to the hospital and turned myself in."

"Did she hit you first?"

"No . . . Is she okay? Did you check on her?"

Check on her? Why would I check on her? Luxury was my friend. I knew what he did was wrong, but she wasn't my concern. He was.

"No, not yet."

"Can you, please? I gotta know. Shit, I fucked up." Tears fell from his eyes, and he quickly wiped them away. "A man should never, ever let his anger do no shit to a woman like that. You should've kept my ass in there."

"Listen, what you did was wrong, but don't talk like that. You got people that genuinely care about you."

I wanted to blurt out that I loved him. I never would've done what Desire did to him. For a few short seconds, he looked up at me. I tried to see what was behind his eyes, because I wanted to know that he was done with her.

"I think it's nice that you worry about me," he said. "It's like I got the sister my mama could never have, you know."

How could he look at me like a sister? He was out of his mind.

"Well, I'm here for you, Luxury. Always will be."

He nodded, and his eyes left mine. He took his cell out of his pocket and tried to turn it on, but it was dead. I started up the car and started heading to his house.

"Hey, can you not take me home right now?" he said. "I can't even go in that house, with her fragrances and stuff everywhere. It will just fuck me up even more."

"Where you want to go? Lav's?"

"Nah, I'll check into a hotel somewhere. I'm trying to lay low."

"You think that's a good idea? I mean, paparazzi will be everywhere. We can go to my place. That way you won't be bothered."

"I don't want to impose or nothing."

"No, it's cool," I assured him.

We drove over to my place, which was about twenty minutes away.

When we stepped inside, he said, "You got an iPhone charger?"

"You know I do." I went into the living room and took the charger out of the wall. "Here you go."

"Thanks," he replied as he sat on the couch and plugged the charger into the same outlet I had just pulled it out of.

"You hungry or anything?" I asked him. "I have some leftover spaghetti from Buca di Beppo. I have plenty."

"Nah, it's good. I can't really eat all like that."

Pitiful thing. He was really fucked up over this. Luxury always had an appetite.

As soon as he had power on his phone, he called someone. I wondered who he was calling. Whoever it was didn't answer, and he looked stressed. I hoped he wasn't trying to call Desire.

As I heated up my food in the microwave, I kept looking over at him. He rubbed the top of his head repeatedly, his head down, as he scrolled through his phone.

"Can you call up to the hospital and check on Desire, please?" he asked.

I wanted to scream no, but I replied, "Okay. I'll call up there right now. Will that make you feel better?"

"I just gotta know if she's okay," he answered.

After grabbing my phone out of my purse, I called the hospital.

"University of Miami Hospital. How may I direct your call?"

"Hello. Can I get Desirae Monnahan's room?"

"Let me locate the patient. You said Monnahan?"

"Yes."

"I don't have a Monnahan here."

"Try Fernández," I said.

"One second." She was silent for a moment. "Desirae Fernández?"

"Yes, please."

"She's in room sixty-five forty-three. I'll transfer you now."

"Thank you," I replied.

Luxury was listening carefully, so I made sure to put the call on speakerphone. The phone rang. After about five rings, I started to hang up, but then she answered.

"Hello?" she said, sounding heavily medicated.

"Hey, Desire. This is Egypt. I'm calling to check on you. How are you?"

"I'm . . . in a lot of pain, but I'll be fine. No major injuries . . . Where's Luxury?"

"Just made bail. He's . . . at home now," I lied, looking at Luxury.

I didn't know what else to say. What if she didn't want him to know where she was? I was doing my best not to fuck this up for him.

"I need to speak to him. The hospital won't let him see me, because of the restraining order they made me file, but I have to talk to him."

He looked just as surprised as I did.

"I'll have him call you, and—"

"I'm right here," he said, taking the phone from me. He broke down and cried to her. "I'm sorry, baby. I'll never drink or pop pills again. Now, weed . . . I think I can control how many blunts I smoke, but that other shit, I'm done with."

"I'm sorry too." Desire paused and took a deep breath. "I don't know if I can get over this, but I have to try, because I found out today that . . . I'm pregnant."

My eyes grew wide, and it felt like my heart had just been ripped to shreds. Just when I thought this was over between them, she had to hit him with this shit. *But wait.* Who was she pregnant by? I watched Luxury's reaction to see if he was thinking what I was thinking. He broke down and shed more tears, and I just did not understand his feelings.

"I swear, Desire, I'll never put my hands on you again. We're having a baby? I could've killed . . ." He stopped himself. "I'm so sorry."

"They want me to press charges, but I'm not going to. I can't bring myself to do it. I know you. I know your heart. Just give me a few weeks to deal and heal, okay? Please, don't call up here. I'll call you."

"Yeah . . ." He paused for a long time before he handed me the phone. Then he sat on my couch and cried into his hands for a few minutes.

I stood there in silence. The sound of his crying was breaking my heart. I took a few tissues from my Kleenex box and handed them to him.

"You want some water or anything?" I offered.

"Yeah. Thanks."

I went into the kitchen and fixed him a glass of ice water.

As I handed it to him, he said, "She's pregnant."

"I heard her. You think it's yours?"

He didn't respond as he sipped the water.

I shook my head. His constant denial was killing me. Why wouldn't he think the baby was Nas's?

"I know you've been through this scenario too many times, Luxury. I just feel like this time, you—"

"Except this time, she's my wife," he barked, looking at me like I was crazy. "Desire fucked around, so I gotta consider that the baby ain't mine, but at the same time, even if this baby is his, she's still my wife."

I put my hands up and walked over to the microwave to pull out my food. "You're right. I mean, you know her better than anyone, but you gotta be smart. What happened last night? Why did you do that to her?"

He took a deep breath and replied, "She said she was done with me and wanted to leave me. I was doing stupid shit, flirting with the next bitch in her face, but I was mad. I was on some pills, some drink, and I just lost it. I kept thinking about her leaving me."

"You think she still wants to leave now?"

"I don't know. I hope we can work this out. I gotta give up the drugs. I'm checking into rehab. I gotta do better for my family."

I prayed he wasn't setting himself up for another disappointment. He was too good for Desire. She didn't deserve to have him. I walked over to him and sat next to him.

"That's a great start," I told him.

"Yeah?"

"Yeah."

I rubbed his back and stared into his eyes. For a moment, we stared at one another. I inched slowly toward him, and he didn't move. I felt my lips on him, and he pulled back.

He looked perplexed but didn't say anything. I searched his eyes to see what he was thinking and if there was a small part of him that wanted me the way that I wanted him.

"I'm in love with you," I confessed. I bit my lower lip to stop myself from saying anything else. I hadn't meant to say that much.

"Be for real with me, E. How long have you felt like this?"

"Since we were kids. You remember that time Clarence hit me in the face with that four-square ball?"

"Yeah. I beat that nigga's ass."

I laughed. "That was when I knew I loved you, and the feeling has never left."

"We were in the fourth grade, E."

"I know."

"What you knew about love at nine or ten years old?"

I shrugged. "I can't explain it. Because you've protected me all these years, that's why I'm so overprotective all the time."

He nodded slowly. "Hey, I don't want you to take this the wrong way or fuck up our friendship. You've been there for me through thick and thin, and I appreciate everything that you've done. Why didn't you tell me sooner?"

"I was too afraid. You always had some chick on your arm. I couldn't find the right time."

"And you think right now is the right time?"

I shrugged, feeling tears come to my eyes. "I figured I'd shoot my shot."

He looked me in the eyes and said, "I want you to know that I care about you and I love you . . ."

"But not in the way that I love you."

He shook his head. "No, and I'm sorry, E. You've been my best fuckin' friend ever since I can remember. You're beautiful, and you're the shit. I'll kill anybody for you. I just can't be with you like that."

My tears fell down my cheeks. I wiped them away and sniffled. "It's okay. Hey, listen, I can't work for you anymore. It's getting too hard for me."

"You for real?"

I nodded. I was hurt and upset that I had put my feelings out there, and Luxury had dismissed them like what I was feeling was just some childhood crush. I was driving myself crazy by continuing to work for him. I couldn't assist Desire when I couldn't stand looking at her.

"I don't want you to quit because of this, but I think I understand why. You know if you ever need a job, I got you. You know what you want to do?"

"Go back to school and just do some new things. I need a vacation, for starters . . ." I stood up. "I'm going to go rest a little now. You know where everything is." I headed to my bedroom, fighting my tears.

As soon as I was in my bedroom and the door was closed, I couldn't stop myself from crying. Why couldn't he be with me? I didn't understand. He would rather be with someone who treated him like shit? Through the years, I had had to sit back and watch bitches do this to him. I was tired of it. I wasn't going to sit back anymore and watch the man I loved waste his time.

37

DESIRE

Love Can Still Thrive

After the doctor told me I would be released in a few hours, I closed my eyes to get some sleep. I hadn't slept much since my arrival, because I just kept replaying the night in my head, thinking about what I could've done or said differently. Luxury on drugs wasn't the same Luxury I knew. We had both realized that. I wasn't trying to make excuses for his behavior, because he was foul for what he had done, but I also owned my shit. But at the end of the day, I loved him. I wasn't some stupid bitch who let a nigga pound on her just to stay in a relationship. If he ever did this shit again, we were done.

My cracked cell phone chimed from the table on the side of the hospital bed. Though I was sleepy, I reached to see who had texted me. Even though my screen was all messed up from my cell hitting the concrete, I could still read my messages.

N: Are you okay?

My heart felt like it stopped for a moment. What if I was having Nasim's baby? What was I going to do? Luxury would leave me and wouldn't want to have shit to do with me.

Me: I'm okay. Going home in a few hours.

N: Can I see you?

Me: Not a good idea. I have to tell you something, though.

N: Okay. What's up?

Me: I'm pregnant.

N: Can you call me?

Me: I don't want to talk right now.

N: Okay. Does your husband know? Is that why he flipped out?

Me: He knows, but that's not why we got into it. Look, I'm tired, and I need to get some rest.

N: Okay. Call me as soon as possible. I don't like to talk about this kind of thing over the phone.

I put the phone back on the table. I had already made up my mind that Luxury was going to pay to buy a new one since it was his fault it was broken. I had closed my eyes to try to get some sleep when my hospital door opened. I could not believe my eyes when my mother walked in. She was alone. I hoped she wasn't here to start no shit with me. I wouldn't be able to handle that.

Her hair was pulled back into a bun, and she was wearing a cute pair of jeans and a red blouse. She stood at the foot of the bed and didn't come any closer. She saw my bruised face and busted lip. As tears welled up in her eyes, I didn't know how to react. This was the most emotion I had ever seen from her. Her mouth had wrinkle lines, and her forehead was covered in wrinkles from frowning so much. Now she looked as if she were permanently frowning.

"Are you okay?" she asked, looking into my eyes.

I heard her say the words, but I couldn't believe she was asking me if I was okay.

"I'm okay. How are you?"

"I'm doing fine. Javier left for Orlando a few weeks ago. He moved with some guy. Crazy how he thinks he can't talk to me. I know he's gay, but he still hides it."

"Yeah, it's tough to talk to you sometimes."

She looked around the room, at the flowers, the balloons, and the cards Nia and Lala had sent, before her eyes landed back on me.

"I came here to tell you that I don't hate you. You asked me why I hated you when your father was dying, and I didn't know how to respond. I see so much of me in you. I've been too hard on you, because I didn't want you to end up like me, without work experience, without any skills other than taking care of kids and being a wife. I had dreams, too, you know. Diego treated you like the golden child. He always doted so proudly on you, no matter what kind of mess you were in. My father never did for me what Diego did for you. I guess you can say I was so jealous . . . " She paused, as she had started to cry.

"Ma, don't cry. I—"

"No, I'm okay. I won't cry. I said I wouldn't cry. I thought that if I was hard on you, you would be tough and ready for this ugly-ass world. Now I'm all alone. My husband is dead. My son has moved away, and my daughter thinks that I hate her. I do not hate you. I love you, Desirae, and don't you forget that."

Tears left my eyes, and I couldn't stop them. I had waited all my life to hear her say that to me. She came to the side of the bed and hugged me. We cried together. Felt good to let go of all the years of frustration and all the times we had bumped heads.

She wiped my tears with her hands. "Don't you ever let no man do this to your beautiful face again. I don't know if you plan to stay with him, but you make him pay in the worst way the next time."

"There won't be a next time, Ma."

"You be sure of that. He bruised you up."

"I know. It was one big misunderstanding."

"Listen, there will always be a misunderstanding, but the moment a joker puts his hands on you, you gotta fight back. I wasn't there, and I'm not judging you. I just hope this never happens again."

"It won't." I paused, debating whether I should tell her my news. "I'm pregnant."

She smiled and hugged me again. "Really? Is the baby okay?"

I nodded. "Yeah. I'm six weeks along. I found out when I got here."

"Everything is going to be okay." She hugged me tighter and held me for a little while. "I'll let you get some rest. You can call me anytime. The number is still the same."

"Okay. I love you, Mama," I said.

"I love you too, honey. Get some rest. Oh, and another thing, when I see you on TV, I feel so proud of you. I may not care for the music, but that's okay." She kissed my cheek before she walked out of my room.

My heart was warm. I was glad she hadn't said, "I told you so," or tried to belittle me. I was delighted she could accept me for the woman I had become rather than the problem-creating teenager I used to be. To know that she had reflected on my words and my truth made me feel so good. No longer would we hurt one another with our mean comments. I just wished Papi and Mina were alive, so I could tell them all about it. I was sure they were smiling down at me from heaven.

38

DESIRE

Torn

I was in a little bit of pain for a few days while I recuperated at home. Luxury hadn't been to the house, because he was giving me some space, which I needed. I had a lot on my mind. This whole pregnancy thing was too much. I pulled out my cell phone to look at my calendar and counted back nine weeks, which included my period. The week after my period had been when I was in Spain, which was when Luxury came to visit, and a few days later, Id slept with Nasim unprotected. I hadn't given it any thought, because I had never had a pregnancy scare in my life. The idea of not keeping the baby came to mind, but then again, it didn't matter who the father was. This was my baby. I did some research and found out that I could have a paternity blood test done as early as eight weeks. The sooner I got it done, the better.

I had to go to Luxury's court hearing, and since I didn't file any charges, the judge gave him community service hours, and he agreed to go to rehab and anger management. I had to go to another court hearing so the judge could lift the restraining order. I explained to the judge that I didn't feel like my life was in any danger and that it had been a domestic dispute. The judge made the final decision and lifted the order. I left before Luxury could make his way over to me. I wasn't ready to talk to him yet.

As soon as I made it home, Nasim was calling. I hadn't contacted him since I left the hospital, so I decided to pick up.

"Hello?"

"So, you left the Range sitting in front of my house this morning, but you didn't come in or let me know? Where're the keys?"

"They're behind your big ceramic pot. I felt it was better to give it back."

"Yo, you could've just knocked on the door and put the keys in my hand. I thought you wanted to talk, anyway."

"I do. Look, I did some research and found out that we can do a paternity blood test while I'm pregnant. I want you and me to do this so that Luxury and I can know for sure."

"Oh, so you working things out with Luxury? After what he did to you?"

"Don't say it like that. This is hard enough."

He blew air out of his mouth as he sighed. "So, when and where do you want me to meet you?"

"I'll send you the address. The appointment is tomorrow, at nine a.m. Can you make it?"

"Yeah, I can. What if the baby is mine, Desire? You still want to be with him?"

I paused. I loved Luxury, and he loved me. This fling I had had with Nasim was only a fling.

"We just have to wait and see."

The phone went silent.

"Hello?" I said.

When he didn't say anything, I pulled my cell away from my ear and saw that he had hung up on me.

I pulled up the address to the DNA diagnostic center and sent it to him. He texted back that he would meet me there. I started to feel dizzy, so I walked up the stairs to the bedroom. As soon as I made it to the top, I felt the urge to throw up. I put my hand over my mouth to stop it all from coming up until I made it to the bathroom. After I puked, I washed my hands and mouth. I looked at myself in the bathroom mirror, wondering if I could really go through with this.

I showed up at the DNA diagnostic center on time, and to my surprise, Nasim did not show up. I blew his phone up, demanding to know where he was, and my call kept going straight to voicemail. Either he had blocked my calls or his phone was turned off.

After waiting for thirty minutes, the receptionist said, "Mrs. Monnahan, you'll have to reschedule."

"Okay. No problem."

I walked out of that center, feeling pissed off. I wanted to get this shit over with. Now I was going to have to wait on Nasim. This was bullshit. I could have Luxury do the test, but I hadn't talked to him much about the pregnancy. Since Nasim wasn't answering my calls, I drove over to his house.

While heading that way, I received a call from Luxury.

"Hello?" I said when I answered.

"Hey. I meant to tell you thanks for coming to court yesterday. You really didn't have to drop the charges."

"I know, but I wanted to . . ."

"Is it okay if I come home now?"

"You can come home. When will you be on your way?"

"I have a few things to tie up, and then I'll be there. So a couple of hours. You at home now?"

"I'll be home by the time you get there."

"A'ight."

"Okay. Bye." I ended the call.

I was happy he was coming home, but I was hoping that I would have all the unresolved issues with Nasim resolved as much as possible by then. Giving back the Range was the first step to ending things. Why hadn't he shown up for the DNA test? Didn't he want to know if he was the father?

When I pulled up to his spot, I noticed the Range and his Porsche were gone. I got out of my car, anyway, and walked up to the door. I knocked and waited. No answer. I hit the door harder and waited. Out of the corner of my eye, I saw his sister walking up the driveway, looking like Felicia on *Friday*. Hair frizzy and clothes hanging off her skinny body.

"Hey," she said.

"Yeah?" I scowled.

"He ain't here. He's been gone since last night."

"You see him when he left?"

She shook her head. "No, but his car has been gone for a while."

"Okay. Thanks. If you see him, can you tell him that Desire came by?"

"A'ight . . . You got any spare change? I need to get these kids some hot dogs or something. Nas usually brings them lunch every day."

I reached into my purse and handed her the only cash I had, which was a few one-dollar bills and some change. It was about four dollars in all.

"This is the only change I have."

"This good," she said and quickly walked down the driveway and then down the street.

I walked down the driveway and got back in my car. I sat there for about ten minutes, hoping I would see him. I wondered if he had got rid of the Range since I didn't want it. I started up my car and headed home.

39

LUXURY

A Man of My Word

For two weeks, I stayed in a hotel, and I didn't go anywhere other than to AA meetings in the evenings. I stopped sipping Lean, and I quit taking Ecstasy. Once I ran out of tree, I didn't go get none. So, surprisingly, I hadn't smoked a blunt in a few days. I needed my mind to be clear. My nights were filled with delivered meals and XXXVideos.com. I guessed my brothers got tired of me not answering their calls, because they showed up at my hotel room one day.

"Damn, nigga. I know you tryin' to get ya shit together, but you ain't gotta ignore us," Frill said as they walked in.

"I know. Just been trying to get my mind right."

They hugged me before we sat on the couches.

"How you really doin', though?" Lavish asked.

"I'm just taking it one day at a time. Desire had those charges dropped."

They nodded.

"What about this nigga she been fuckin' with? We know him?" Frill questioned.

I shook my head. "Some New York nigga. Charity told me he works for Bo."

"He works for Fat Man?" Lavish scowled. "Desire know that?"

I shook my head. "Nah, I don't think she does. She doesn't even know Fat Man is behind Mina's murder, remember?"

Lavish frowned. "That's right. Damn."

"Listen, though, so I did some calling around and I found out that this nigga pulled the fuckin' trigger. He killed Mina," I revealed.

"Nah, don't say that," Lavish said.

I threw up my hands. "I'm sayin' Desire was fuckin' with the nigga that killed her best friend, and she don't even know it."

"*Fuck*. That shit is crazy," Frill commented. "You plan on rollin' up on the nigga or what? You know we ride."

"I feel like I got to, but Desire says she's not fuckin' with him anymore. She's pregnant, though, so I'm, like, lightweight trippin' on that."

"She keepin' it?" Lavish asked.

I nodded. "That's what she says."

"So, what if it's that nigga's baby? Then what?" Frill questioned.

"I really don't know. I need to talk to her, see where her head is. For now, I'm gonna get shit right with her and take it from there."

They both nodded.

I had every intention of finding out where this nigga lived, so I could holler at him. I needed to know how he and Desire had met and if he had been sent by Fat Man Bo to fuck with her. If that was the case, we would have more of a problem than I initially thought.

***

Desire was watching *Martin* reruns when I came through the garage. I had missed her, and I hadn't liked being away from home and away from her one bit.

"Hi," she said as she stood up.

I went over to her, and she opened her arms for a hug. We embraced, and I didn't want to let go. I squeezed her.

"Baby, I missed you so much," I said.

"I missed you too. Watch TV with me."

I sat on the couch with her, and she flipped through the channels.

"What you want to watch?" I asked.

"I don't know. I'm trying to see what's on. I've seen all these *Martin* episodes a million times. How you been?"

"I've been better, but I started going to counseling and stuff," I told her.

"That's good."

"Next week, I have anger management."

She looked at me. "I'm proud of you." She turned off the TV. "I think we should talk about my affair."

I didn't want to talk about the affair. I wanted to find out if she knew who he really was.

"Uh, I don't care about your affair, and I don't know the details. A nigga was just ready to start all over."

"Luxury, he could be the father of the baby."

I swatted the air, as if a fly was hovering in front of my face. "Man, fuck all that. I don't give a fuck. It doesn't matter who the father is. Regardless, I'm going to be that child's father. What I want to know is, How did you meet him?"

"The day I went to the bank and opened my account, he was there, handling a transaction. That same day, after the shoot, you went to bail Frill out of jail, I saw him at the soul-food joint I like. We exchanged numbers because I was in my feelings about you and the baby mama rumors."

"So, was it your idea to bring him to Spain or his?"

"He was in Paris for my show, and that shocked me. We linked up. When I found out about you not coming, he offered to keep me company. I offered to pay because it was a long way for him to come just to keep me company since you weren't there."

I shook my head and took a deep breath. "Do you know what he does for a living?"

"I don't really know. I think he sells dope, but I'm not sure. I gave the car back to him, and I'm done. I'm not seeing him anymore."

"Good. Look, I'm glad you gave him the Range back. When I say we're starting over, that's what the fuck I mean. We're selling this house, and I'm getting you that penthouse overlooking South Beach."

"That's cool with me," she said. "What if he wants to be involved with the baby? Do you want to get a paternity test?"

"Nope. I told you, it doesn't matter. I will raise this baby, along with my son. Is that cool with you, or do you feel like the nigga needs to be involved?"

"I just feel like we should know."

"If you feel it's that important, then have him take the test, and you let me know the results," I told her.

I was serious about not wanting to know. I loved Desire, and I was going to love the baby. I could care less about the next nigga, who was just a fling because I couldn't be there for her.

She looked worried, but she didn't need to be.

"Look at me." I turned her face to me. "I made an appointment with a good Realtor. We can go look at a few penthouses and condos today. I'm gonna get you another Range Rover."

"You don't have to try to buy me, Luxury."

"How can I buy something that already belongs to me? You're my wife. These are the things you've always dreamt of. I'm just making sure you have it all."

Running her hand down my cheek, she stared into my eyes. "I love you, and I'm sorry for betraying you like that."

"Don't worry about it. In life we all make mistakes. The love I have for you outweighs any problems we ever have. When I said, 'Till death do us part,' I meant that shit." I looked at my watch. "Let's get ready to meet the Realtor. I'm sure you'll love what he has to show us."

"Oh, we're doing this right now?"

"Right now."

She smiled. "Of course right now. That's how my baby rolls."

"You know it."

The very first condo we were shown had the best location in South Beach, and it was on the oceanfront. It was a beautifully updated penthouse, fully furnished, with a mind-blowing view of the ocean. It was within walking distance to shops, restaurants, and theaters, and it had twenty-four-hour security, a valet parking service, concierge service, a fitness center, and a heated pool. Desire was in love at first sight.

"How much?" I asked as we walked through the penthouse.

"One point seven five million," said the Realtor.

I nodded. "Not bad, but I was thinking more like one point five. Any other bidders?"

"Not yet. It just went on the market this morning."

"What you think, baby? You like it?" I asked.

Desire smiled. "I love it. This is exactly what I dreamed of, only better in real life."

"We'll take it. We don't need any bank loans, because we're buying it straight out. One point five is our offer."

I shook the young Caucasian man's hand, and he nodded. "You ready to make an offer?"

"You take a check?"

"Yes, absolutely, but first I have to see if the owner will accept your offer. Then, I'll be in touch with you."

"Thank you . . . Also, we're putting our current house on the market. Can we use your services to sell it?" I said.

"Absolutely. Give me a call later, when I get back in the office, and we'll discuss your asking price and get someone out to appraise your home."

I shook his hand again. "Thank you."

"I'll talk with the owner, and the penthouse should be all yours."

"Good. We look forward to hearing the good news," I told him.

Desire was glued to the view overlooking South Beach. She was in heaven. I took a picture of her in my mind. I wanted to remember that expression for the rest of my life. She walked backward from the window with a huge smile on her face. If everything worked out, this place would be all hers.

40

DESIRE

Never Be the Same

The owner took our offer. It took a little over a month, and after much paperwork, we moved into the penthouse. I bought my own Range Rover with customized red stitching in the headrests. I wanted to do something nice for myself, and I didn't need Luxury to buy everything for me.

As much as he wanted me to forget about the baby's DNA, I couldn't help but think about it. I was starting to feel flutters in my tummy from the little movements of the fetus. I was still trying to find Nasim. He hadn't returned any of my calls.

Spending time with Luxury was a beautiful thing. It honestly felt as if we had hit the reset button. The changes in him were what he'd needed to make himself a better person. He hadn't pressured me to get back in the studio, and I had noticed he hadn't made any mention of Egypt or his brothers. I hadn't heard from Egypt, Nia, or Lala, which I thought was strange.

"Babe, you taking a break from the label?" I asked him one afternoon. "When's the last time you went over there?"

"I haven't been there since we got into it. I needed a break from it all, but I have to be down there in, like, twenty minutes."

"Will Egypt be there? I was wondering if she could tell me what's up for me next. Am I recording my next album? I want to get things going before I start showing."

He took a few seconds to answer. "Egypt won't be assisting you anymore. She's moving on to a new career."

"Really? Was this sudden?"

"Yeah, she sprang it on me when she picked me up from jail."

"She bailed you out?"

He nodded. "Yeah. She feels like she's outgrown the company. She's on to bigger and better things."

"I see. That's understandable. I wish her the best."

"Me too. You going to be okay while I'm gone? You need anything before I leave?"

"No. With us being so close to everything, I'm cool."

He kissed me on the lips. "I'll probably be gone for a few hours."

"Okay. You want me to cook dinner?"

"No. Let's go somewhere. You pick the spot."

"Okay," I replied.

He walked out of the penthouse, and I sat down on the couch, turned on the TV, and kicked my feet up. As I was scrolling through the channels, I stopped on a news program to watch a story about a young kid who had been killed in a hit-and-run.

"So sad," I said, shaking my head.

His mother was crying, talking about how he was a straight-A student and everyone at his high school loved him.

As I walked to the kitchen to get a cup of ice water, I heard the reporter say, "A man has been reported missing. Nasim Rhodes was last seen in the late afternoon of October thirteenth at his home in Miami, Florida. The Dade County Sheriff's Office is investigating his disappearance. There has been a break in this case. Nasim Rhodes's car was found parked in a parking lot at Fort Lauderdale–Hollywood International Airport this morning. His sister is desperate for answers. If you have any information surrounding Nasim's disappearance, please call the Dade County Sheriff's Office."

I took a glass from the kitchen cabinet, trying to process this information. As soon as I turned my head to look at the TV, a picture of Nasim popped up on the screen. I dropped the glass in my hand, and it shattered on the kitchen floor. No wonder he hadn't shown up for the appointment or returned any of my calls. I prayed that he was okay and that nothing bad had happened to him. My heart was racing, and I felt faint. There was a fluttering in my stomach, but I couldn't tell if it was nerves or my baby moving.

I sat on the couch and pulled my knees up to my chest. I wrapped my arms around my knees, trying to curl myself up into a ball. I felt like I needed to protect myself from the world, because it seemed as if everyone I adored or had allowed myself to get close to wound up dead.

What if Nasim is dead? Lord, please, no.

I prayed Nasim wasn't dead. What if something happened to Luxury next? I just wouldn't be able to deal with it. These sad memories of Mina and my papi were swirling around in my head. Tears had welled up in my eyes, and I shut them. Tears managed to escape. I allowed my head to fall on my knees, and I pulled my legs closer to me.

Nasim. Nasim. Nasim.

I prayed, "Please, Lord, let him be all right."

I must've fallen asleep, because I woke up when I heard Luxury come in the door. He came and sat next to me on the couch.

"Sorry if I woke you up, baby."

"It's okay. I hadn't realized I fell asleep. I was tired from moving and everything."

He nodded. "You've been crying?"

"A little bit earlier. Just missing Mina and Papi," I said, playing it off. "How was everything at the office?"

"I know how that is." He paused before answering my question. "Well, we're working on a date for you to start working on your new album."

"That sounds good."

"Yeah. Everyone is ready to go. It's your time. If we play everything right, your pregnancy won't be a factor one bit."

"I am a little nervous about being a mommy, though."

"That's to be expected. You eat anything for dinner?"

"No. I was watching the news and fell asleep."

"You feeling up to going out for dinner?" he asked.

"I'm not in the mood, to be honest."

"I can order something," he said.

I got up from the couch and said, "Yeah, just get whatever. I'm going to lie in the bed. I don't really feel good. I think I'm having morning sickness. Even though I don't know why they call it morning sickness. I'm starting to feel sick in the middle of the day. I don't even know if I can take any medication without harming the little seed."

"You call the doctor?"

"Not yet, but I will first thing in the morning."

"A'ight, babe. Go lie down. You need some water or anything?"

"You can bring me some ice water."

He stood up and walked into the kitchen. As I walked to the bedroom, I heard him call, "Desire, baby, you dropped a glass?"

I had completely forgotten about that.

"Oh, yeah."

I heard his footsteps coming down the hall. I got into the bed and pulled the covers up to my neck.

"What happened?" he asked as he stood in the bedroom doorway.

"I was feeling faint and dropped it. I meant to clean it up, but I fell asleep."

"Okay. I'll get it cleaned up for you."

As he stared at me oddly, I wanted to blurt out that I was distraught because Nasim was missing, but I didn't want to make him feel any kind of way about it. Luxury had already made it clear that we were starting over, that it didn't matter if Nasim was the baby's father, and that he didn't give two shits about Nasim.

"Why are you looking at me like that?" I asked.

"I feel like there's something you're not telling me. It's the same look you had on your face when I popped up on you in Barcelona. What's going on?"

"I saw . . . on the news . . ." I paused. "Nasim is missing. They found his car at the airport, but nothing else."

He looked unaffected by what I'd said. As he turned and walked back down the hall to the kitchen, a chill swept over my body. I sat straight up as I got to thinking.

Did Luxury do something to Nasim?

41

LUXURY

Ending What Never Should've Started

As I cleaned up the broken glass on the kitchen floor, I thought about when I had finally met Nasim face-to-face. I hadn't known this nigga would end up on the news. Now this shit looked funny. What was he doing? Trying to set my ass up or something?

Back when I'd checked out of the hotel, before I'd gone home and found Desire watching *Martin* on TV, Frill and Lavish had rolled with me to Fat Man Bo's pool hall. There'd been no way I was going back home without figuring out what the deal was with this Nas nigga. To my surprise, Fat Man had been alone at the pool hall. It hadn't opened for business yet, but the door had been wide open. He'd been at the bar, counting the drawer.

"Luxury, Lavish, Frill," he'd announced. "We closed right now."

"We can see that," I said. "I got a few questions."

His fat ass shook his head. "Don't come here asking me about Mina."

"Nah. I mean, it's related, but I have an issue with ya hitta."

Bo leaned up against the bar as we got closer. We stopped right at the front of it.

"A'ight. What about my hitta?"

"This nigga Nas you got on ya team, the nigga who pulled the fuckin' trigger, was fucking my wife. I need to know if you sent him to fuck with her," I said.

Bo looked confused. "What you talking about? When you came in here asking me those questions about the shit, that was supposed to be the end of it. Why would I send a nigga after ya bitch?"

I shrugged. "That's what I want to know. If you didn't send him, then I need to holla at the disrespectful muhfucka. You know where I can find him?"

"Hey, look, if I help you out, what's in it for me?"

"What you want?"

"My brother is looking for a record deal," he said.

"How he sound?" I asked.

"He got talent. The next big thing out of Florida."

I nodded. "Send him my way, then."

"Cool. Look, Nas is my best hitta right now. The nigga knows how to get shit done."

"We see that. What would you do if a nigga fucked ya wife and didn't give a fuck, though?"

"I'd kill the fuck boy. No questions asked."

"Put yourself in my shoes right now."

Fat Man nodded his head. "I want you to know that I didn't have anything to do with him fuckin' with ya bitch. If I knew anything about it, I would've deaded that shit. It ain't cool to fuck around, especially with you."

"Respect. You know where he stays?"

"I don't know his exact address, but I hear he stays near the liquor store on the corner of California Street and Ives."

"Bet."

We turned to walk out.

"Hey, you weren't here," Bo said.

I turned back. "I already know."

"I'll have my brother hit you up."

"A'ight." I turned back to my brothers, and we strode out of the pool hall.

We got in the car and headed to where this nigga might be. The whole time everyone was quiet, preparing mentally for what could go down.

As soon as I hit the corner of California and Ives, I saw the Range parked in front of a house.

"That's his crib right fuckin' there," I said.

"Mmm-hmm, there the Range right there," Frill noted.

I parked behind it and looked at the Porsche in the driveway. I took my Glock out of the center divider and tucked it in my waist. "Y'all stay in the car. I'm gone knock on the door and get him to come out to talk to me."

"A'ight," they said in unison.

I got out of the car and walked up the driveway to the front door. I knocked three times and waited. I heard someone unlock the door. He opened the door, and we stood face-to-face. I sized him up, wondered if he was strapped. He was slightly taller than me but thinner. I could take him fist to fist if I had to, I was thinking. He looked exactly the way he did in his Instagram photos. Looking at him, I wouldn't think he was a killer. He looked more like a model or some shit like that.

"You Nas?" I asked.

"Yeah . . ." He looked at my car and saw my brothers sitting there. "Luxury?"

"You the nigga that was fucking my wife, huh?"

He took a deep breath and exhaled. "You left her alone to travel overseas right after losing her father, you beat the fuck out of her, like she was some nigga off the street, and now you here asking me if I was fucking her. You came over here for what?"

"Hey, nigga, don't get at me like that. I'm the one that's asking the questions, and I expect you to respond. I don't need all the extra shit."

He lifted his hands. "Look, I don't want no problems with you, Luxury. What's done is done. She gave me back the car, and she said we're done. I'm not your problem. Yo, you have my word."

"Nah, nigga, you will always be my fuckin' problem unless we set some shit straight."

Nas walked out of his house, closed the door behind him, and folded his arms across his chest. "A'ight, I'm listening."

"I know you were paid to murder her best friend, and then you started fuckin' with her when she was vulnerable. What I want to know is, Were you paid to fuck her?"

He shook his head. "Listen, that theory you got going sound mad crazy. Yo, I didn't kill her best friend, so whoever told you that shit got me all wrong. When I met Desire, I didn't know anything about her. I didn't even know she was a rapper. My intentions with her wasn't on no paid shit. We started out as friends."

"Friends, huh? Yeah, okay. So you just gone lie to my face and tell me you ain't kill Mina? Everybody knows that you're Fat Man Bo's new hitta. Don't play with me right now, nigga." I was two seconds away from taking my gun out and ending his life. "This ain't no muhfuckin' game."

"A'ight, look, I was introduced to Fat Man through some broad that's cool with ya baby mama, Charity. I was looking for work out here, and she said he could put me on. I let him know what I used to do in New York, and he said he had a job for me. I had no idea they were friends. I wouldn't have did it if I knew. It wasn't until Desire talked about what had happened to Mina when we were in Spain. Desire loves you, Luxury. You and Desire can work y'all shit out and leave me out of it."

"Did she tell you she's pregnant?"

He nodded. "Yeah . . . I was supposed to meet her this morning at the diagnostic place to take a paternity test, but . . . I feel like that's between y'all."

"You say that, like, even if the baby was yours, you don't want shit to do with it."

"It's complicated. We were just fuckin' around. Nothin' serious. I thought she was on birth control. She even told me she took the morning-after pill. I don't want these kinds of problems in my life. I got my own shit going on. I think it would be better for her not to keep it."

"Well, nigga, it ain't up to you. You love her?" My heart was beating fast when I asked that. If he loved her, it would be hard to erase him. I didn't need him applying pressure and coming back to claim what he thought he could have.

He shook his head. "Nope, I don't, and she knows that."

"Listen, the only reason I'm not killing ya ass right now is the gun will ping the muhfuckin' police. Your best bet is to get the fuck outta my city by tonight. Go back to wherever the fuck you came from, nigga. Never call my wife again. Matter of fact, don't even tell her you leaving. If I find out you hit her up on your way out, it's a fuckin' wrap."

He looked at me as if I were crazy, but then he said, "A'ight. I'll leave. Like I said, I don't want these problems."

I gave him one last hard look before I walked back to the car. That shit was easier than I had thought it would be. I'd seen the look in his eye. He was ready to get out of town, anyway. He didn't want to take care of his responsibility with Desire. Plus, with everything swirling around that he was a hitter, he didn't want no smoke with the police.

As soon as I was in the car, I said, "He's leaving town. I told him if he ever contacts Desire again, I'll kill him."

"You think he gonna leave?" Lavish asked.

"We'll see."

I snapped out of the memory and sighed as I stood in the kitchen, a few shards of glass still at my feet. Something wasn't right here. Nas had said he would get out of town and disappear. He could've at least told his sister he was leaving, so she wouldn't file a missing person's report.

Desire was afraid that I had killed the nigga. I'd seen how she looked at me. After I swept up the rest of the broken glass and put it in the trash, I took my phone out of my pocket. I went to Nasim's Instagram page and shot him a message.

I wrote: Nigga, you're all over the fucking news. Call your sister and tell her you're good.

I got a glass out of the cabinet and put ice in it. I filled it with bottled water. Then I walked to the bedroom. Desire had a wild look in her eyes. After placing the glass on the night table, I sat down.

"I went and hollered at Nas," I said.

"When?"

"The day I came back home. There's something you should know."

"What did you do?" she asked, starting to panic.

"Calm down and listen, babe. I'm going to tell you everything."

She folded her arms across her chest and waited.

"You know Mina was fucking around with Fat Man Bo, and remember when I came back from the pool hall and told you he had said he didn't do it?"

"Yeah."

"Well, the nigga lied. He paid Nasim to kill her. Now, before you start asking questions, just listen . . . When you met Nasim, he didn't know you were Mina's best friend. That was a coincidence. Fat Man Bo told me where he lived, so I went over there. We talked. He said he would leave town."

"Can I talk now?" she asked.

"Go ahead."

"What do you mean, he killed Mina?"

"He admitted it to me. Bo paid him to get rid of her."

Tears fell from her eyes. I put my arms around her and pulled her close to me.

"It's over with now, baby. Fuck him. That nigga don't even want you to keep the baby. I can't share a city with a dirty-ass nigga like that."

"He told you that too?" she asked.

"Yeah. It's all good, though, because I got you and the baby."

Just then, my cell vibrated against my hip. I took it out of my pocket and read the message from Nasim: I just got off the phone with my sister. I didn't think she would call the police. She said they found my car at the airport. I left it there because somebody is supposed to come and get it. I sold it.

"That's him," I said, showing her the message.

She replied, "I really hope that from this day on, you don't hide shit else from me. You could've told me that you thought that Bo was lying to you."

"True. You're right, baby. I'm sorry."

"My only thing with you is that you just like to keep shit to yourself. As my husband, you can't do that, so promise me you won't do it again."

"I promise never to keep or hide anything from you, no matter how I think you will react."

"That's all I ask." She paused and thought for a moment before she continued. "When I talked to him about Mina's death, he looked spooked. I feel so stupid."

"You okay?"

"No, but I'll be fine. This is just a lot to put on me right now. Why would I keep a baby if I don't know if I'm giving birth to that killer's baby?"

"Well, like I told you before, it don't matter if it's his or not."

"It *does* matter, Luxury. I won't have a baby by a nigga who killed my best friend. I don't care if he was hired to do it or not. He should've found a way to tell me."

I didn't blame her for not wanting the baby if it was his.

"At the end of the day, it's your body and your decision. I'm here for you, no matter the decision," I assured her. "I'll let you get some rest. Let me know if you need anything."

She nodded, and I got up from the bed and headed out of the room. I closed the door behind me.

I hoped that my telling her everything would help her get through it. I would follow Desire into hell if that was what it would take to keep her safe. It was my responsibility to take care of her, because she was my wife. I would protect her, even if that meant protecting her from myself. Not a single soul was going to come before her. I was going to stay with her if she would stay with me. I wanted us to ride through everything, good or bad. I wasn't sure about what was going to happen next, but I was going to do my best to take care of her no matter what.

42

DESIRE

Starting Over

When Luxury loved, he loved hard. Though our love was not perfect, it was ours, and we had figured out how to make things work in our crazy world. When I woke up the next morning, I cuddled up next to Luxury, pressed my nose into his chest.

"Good morning," he said.

I looked up from his chest and said, "I'm going to the clinic. I've decided not to keep the baby."

There was a little sadness in his eyes when he asked, "You sure?"

"Positive."

He kissed my forehead and replied, "Say less. Tell me what you need for me to do, and I'll do it."

"I want to be discreet, so is there a way to enter the clinic without anyone knowing? I don't want this story to get out."

"I hear you. I'll make some calls. How soon you want it done?"

"As soon as possible."

"I got you." Luxury sat up and reached for his phone.

I put my hand on his to stop him. "Hold up. Before you call, let me say this . . . I want things to be different between us, babe. I want to feel secure in this marriage, and I want you to trust me. I will never cheat on you again. Do you believe me?"

He looked into my eyes and said sincerely, "I believe you. Do you believe me when I say that I will never put my hands on you?"

I nodded. "Yes. I know it was the pain I caused, along with the intoxication."

"No more drinking and drugs for me, I swear. I want things to be different for us too. We need to slow things down and enjoy one another. I'll put you first always."

"I believe you. Thank you."

I forgave Luxury, and I forgave myself for my flaws. For us to start over, we had to let go of all the negative emotions and memories. It was time to move on with positive thoughts. If we couldn't do that, our relationship would be negative and abusive. I couldn't punish myself for my wrongs, and I wasn't going to punish him for his. With true forgiveness, I could love Luxury fully, and our love was going to blossom like we never knew it could. Luxury and I were learning what forgiveness meant and our future looked bright. It would take time for us to heal our hearts, souls, and minds, and we were willing to go for it because we loved one another. This was our chance to begin anew.

I puckered up my lips to kiss him, and he received me. We kissed passionately, despite our morning breath, and we didn't care. As he picked up his phone to make arrangements for me, I felt confident. There was a tiny part of me that wondered if I was carrying Luxury's baby, but deep inside, I felt it wasn't his. This was the best decision to make. While he talked on the phone, I took a shower, washed my hair, and thought about when would be an appropriate time to have babies. I decided to hold off on kids until I had at least one more album under my belt. There was no rush to start a family. I entered the bedroom with a towel wrapped around me.

"Tomorrow morning you will be the first and only one there. No cameras. We'll have NDAs signed. You okay with that?"

"Yeah." I nodded, putting lotion in my hand.

"Good."

"In about a week, I'll be ready to start recording my next album." I smiled.

He smiled and nodded. "I like the sound of that, but you sure? I don't want to put any pressure on you."

"We gotta keep it going. I want that platinum plaque," I said.

"I got you, baby. Let's do it."

"Oh, and you think we can go to the beach today?"

"We can do that. You want one of those fruity smoothies, don't you?"

"Yup, and it's called a batido, babe," I said.

"I know what it's called. It's a smoothie, right?"

"No, it's a Cuban milkshake, and I want a large, with extra mangos and pineapples."

He came over to me, put his arms around my waist, and smiled with those incredible dimples. "You can have whatever you want, Mami. Maybe I should try one this time. Which flavor would you suggest for a first timer?"

"You like strawberries. Get that one."

"Can they put some banana in there too?"

"They can put whatever you want in it," I promised.

"Hmm. You know what? I actually Googled this spot for the best batidos in Miami yesterday, and I was going to surprise you with a little outing, but why not go there and then go to the beach?"

"Ooh! Where?"

"Let me see." He pulled up Google on his phone. "It's called Bocas House. It's in Doral. Brand-new little spot. You heard of them?"

"No. What time they open?"

"It says eleven thirty. I'm going to take a shower, get dressed, and we can get some breakfast. Then we can head over there. The rest of the afternoon, we can chill on the beach."

I smiled and kissed him all over his face. "Sounds like the perfect day and exactly what I need before tomorrow."

Biting his lower lip, he palmed my behind with both hands. "I love you so much, Desirae."

His loving words were the sweetest melody. I could wrap myself in his arms and stay that way for eternity.

"I love you too."

The End